PRAISE FOR A[

A Conflict of Interest

"A Best Book of the Year"

—*Suspense Magazine*

"A heady combination of Patricia Highsmith and Scott Turow, here's psychological and legal suspense at its finest. Adam Mitzner's masterful plotting begins on tiptoe and morphs into a sweaty gallop, with ambiguity of character that shakes your best guesses, and twists that punch you in the gut. This novel packs it. A terrific read!"

—Perri O'Shaughnessy, *New York Times* bestselling author

"Mitzner combines the real-world insights of an experienced litigator with the imaginative flair of a fine novelist to produce a page-turner with deeply flawed heroes, sympathetic villains and totally unexpected twists. I loved it."

—Alan Dershowitz, author of *Trials of Zion*

A Case of Redemption

"Head-and-shoulders above most . . ."

—*Publishers Weekly*

"*A Case of Redemption* is engaging and compelling—a story that literally challenges the reader to move on to the next chapter rather than setting the book down. With plenty of plot twists and turns as well as a hugely unexpected turn of events at the end, Adam Mitzner's legal thriller is fresh and satisfying."

—*New York Journal of Books*

"This noirish tale . . . is sure to keep you riveted from start to finish."

—*New York Observer*

Losing Faith

"Mitzner provides a surprise ending that will leave fans gasping in shock . . ."

—*New York Journal of Books*

"A worthy courtroom yarn that fans of John Grisham and Scott Turow will enjoy."

—*Kirkus Reviews*

"If looking for a good, solid legal thriller, this is the one to read."

—*Suspense Magazine*

The Girl from Home

"An engrossing little gem."

—*Kirkus Reviews*

"This inside look at underhanded Wall Street dealings dramatically explores the things that matter most."

—*Publishers Weekly*

"Readers will thoroughly enjoy this story of the Wall Street wealthy and just what happens when everything falls apart. A definite '5-star' read!"

—*Suspense Magazine*

"Mitzner's finest work to date, and I won't be surprised to see it up for award consideration this year."

—*newmysteryreader.com*

DEAD CERTAIN

DEAD CERTAIN

A NOVEL

ADAM MITZNER

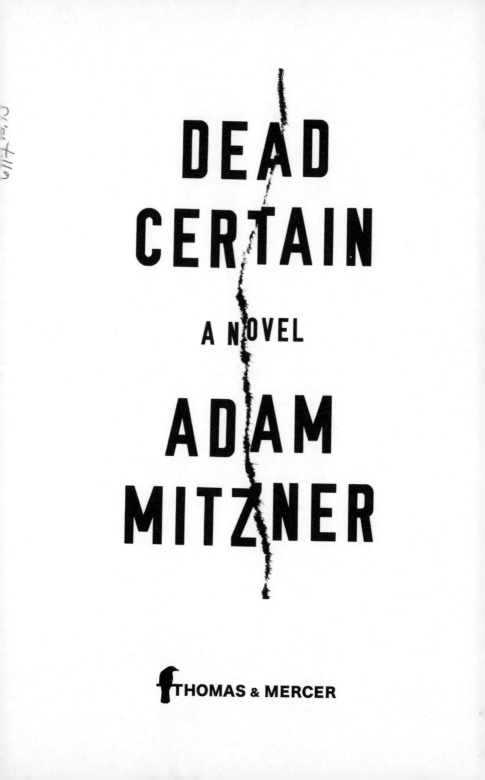

THOMAS & MERCER

Published by Thomas & Mercer, Seattle

www.apub.com

Amazon, the Amazon logo, and Thomas & Mercer are trademarks of Amazon.com, Inc., or its affiliates.

ISBN-13: 9781477822593
ISBN-10: 1477822593

Cover design by Faceout Studio

Printed in the United States of America

To my daughters, Rebecca and Emily, because . . .
because

PART ONE

DAY ONE

TUESDAY

Ella Broden

1.

I have news!!!

For someone who fancies herself a writer, Charlotte's texts are extremely heavy on exclamation points.

I text back, **wat**—no question mark. My sister and I have used this shorthand since texting began, even though it's actually more difficult because my phone autocorrects to *what*, and then I have to manually change it back.

No! In person! Tom's!

That it's the middle of a workday didn't seem to enter Charlotte's consciousness. Nor did the fact that she's asking me to go to 112th and Broadway, a few blocks from her apartment. She undoubtedly knows that I'm in my office in Midtown, at Fifty-Seventh and Madison. In other words, a two-minute walk for her and a forty-minute commute for me. But my sister and I long ago established that when she asks me to come to her, I come, no questions asked. One of the privileges of being the baby, I suppose.

KK. We always text that too, even though that autocorrects to **OK**, and then I change it back.

Leaving in 10.

C u there at 2!!

On my subway ride to the Upper West Side, I consider the possibilities regarding my sister's news. Given that we are both of *that* age, marriage is always what I suspect by default when a single friend says she has news, or a baby if she's already wed. Charlotte is unmarried and enough of a traditionalist that I reject pregnancy in favor of nuptials. I know I should be happy for her if that is her big reveal, but I hope to God it's something else. Not because Charlotte is six years younger than I am and I don't even have a boyfriend—it's because I'm not a fan of her current beau, Zach.

Zach is the kind of guy you date in your twenties because he's beautiful and damaged and you think you can change him. The problem is that when you reach your thirties, you realize he's not always going to be beautiful, you're never going to change him, and being with him has already damaged *you* so profoundly that you can't even imagine the wreck you'll be if you remain together even one more day, much less 'til death do you part.

When Charlotte and I last discussed Zach—which was only a few weeks ago—she seemed ready to end it, so I doubt that she's suddenly decided to marry him. Then again, stranger things have happened after a man proposes. And Charlotte is nothing if not a romantic in that way.

The next possibility my mind runs to is that Charlotte's news might be employment related. But here there really couldn't be much for her to say. She just finished her first year of a two-year MFA program in creative writing at NYU—all on our dad's nickel. I couldn't imagine her giving up that cushy life for an entry-level job anytime soon.

It isn't until I'm coming up from the subway at 110th and Broadway that I consider the possibility that her news might not be good. Could she want to tell me that she's got some health issue? That she's pregnant and doesn't know what to do?

I shake off the idea that it could be negative. Bad news doesn't come with three exclamation points.

———

Even though clients pay $750 an hour for my time and all Charlotte has *is* time, she isn't at Tom's when I arrive. So I take a booth in the corner and wait.

A note about Tom's. It's the most famous diner in the world because its exterior was used for the coffee shop on *Seinfeld*. The sign shown on television was on the 112th Street side, where it only says the word *Restaurant*, but from Broadway it reads TOM'S RESTAURANT. Before *Seinfeld*, though, Tom's was immortalized in Suzanne Vega's eponymous song, and even before it made A-list connections, Tom's had been a haunt of the Columbia University crowd for years.

At a quarter after, Charlotte bounds into the restaurant. She's absolutely beaming. If anyone else made me travel for close to an hour and then showed up fifteen minutes late from a location two minutes away, I would have been furious. But I've never been able to be mad at Charlotte. Not when I was nine and she was three and she cut my hair when I was asleep; not when I was thirteen and she was seven and she poured chocolate milk in my favorite boots; not when I was sixteen and she was ten and she told Bradley, who was my boyfriend, that I wished Ryan would ask me to the junior prom.

Charlotte slides into the booth and sits up straight. When we were younger, my sister's main ambition in life was to be taller than me. It wasn't a very lofty goal considering I'm all of five three, but our parents' short genes caught up with her too, and she topped out at five two.

"Sooooo . . . ," I tease out. "What's the big, exciting, three-excla-mation-point news?"

A delicious smile comes across her lips. As if she wants to savor her news before letting it out into the world.

"Well," she finally says, "your . . . sister . . . has . . . just . . . ," and then she quickly runs through the rest of it, "sold her first novel!"

"What?" I say, although I understand completely. I just can't get my head around it.

"Our major assignment is to write a novel. You submit the first half of the manuscript as your final first-year project, and you're supposed to finish it your second year. My advisor loved mine so, even though it was unfinished, he sent the chapters I'd written to a friend he knows over at Simon and Schuster . . . long story short, they're going to publish it!"

It takes me a moment to scan through my emotions. It feels a bit like watching the wheel spin on *Wheel of Fortune*—jealousy, envy, and anger click by, but I don't come to rest on any of those things. I finally stop on shame.

I'm ashamed of myself. Charlotte has followed her dream, and now it's coming true. And I, who could have done likewise, chose a safer course. I'm left wishing with all my might that I could go back and redo everything in my life.

My dark emotion quickly lifts, however. Sitting across from Charlotte, with her glistening eyes and a smile whose wattage could illuminate the city, I am quickly consumed with pride. My baby sister is going to be a published author.

"That's amazing! I don't even know what I'm supposed to ask. What's the book about?"

"The pitch was *Gone Girl* meets *Fifty Shades*. But at its core, it's a story about these two sisters—"

This sounds an alarm bell. Over the years, Charlotte has written many a *roman à clef*, including family and friends among her thinly veiled characters. When pressed about the similarities to real people and events, she's always leaned on the standard disclaimer: "Any similarity to actual persons, living or dead, is purely coincidental." Despite that, the circumstances leading up to the loss of my virginity were memorialized for all time in a story about a girl named Ellice that Charlotte published her senior year in the high school literary magazine. Another time, the older sister was named Gabriella; and once Charlotte thought that by adding a *B*—Bella—she'd throw people off the scent that her protagonist's older sister was me. As for her own doppelgängers, Charlotte was only slightly more creative. She went through a phase of cycling among the *Sex and the City* characters; instead of Charlotte, her stand-in was named Carrie or Samantha or Miranda. Once she even called her fictional counterpart Wilbur, a *Charlotte's Web* allusion.

"Wait a sec. This isn't your blog that no one ever looks at. This is a real book. People are going to read this."

She laughs. "That's kind of the point. For people to read it. But, to put you at ease, no . . . it's not about us. It's fiction. Any similarity to actual persons, living or dead, is purely coincidental."

"Of course it is," I say with an eye roll. "Are the two sisters named . . . Charlemagne and Eleanor?"

"No. Emily and Clare."

"Great. So you used our middle names. Very creative."

"I'll change them if you want. But you should be honored that I think you have the makings of a great literary character. Besides, it's the younger sister who's really messed up. The older sister is the moral compass of the book."

This much I believe. Charlotte always paints her alter egos with harsh colors, and the characters based on me always seem too good to be true.

"You must be ecstatic," I say.

"I don't know about *ecstatic*, but I am very excited . . . and also more than a little scared about the prospect of having to finish it. But it comes at a time when I really needed some good news in my life."

This revelation stops me short. I hadn't realized anything was troubling Charlotte, aside from the usual ups and downs with Zach.

"Is something wrong?" I ask.

"No . . . no. It's just . . . I don't know. Sometimes I feel like I'm the family screwup, and now I have some small measure of validation that I've done something right. You know what I mean?"

I do. All too well, in fact. It's part of the roles that Charlotte and I have been assigned in our family drama. I'm the steady one, the sensible one. She's the free spirit, the dream chaser. I have long wished we could switch parts. Oddly, it never occurred to me that Charlotte might feel that way too.

"Char, you're twenty-five years old and about to be a published author. You're way ahead of the curve. When I was twenty-five . . . I was doing arraignments in traffic court."

She smiles, but I know I haven't alleviated whatever is bothering her.

"Thanks," she says as my consolation prize.

"No, I'm serious. I'm so proud of you, Char. Such an amazing accomplishment. And Mom would be over the moon."

Our mother died when I was nineteen and Charlotte was a month away from becoming a teenager. She had been diagnosed with cancer a year before and underwent the most brutal form of chemotherapy in hopes of surviving long enough to attend Charlotte's high school graduation. I suspected she knew this was asking too much, and that surviving long enough to see me graduate from college was her true goal. She didn't come close to either.

Had my mother lived, I imagine that both my sister and I would have taken vastly different paths in life. For starters, I'm quite certain I wouldn't have gone to law school. My mother's almost-constant mantra was that I possessed a special musical talent.

"You don't realize it now, Ella," she'd said, "but a voice like yours is a gift from God. There's nothing sadder than turning your back on the thing that makes you great."

She had high hopes that, after college, I'd take a year or more and live the life of a singer. A struggling one, at least. Waitressing, auditions, the whole nine yards.

When she died, so did that dream. Instead, I gravitated toward pleasing my father, which meant following in his footsteps. And so, after college, rather than auditioning for Broadway, I went to law school.

But my detour was minor compared to Charlotte's. Before our mother died, the long-running joke in our family was that Charlotte was the only creature on earth happier than our dog. Nixie would run around the house with her tail wagging for no reason at all, and Charlotte always seemed even more joyous than that. By the time I graduated from college, however, my sister had been fundamentally transformed. The happy-go-lucky tween who sang out loud without realizing it suddenly became closed off and moody. She wore nothing but black and applied her makeup so heavily it was almost like a mask. For as long as I could remember, Charlotte had talked about plans for becoming a doctor—and not just any kind of doctor. By twelve she knew she wanted to go into pediatric cardiology. But after witnessing our mother's demise, it was apparent that being around death was the last thing she wanted, so she declared herself a writer.

My reference to our mother is enough to bring both of us to tears. We wipe them away with the same motion—mirror images.

"So, when can I read this masterpiece?" I ask.

"I've got it right here."

Charlotte reaches down into her backpack, a green canvas one that she bought at a thrift store—that's where she buys all her clothing, usually paying a price by the pound. Out of it she pulls a white, loose-leaf binder of the two-inch variety and hands it to me.

"Normally I'd just e-mail it, but I know you prefer reading actual paper books," she says. "So I went to OfficeMax and had them print it out."

I open the binder to the title page, which reads in large, bold font:

Dead Certain, by Charlotte Broden

I turn the page: *To my sister, Ella, because . . . because.*

"Aw," I say. "You dedicated it to me?"

"Who else? Like I said, I've only written the first half. So what you have are the events leading up to the crime, but the identity of the murderer is still unclear. After you're done, if you want, I'll tell you who did it."

I flip through the pages. "What's the second half going to be about?"

"The older sister. She's going to solve the crime."

"Of course she will. But aren't you afraid the murderer will slip town while you're writing the second half?" I say in my snarkiest tone.

"Spoken like a true lawyer," she says with a laugh.

I'm sure she didn't mean it as a rebuke. After all, I *am* a lawyer. Still, it stings. A bit of self-loathing on my part.

"This moment requires memorialization." I say, pulling out my phone. "Smile, Char-bar."

She wipes her eyes again and then flashes her smile. The frozen image on my phone captures my sister perfectly. A woman on the verge of greatness.

I turn my phone to show it to her. "This is the shot you'll use on the book jacket."

The server arrives to take our orders. A salad for me, and what I wished I'd ordered for Charlotte—grilled Swiss on rye and french fries. The moment he leaves us, my ringtone sounds.

"Work," I say, not wanting to tell her that it's actually our father. "Yes. Yes. I can do that." I pull the phone away from my ear to check the time. "It'll take me forty minutes or so to get back, but I'm leaving now . . . Okay . . . Bye."

I tuck away the phone. "Sorry. Duty calls. I have to get back to the office."

"Your boss sounds like a real piece of work," she says with a knowing grin.

"You don't know the half of it. I'm really sorry I can't stay for lunch. Do you mind canceling my order?"

"Sure. And I'm sorry too that you have to leave, but I get it. We can't all live lives of leisure. I'm really glad you came up here, though. I wanted you to be the first person I told. Call me as soon as you've read it, okay?"

"I will."

"Promise?"

"Yes, I promise."

"Oh, and don't tell Dad, okay? I want to tell him myself."

"I promise that too."

I've never broken a promise to Charlotte. Not once in my entire life. But this time I don't keep my word.

On either score.

2.

Although my father is not quite a household name, he's plenty famous in households that have a lawyer in the family. It's not an overstatement to say that he's universally regarded as the guy you go to when money is no object and you're up to your eyeballs in criminal sewage.

He's often asked to speak at law schools. When he does, he always starts with the same story. He usually says it happened when he was in kindergarten, although I've heard iterations where he's in first grade, and sometimes as old as a fifth grader. It's career day, and the teacher is going around the room asking the kids what they want to be when they grow up. By the time they get to my father, nearly every boy has laid claim to being a future athlete of some type, the girls actresses or singers.

When it's my father's turn, he announces that he dreams of someday becoming a garbageman. The disclosure gives rise to snickers among his classmates, and the teacher is horrified that such an intelligent child aspires to a career in waste management.

"Why do you want to be a garbageman, Francis?" the teacher asks.

My father now goes by "Clint," but as a child he went by Francis—the *F* in F. Clinton Broden.

"Because it would be fun to get all dirty and hang off the back of the truck," my father claims he replied to the teacher. In his retelling, this never fails to evoke laughter from his law-student audience.

"Well, you can't be a garbageman, Francis. Pick something else," the teacher scolds.

"Then I want to be a lawyer," says my father. "Because you get paid to fight with people."

The law students tend to laugh even louder at this, but my father is not joking. He absolutely loves the fight.

I suspect he's summoned me back to the office to gird for a new battle. When I arrive, I'm greeted by Ashleigh, the firm's receptionist.

"He's in his office," she says.

I like Ashleigh and she certainly seems competent, but she looks like a stripper. Teased-up blonde hair, a chest that makes you wonder how she doesn't tip over, and spindly legs. I would have thought that my father would be sensitive to the impression she makes on clients. Then again, maybe that's something his clients—who are virtually all male—like.

My father's office is, of course, in the corner. Because we are on the fifty-seventh floor, the view captures the entire city to the north and west. My father once told me that he chose to go into criminal defense rather than civil law because clients facing jail time are happy to pay through the nose in the hope that they can buy their freedom. His office shows that he was correct. It's almost as large as my entire apartment and more opulently appointed than any five-star hotel.

"So nice to see you, Ella," he says when I enter.

The undertone of sarcasm is hardly even an undertone. My father's passive-aggressiveness, front and center.

I could have told him that I'd gone to have lunch with Charlotte and still kept her news a secret, but I learned long ago to deal with my father the way he advises clients to act with prosecutors—by saying as little as possible. My father is probably the world's foremost cross-examiner, and he does not restrict his talents to the courtroom. He has an almost preternatural ability to detect not only lies, but even half-truths and meaningful omissions. Yet like any state-of-the-art detection device, his powers only work when they're turned on. For much of my life, my father's interest in me has been stuck in the "Off" position. Still, I've always adopted a less-is-more approach when providing him with information about me or Charlotte.

"Am I not allowed to take a lunch hour now?"

"Not when I need you."

He says this with a smile, but that only reinforces that he's deadly serious. My father is well aware that he calls the shots with everyone, especially his daughters. Correction—*me*. Charlotte is too strong-willed, which is why she's a writer and not a lawyer.

I take a seat in one of the many guest chairs opposite my father's desk. "So, what's the emergency?"

"It's about Garkov," he says.

Nicolai Garkov is my father's marquee client of the moment. Garkov is . . . There's no delicate way to put this. He's a terrorist and a murderer. The Red Square Massacre is his crowning achievement, if you measure such things by body count. My father has been retained to defend him in connection with charges relating to money laundering, which, ironically enough, is the only unlawful act for which Garkov has been indicted. If you believe my father, it's also the one crime of which he is innocent.

The defense strategy for Garkov from day one has been to delay, delay, delay. My father boasted back then that it would be four years before Garkov saw the inside of a courtroom. I thought he was being hyperbolic, but he's kept Garkov from his day of reckoning for nearly five.

The string appears to be finally played out, however. At the last pretrial conference, Judge Koletsky told my father that he'd had enough. "Come hell or high water," the judge said, "we're going to start this trial next week." And then, as if that weren't clear enough, he added, "And if it's high water then you all better bring wet suits, because we're still picking a jury."

"Okay . . ." I say in a noncommittal tone.

"I'm thinking of putting Garkov on the stand. He's got a story he can tell to defend himself." My father pauses and then clarifies, "On the money-laundering charges, at least."

Most criminal defense lawyers keep their clients *off* the stand. The conventional wisdom is that, once the defendant testifies, the jury's verdict is a referendum on that testimony. If they believe him, they acquit; if not, they convict. And that means that reasonable doubt—the defendant's ace in the hole—becomes irrelevant. My father is one of the few criminal defense attorneys of the first rank who disagrees, and I stand with him on that issue. When I was prosecuting, I always knew I had a winner when the defense rested without the defendant telling his story.

"The problem is," my father continues, "I'm worried that they'll get into Red Square on cross."

My father never calls it the Red Square Massacre, which is how it's referred to in all other circles. For him it's just Red Square. The place, not the murders.

I've heard my father say on many occasions that there are only three circumstances in which a defense lawyer should not put his client on the stand. The first is if the client has admitted guilt. In that case, allowing the client to testify to his innocence violates ethical rules and crosses the line into suborning perjury. The second is when the testimony to be proffered is so preposterous that no juror will buy a word of it. Neither scenario applies very often. That's because most clients swear their innocence—even to their lawyers—and are usually adept enough liars that their stories have at least a whiff of believability.

It's the third reason that comes up most often: the client has a criminal record. Once the jury learns that the defendant is a convicted felon, it votes to convict nine times out of ten.

It's a quirk in the law of evidence that prior bad acts—including prior criminal convictions—are normally inadmissible at trial. The theory is, if you've been previously convicted of a crime, with limited exceptions, that conviction is irrelevant to your guilt or innocence in relation to the pending charges. However, if a defendant testifies, the prosecutor can tell the jury about the defendant's prior convictions—not to show the defendant's proclivity to commit crime, but because the law views a felony conviction as probative that the perpetrator's testimony might be untruthful. In other words, the jury can't *assume* that because the defendant committed a prior crime he's guilty as charged, but they are allowed to make the *logical deduction* that because he's a convicted felon, he might be lying when he says he's innocent.

Like I said, it's a quirky thing and makes no logical sense. But the bottom line is, if your client has a prior criminal conviction, you keep him off the stand.

Garkov has not been indicted for the Red Square Massacre, however. The official law-enforcement position is that he remains a person of interest and that the crime is still under investigation. Nevertheless, I'm quite certain the prosecution will argue that Garkov's role as a terrorist is an integral part of the motive behind the money-laundering charges for which he stands accused—the reason why he had to move money surreptitiously. And if Judge Koletsky buys it, evidence about the Red Square Massacre comes in whether Garkov testifies or not.

"Why don't you make a motion *in limine*?" I suggest.

A motion *in limine* is a pretrial request to preclude certain evidence. You ask the judge ahead of time to rule that certain evidence cannot be presented to the jury, so you know how to prepare your case.

"Already did," my father says. "More than a month ago. Judge Koletsky hasn't ruled on it yet. Knowing him, he may not rule until well after the trial begins. If I'm going to have Garkov testify, I want to tell the jury about it during my opening—it keeps them from coming to any conclusions when the prosecution makes its case because they know they're going to hear the other side. But if I promise Garkov's testimony and then Koletsky rules that Red Square is fair game, I can't put Garkov on the stand. The jury will hold it against *him* that I didn't deliver on my promise."

Garkov is not one of my cases. By the time I joined my father's firm three months ago, too much had happened for me to get up to speed in time for trial. I was tasked instead with minding my father's other clients for the two months or so that he would be trying to persuade a jury to let Garkov go free.

It's not uncommon for my father to share his legal strategies about Garkov, or use me as a sounding board. But I get the distinct impression that something different is in play. The fact that he's now silent is the biggest tip-off. He most definitely has an agenda.

"Are you asking me what I'd do?" I finally say.

"Not exactly . . . you told me a while back you have a law-school friend who works in Judge Koletsky's chambers, right?"

For the umpteenth time, I regret having shared that bit of information. My friend Abby Doft does not merely work in Judge Koletsky's chambers, she's his head law clerk. She had been a paralegal in the DA's office back when I started there, and we kept in touch when she went to law school. She graduated two years ago, and I actually wrote one of the letters of recommendation that got her the clerkship, even though I told her at the time that my father had a particularly notorious case pending before Judge Koletsky and warned her that a Broden singing her praises might be seen as a negative.

"Right," I say. "But I told you from the start that I'm not going to talk to Abby about the case."

"Not about the case, Ella. About getting Koletsky off his octogenarian ass so he rules on the goddamn motion. I frankly don't care which way he decides, just so long as he does it before opening statements."

The oldest lie in the book. Like when you're waiting to hear your medical test results and you tell people that the uncertainty is the worst part. Same thing here. The substance of Koletsky's ruling matters much more than the timing.

"Why don't you tell him that yourself, then?"

"Ella . . . Believe me, I respect your ethics. I would never ask you to do anything to compromise them. But I'm not asking for help in the case. I'm asking you to see if that motion can be pushed to the top of Koletsky's to-do list. That's all."

I've always found it difficult to say no to my father. That's probably the biggest difference between Charlotte and me—and in some ways, it's made all the difference.

3.

Before joining my father at the Law Offices of F. Clinton Broden, I was an Assistant District Attorney in Manhattan for six years, rising to become the deputy chief of the Special Victims Bureau. Three months in, I'm still not completely comfortable at my father's firm. Putting away the bad guys was far more satisfying than defending them.

My office in the private sector is actually smaller than the one I worked out of at the DA's office. This one is nicer, though. Views that go for miles and expensive built-ins. My high-back, ergonomic leather desk chair cost more than three grand. The computer is also a step up. My desktop at the DA's office was forever buffering, but my new PC fires up as fast as lightning.

I still haven't put anything on the walls. I wanted to hang a plaque the District Attorney gave me for outstanding service, but my father suggested that I not seem too beholden to my former employer. "It's one thing," he said, "to tout to clients that you know the enemy's secrets; it's quite another to indicate that you actually enjoyed the time you spent behind enemy lines."

My father offered to move the Miró that hangs in the hallway to my office, but I declined. I told him that I wanted the space to reflect my personality, and I'd figure something out soon enough. For the last three months, however, my personality has been a blank slate.

Home is a one-bedroom, third-floor walk-up in a Greenwich Village brownstone. I realize that sounds depressing to non–New Yorkers, but it's actually considered to be desirable housing. Up until four months ago, I shared the apartment with my boyfriend, Jeffrey. He lived here before we met and after dating for a year we decided that paying two rents made no sense, so I moved in. That was two years ago.

Jeffrey is a lawyer at Lowell and Pike, one of those megafirms with more than eight hundred lawyers in New York and offices in every major city in the world. He's a tenth-year associate, which means he's been passed over for partner once and this year is his last shot at that Holy Grail. If he doesn't make it, he'll end up in the lawyer-purgatory known as "of counsel" and watch more junior lawyers—lawyers he now commands to give up their weekend plans or work all-nighters—become partners, and thereby gain the authority to boss *him* around.

Four months ago, Jeffrey came home and matter-of-factly told me that he owed it to himself to give his full-time attention to making partner. I tried not to laugh. Ever since we'd started dating, he'd made it quite clear in word and deed that I took a backseat to that quest. Apparently he'd decided that more drastic measures were required than merely working ninety-hour weeks, because the next day he moved to a furnished studio apartment a block from his office. He left behind virtually all his worldly possessions aside from his clothing.

Jeffrey was the latest in a long line of decisions I'd made about my life because they seemed right on paper. I never met a single person who didn't think Jeffrey and I were perfect for each other. He's handsome, but not so much that I worried about his fidelity, and the kind of person the phrase "smartest guy in the room" was coined to describe.

But even in the early days, I knew that I didn't feel the head-over-heels passion for him that I'd always craved. What I had instead was a talent for convincing myself that lacking a little spark didn't matter because Jeffrey possessed so many other important attributes. Deep down, of course, I knew it was a lie. When he told me it was over, I felt relieved more than anything.

Even before Jeffrey left, I'd already begun thinking about my next professional act. Most Assistant District Attorneys cash out after three or four years, as soon as they've tried enough cases that headhunters representing Wall Street law firms and investment banks start calling with offers to triple their salaries. The true believers—like me—stay longer, eventually moving to a supervisory role because the grind of trying a case every few months is brutal. But life as a supervisor is like being a shark—you either constantly move ahead or you die. And I had stopped moving. My ex-boss at the Special Victims Bureau was a lifer like me, which meant that becoming bureau chief of Special Vics wasn't going to happen for me for another ten years, minimum. I saw no other division that I would be a natural fit to lead, and even if I did want to go to General Crimes or Forfeiture, deputy chiefs in those groups were already waiting in the wings.

So when Jeffrey left me with a monthly rent I couldn't afford on an ADA's salary and my father reiterated for the millionth time that it would be the perfect moment for me to come aboard and practice "real" law—by which he meant for clients who pay—my resolve finally cracked and I accepted.

I've wished I hadn't every day since.

Tonight that regret is hitting me hard. I can feel the pull toward Lava, but that will have to wait one more evening. More and more, I've begun to feel that my secret life is becoming as addictive as a drug habit—and perhaps just as dangerous to my long-term well-being. I know that Charlotte's news is the reason I feel like I need just a little hit, and I'm also self-aware enough to appreciate that it will be an increasing problem as my sister becomes more successful by following her passion and I'm left with the harsh truth that my life is, for lack of a better word, passionless.

I open a bottle of white wine and take it, a glass, and Charlotte's manuscript over to my sofa. My plan is to start Charlotte's book after I unwind a bit, but half a bottle later, in the middle of some ridiculous pay-for-view rom-com that I have no idea why I selected, I pass out on my sofa.

If I hadn't been wallowing in my own self-pity, I might have paid more attention to the fact that I hadn't heard from Charlotte that evening. It's not unprecedented for us to go twenty-four hours without any type of contact, but it's much more the exception than the rule. Usually I'll get a text of her toes or something before bed, or I'll see that she's posted something on Facebook or Instagram or tweeted something that I'll "like," or vice versa.

But on that night, I don't hear a peep.

DAY TWO

WEDNESDAY

4.

I'm still feeling a little hungover the next morning. As I walk through the glass double doors leading to the Law Offices of F. Clinton Broden, all I can think about is getting some coffee in my bloodstream.

Unfortunately, before I can get my fix, Ashleigh says, "Your father's in the conference room with a client. New business. He wants you to join them."

New business is the siren song that no lawyer can resist. Even the receptionist knows it's the lifeblood of any law firm.

"For the love of God, please tell me that there's coffee in there?"

"Yes." Ashleigh laughs. "Freshly brewed, in fact. And muffins. I ordered them from Angelina's."

I take a deep breath and push open the conference-room door. My father is sitting with his back to the window, allowing the client to enjoy the helicopter views.

"We've been waiting for you, Ella," my father says.

The client turns around. For the second time, I suck in a mouthful of oxygen.

"Hi Ella," he says. "It's been a long time."

Indeed it has. I last laid eyes on Paul Michelson ten years ago, when he was breaking up with me, a week after we graduated from college. I had had hopes of spending the summer together and then giving a long-distance relationship a chance, with him staying in New York to start a job on Wall Street while I went to law school at Stanford. He said that he wasn't aware of any relationship that survived in different cities, much less on different coasts, and that it would save us both a lot of heartache if we just made a clean break.

I spent the summer in a fog of depression. Paul went backpacking in Europe. While there, he met up with Kelly Nelson, a fellow classmate of ours. I had been somewhat friendly with her during our junior year, when we sat next to each other in some poli-sci class. I didn't think Paul even knew her, and it was never clear to me whether he had prearranged their supposedly coincidental rendezvous, which occurred in front of the Louvre.

"Oh my God," I say. The moment the words come out of my mouth I realize I sound like I'm still the twenty-one-year-old he dumped a decade ago. In an effort to regain some professionalism, I add, "It has been a long time."

It looks as if time has stood still for Paul. He hasn't gained more than five pounds since college or lost a single strand of the jet-black hair that first made me notice him, although it's now neatly cut, whereas back in the day he wore it shaggy and past his collar. The only other thing that's different about him is that he now looks to be wearing a $5,000 suit, and the Paul I knew was strictly a sweatshirt-and-jeans kind of guy.

My eyes glance down to his hand. No wedding band.

All of which makes me more than a little self-conscious that I'm not looking my best. Not only is my face puffy—the way it always gets after I drink too much wine—but I'm also wearing an old suit, one of the last vestiges of my public-sector wardrobe.

The coffee and muffins are set out on the buffet along the back wall. I go there as if pulled by a magnetic force and quickly pour myself a cup of coffee. The aroma soothes me with the thought that I'll be consuming it soon. I want to take a muffin too, but think better of eating in front of Paul.

Coffee cup in hand, I make my way to the chair beside my father, which requires walking around Paul. As I pass him, I can't help but breathe in his scent. More intoxicating than the coffee. I would have recognized it if I'd been blind.

Once I'm seated, I take in a few strong sips of coffee. Then I reach across the table for a yellow legal pad, write the date on the top of the page, and wait for someone to fill me in.

My father does the honors.

"Your old friend Paul is now the head of the derivatives desk at Maeve Grant."

Maeve Grant is one of the biggest financial houses on Wall Street. Running a desk there means that Paul's done quite well for himself.

"As it happens, one of the newest employees on that desk is Jennifer Barnett," my father continues. "Does that name ring a bell?"

I wonder if my father is being sarcastic. Every person in the English-speaking world has heard of Jennifer Barnett. Her pretty face, bright blue eyes, and blonde ponytail have been a ubiquitous presence on television, the tabloids, and social media since she vanished without a trace.

"Yes, the missing woman," I say.

The fact that Paul is meeting with a lawyer of my father's caliber only days after an attractive young woman who works for him went missing means that there's only one place this is heading: a place no one wants to go.

My father is in full defense-lawyer mode. A happy-go-lucky expression fills his face—even as we sit in the presence of a potential murderer.

"So I'm sure you're well aware that, at the moment, there's no evidence of any foul play regarding her disappearance," he says. "Nevertheless, Paul made the decision—the right one, in my opinion—to get out in front of things. The police made a visit to interview everyone on the desk. As luck would have it, Paul was traveling that day so he hasn't yet spoken with them. He's now wisely decided that he'd benefit from some top-shelf legal advice before deciding whether to sit down with law enforcement."

I don't react to my father's assertion that the proper response to a routine police inquiry regarding a missing woman is to lawyer up. In my experience, that's what guilty people do. Innocent people offer to help.

"I was just telling Paul that since you've come over from the dark side, we've been tag-teaming most matters, and that we would handle this matter in the same fashion. I've also just shared with him that I have a very busy trial schedule for the next two months, which means that you'll be the point person. I've assured him that if something material were to happen with the investigation, I'd drop everything."

I nod reassuringly, like a political spouse. My father has made this pitch to many a client since I've arrived—it's a classic bait-and-switch. The clients hire him but they get me, with the promise that if they really need him, he'll be there. What he always leaves unstated is that he's the final arbiter of whether they *do* really need him, and he almost never decides they do.

"What my father so lovingly describes as my time on the dark side," I say, "was actually six years as an Assistant District Attorney here in Manhattan, where I rose to become the deputy chief of the Special Victims Bureau. So although I'd be the first to admit that I don't have my father's standing in the courthouse—honestly, no one does—I'm intimately acquainted with the methods used in the DA's office."

Paul's response to me touting my credentials is an ambiguous smile. It isn't clear to me if it suggests that I have his complete confidence or that he is thinking solely about getting me back in bed. Truth be told, it's the reaction I get from a lot of the male clients.

"Very good," my father says. "So, let's get down to it, shall we? I'm going to start by giving you some rules for the road. The gospel according to F. Clinton Broden, as it were."

My colleagues in the DA's office had always suspected that criminal-defense lawyers gave this speech. Call me naive, but I disagreed. Until, that is, I heard my father deliver it.

"I'm not about justice," my father's gospel always begins, and this time is no exception. "And you shouldn't be either. It is my professional obligation—what we in the law business call a *fiduciary duty*—to do everything I can to make sure that nothing bad happens to you while you're my client."

I've pointed out to my father on more than one occasion that a lawyer's obligation to a client has limits. For starters, you're not allowed to suborn perjury or destroy evidence. But my father firmly believes that any qualification of his sweeping assertion sends the wrong message. So in his telling, a lawyer's duty to his client is boundless.

"The best way to make sure that nothing bad happens to you is for you to hunker down and let the other side play their hand," my father continues. "I've been doing this for a long time now, longer than you've been alive, so I know that clients hate the hunkering-down part. They want to go in there and tell their story. They want to *prove* their innocence. But under the laws of our great nation, the prosecution has to prove guilt beyond a reasonable doubt, and you, Paul, don't have to prove a goddamn thing. Don't forget that. I'm emphasizing this point because, early in my career, I wasn't so strident about it and I let a few clients try to prove their innocence to a prosecutor. And you know what? There's not a single client I've had—not one—who talked a gung ho prosecutor out of filing charges. Of course we still beat them at trial all the time, but that's before a jury. I hate to say it, but the sad truth is that prosecutors are in the business of prosecuting and if they don't bring cases, they're out of business. After all, nobody ever became famous *not* bringing a case. Bottom line is that there's no way to convince a prosecutor that you're innocent, and trying to do so always comes back to haunt you."

My father takes a break from his narrative and turns to me. As the ex-prosecutor in the room, he expects me to vouch for his description of the inner workings of the DA's office—even though I've told him repeatedly that his version isn't even remotely true. When I was an ADA, many a person of interest convinced *me* not to prosecute. If they had an alibi or lacked motive or provided evidence pointing to someone else, I'd go in a different direction.

But now I play my role.

"That's right. The mind-set over at One Hogan Place is that everyone is *guilty until proven innocent*." Then I smile. "But of course that does not apply to former ADAs."

Like every client to whom I've seen my father make his pitch, Paul takes it in hook, line, and sinker. "Clients are like children," is one of my father's many pithy expressions about the practice of law. "They just want to know that there's a grown-up in the room who's going to make sure they survive. And we're that grown-up."

"It all sounds good," Paul says. "What do we do next?"

"Nothing," my father says. "I don't want to know any facts. Let the District Attorney's office do its digging. If they have something worth telling us about, we'll consider at that time whether to respond. What we will do now is shadow their investigation so we know where they're going before they get there. That's where Ella's connections become invaluable. They'll give her the straight skinny."

I again nod to confirm the truth of my father's assertion, even though, like his other pronouncements, it's not true. My former colleagues will be courteous to me and they'll listen to what I have to say, but they're not going to give me any more information than they'd provide any other defense lawyer.

"I already feel better," Paul says.

"Then this is a perfect time to discuss the terms of our engagement," my father says with a smile.

5.

After the meeting ends, my father suggests that I walk Paul out. As we wait for the elevator, I resist the urge to assure him that everything is going to be fine, or even that I believe he's innocent. I don't know whether either is true.

I half expect him to kiss me good-bye. But when the elevator doors open, he extends his hand instead.

"Good seeing you again, Ella. You really look great."

"Thank you. I'm sorry we're not meeting under more pleasant circumstances."

As the elevator doors close, blocking him from my sight, I consider whether Paul Michelson is the kind of man who could commit murder. The Paul I knew was a narcissistic womanizer to be sure, but most handsome, smart boys in college fell into that category. I don't remember his having a temper—in fact, the few times I recall Paul even raising his voice, he did so to be heard over my screaming. But the one thing I know for certain is that the Paul Michelson from back then would do whatever was necessary to survive. I can't rule out that it wouldn't now include killing Jennifer Barnett if she threatened him in some way.

I head back to my father's office. I need to know exactly how my ex-boyfriend from college ended up a client of the firm.

"Small world, isn't it?" my father says even before I pose the question.

"A little odd, don't you think?"

"No. Not really. He's got a criminal issue—*potential* criminal issue, I should say—and he knows that your father is a criminal-defense lawyer. He claimed he didn't even know you and I were working together until I told him."

I had been secretly hoping that it wasn't my father who Paul sought out, but me. My father's version of events made more sense, however.

"He didn't blink at the hundred-grand retainer," my father says.

This is another one of my father's theories: the degree to which a client pushes back on the retainer is inversely proportional to their guilt. Clients with nothing to fear try to limit the amount they have to pay. The guilty ones write you a check for whatever amount you want.

"So, what's the story?" I ask.

My father knows that I'm asking whether he thinks Paul is guilty. Rather than answer, he shakes his head to suggest that I should know better than to pose the question in the first place.

"You heard me tell him. I really don't want to know the story. I don't. All I know is that he called me this morning and asked to meet. I told him to come right in. Like I said before, it's not even certain that there's been any crime committed here. For all anyone knows, Jennifer Barnett may just be on vacation."

My father is famous for downplaying the alleged crimes of his clients. He has been known to refer to a multi-million-dollar theft as "some type of bookkeeping issue."

"No one's heard from her in four days," I say. "And there's no activity on her credit card or her cell phone. She's not soaking up the sun on a beach somewhere."

"Fair enough, but it still doesn't mean she was murdered. She could have . . . I don't know, jumped off a bridge. Maybe that's why her body hasn't been found yet."

"They haven't found a suicide note."

"Lots of suicides don't have notes. Besides, even if—let's say for the sake of argument—she *was* the victim of foul play, we're still a long way from establishing that Paul Michelson is the foul player here. And at the risk of pointing out the obvious, we are criminal-defense lawyers, Ella. If it weren't for criminals, we'd be out of work. Which, again, is why I truly don't care if he *did* do anything to Jennifer Barnett."

I know my father's attitude is the correct one—at least to survive in this business. And he's thrived. But even after three months, I still hate the idea that I'm dedicating my life to the wrong side. And now it's my professional obligation to turn a blind eye to the possibility that Paul Michelson might be a murderer.

———

When I return to my office, my first instinct is to call Charlotte to tell her about how I reconnected with Paul. I have to resist it, however. Attorney–client privilege prohibits revealing our client's name, at least until we make a public appearance on his behalf. Even though my father thinks that retaining a lawyer from day one and then hunkering down is the smart move, most people think it suggests guilt.

Given that telling Charlotte about my old flame is a no-go, I decide to spend my free time finding out what my father claims he does not want to know—the facts about Jennifer Barnett's disappearance.

The firm subscribes to several very expensive and specialized legal databases, but I still start most of my research with a good, old-fashioned Google search. I type "Jennifer Barnett missing" into the search engine and, a second later, I have more than a million hits. I click the first one and begin to read.

Other than the town in New Jersey from which she hailed, a tony place called Short Hills, everything else reported is something I already knew. She's twenty-two, started at Maeve Grant only three months ago—coincidentally, the same day I joined my father's firm—has been missing for four days, and the police are not revealing the names of any suspects or divulging any working theories concerning Jennifer Barnett's whereabouts.

I peruse another six articles, but none of them contain any different information. Next I plug Paul's name into the search engine. Google returns some articles from the business press in which he's quoted, but he otherwise lacks a cyber footprint. No Facebook profile. His name doesn't even appear on the Maeve Grant website.

My sleuthing completed, I do a little more lawyer work on behalf of some other clients, managing to somehow show that my pushing paper around amounts to nine hours of billing. At eight I leave the office, full of excitement for the evening to come.

———

My transformation to Cassidy begins the moment I step into my apartment. There's no point in having a secret life if you're going to hold back, so I reach for my tightest jeans and decide not to even bother with a shirt or bra. Instead, I put on a fringy vest and cinch it tight, until I'm reasonably satisfied I won't fall out of it.

Cassidy's makeup also makes a statement: dark mascara and bright red lipstick. And she wears her hair down and loose. I only wish mine were longer, because hers should be midwaist to truly be as wild as she'd like. Cassidy certainly doesn't have to tie it back for work in the morning.

Less than an hour later, she's staring back at me from the full-length mirror in my hallway. I eye Cassidy the way a man would. Slowly lifting my gaze from the floor, up my legs, lingering at my breasts, and then finally smiling at my reflection when we make eye contact.

She looks good. No, *hot*.

Cassidy—no last name, just Cassidy, like Madonna or Rihanna—has a bio on Lava's website and more than eight hundred "fans," the

Lava equivalent of Facebook likes. Charlotte might be the writer in the family, but I've crafted a perfectly convincing alter ego for myself. It says Cassidy's from a small town in Oregon and describes her musical style as indie/pop with a jazz influence. There's a "sounds like" section for people who don't understand what indie/pop with a jazz influence means. For Cassidy's, I've listed Lana Del Rey and Adele, along with Billie Holiday, to lend her an aura of sophistication.

There's also a photo array. Eight carefully composed pictures indicate that Cassidy is worth looking at without any of them actually showing her face. Of course, even with the teased-up hair and heavy black eyeliner that Cassidy favors, anyone who's ever met me would instantly recognize that it was Ella Broden onstage. But so far, at least, in the three months that I've been living my double life, that hasn't happened.

And yes, my first visit to Lava was two days after I joined up with my father. And no, you don't have to be a shrink to realize that the timing isn't a coincidence.

I haven't told a soul. Not even Charlotte, although I've come close a few times. I don't withhold out of shame or embarrassment, however. Charlotte is the least judgmental person I know. Rather, I maintain this secret because, as odd as this sounds, I feel like telling Charlotte—or anyone else, for that matter—would be betraying Cassidy. That she's *not* me is the point. If I blur that line, then Cassidy will cease to exist.

And right now I need her. A once-a-week vacation from my life, and a quick glimpse of the road not taken. What Ella Broden might have been if . . . she hadn't been so Ella Broden. If she had been a little more like her younger sister.

6.

The Lava Lounge—as Lava is officially named—is in the East Village. I'm likely the only person who takes a cab there. It's strictly a subway-and-walking kind of crowd.

Open mic is every Wednesday night. Lava's front room is a traditional bar. No seats, just a ten-foot mahogany counter. There isn't even a kitchen. Sometimes a food truck parks in front, just in case a patron wants some form of sustenance between rounds of alcohol. The moment you enter the back room, however, it's like Dorothy stepping out of her black-and-white Kansan world and into the kaleidoscopic colors of Oz. The stage has blindingly bright spotlights that illuminate a bright, red-lacquered floor. The rest of the space, though, especially where the crowd stands—and it's strictly a standing-room-only situation aside from a few bar stools—is dark as a cave. There's a collection of well-worn musical instruments and amps set off in the corner. Lava always provides a piano player, and more often than not, other musicians are at the ready to back up the singers.

It never fails to smell like a heady concoction of beer and sweat, and it's always loud. Very, very loud. The two-drink minimum makes the crowd enthusiastic and unforgiving. Tonight, the decibel level is already high enough that you need to shout to be heard even though the mic hasn't yet officially opened.

I haven't missed a Wednesday performance since I first took the stage twelve weeks ago. By now I'm on a first-name basis with the regulars. The bouncer, Kareem—a refrigerator of a man—greets me at the door. I ask him where I can find Karen. He points, and I see her at the bar, working at her iPad.

Karen is the woman in charge, although her authority is limited to giving out time slots and introducing the acts. She looks to be in her midforties and she has clearly made it to this point the hard way. There's a world-weariness around her eyes, as if she's experienced things she now regrets. She's rail thin—without any of the musculature of someone who adheres to a workout regimen.

"Cassidy!" Karen calls out when I approach.

We kiss on both cheeks the way Europeans do, and I wonder if it's because Karen might be European. Her voice has a trace of an accent, but I'm not sure if it's foreign or affected.

When we pull away, she scans my body. I am reasonably sure Karen is a lesbian.

"Wow. Look at you. Going to blow the roof off the place before you sing a note."

"Going to do some Donna Summer," I say.

She taps her iPad. "I had a bunch of cancellations tonight. If you want to go on at midnight or so, I can give you four songs."

Sets are at most two songs. Rookies, or anyone who has pissed Karen off recently, only get one. People have been known to offer Karen bribes—usually promises of sex, because none of the performers have any money—for an extra three minutes (and she always declines), which makes Karen's offer tonight to double my time without any quid pro quo virtually unprecedented.

My first thought is that a midnight set means I won't be home until after 1:00 a.m., and I'll be so wired that I won't fall asleep until two at the earliest, which is not ideal considering I have to be Ella

Broden, attorney-at-law, in the morning. But I absolutely hate when Cassidy suffers Ella's thoughts.

Cassidy is a creature of the night. She doesn't have anywhere to be tomorrow, and there's nothing she'd like to do more than throw back a few drinks, listen to some music, and then, as Karen says, blow the roof off the place at midnight.

"Sure. Whenever," I say.

———

At the bar, I order a whiskey because that's Cassidy's poison. I'm midway through it when I spy a handsome man in the crowd. He's dark everywhere. Skin, eyes, hair, and dressed from head to toe in black. His smile is borderline dangerous. The kind of man Cassidy would go for in a heartbeat, but who would scare the hell out of a goody-goody like Ella Broden.

I give him my—I mean, Cassidy's—best "fuck me" smile.

It's enough to reel him in. He heads right to me, and sidles up so he's standing wedged between my bar stool and the one next to it.

He tells me his name, but I don't catch it. When I tell him mine—Cassidy, of course—he repeats it back to me.

"I've never seen you here before," I say.

"I've never been. I came here tonight on something of a lark."

"Are you here to watch or perform?"

"Only time will tell, now, won't it?"

My new friend calls out to the bartender, "I'll have whatever she's having," like they say in the movies. When his drink arrives, he clinks his glass against mine. "To . . . ?" he says.

I complete the toast the way Cassidy would. "To whatever time has to tell."

"Indeed," he says. Then he throws his whiskey back in one gulp.

He looks at me like he's the devil, urging me to match him. I give in to the peer pressure, although my attempt to be cool is thwarted when I gag a bit as the whiskey goes down.

When our glasses are empty, he signals to the bartender that we're ready for more by holding up two fingers and spinning them around. We chat for a while, mostly about music. When I ask him to regale me with his life story, he says only that he lives in Brooklyn and that he's a doctor who most recently worked in Peru with Doctors Without Borders. I consider pressing him for more details, but it's so refreshing to be talking to a man who doesn't go on and on about himself that I'm content to allow him to remain mysterious.

He asks about me like he's truly interested, which is also something of a new experience in my dealings with men. For an instant, his sincerity causes me to consider breaking character, but then I hear myself parroting Cassidy's bio, at one point even going on about the sunsets of the Oregon coast as if I've actually seen one.

The conversation, the alcohol, and his eyes are enough for me to completely lose track of the time. I'm just finishing off my third drink when he raises his hand and shouts out, "Right here."

My focus shifts to Karen, on the stage. She's pointing at me. It takes me a moment to realize what has happened, but then it clicks. She's pointing at him, not me. Mr. Only-Time-Will-Tell has just volunteered to do a set.

He pushes through the crowd and climbs onto the stage. After he makes his way over to the band and whispers his song selection, he returns to the mic.

Some people look lost up there, but not my new friend. He reminds me of a conquering monarch addressing his subjects.

"I'm Dylan Perry," he says, so at least now I know his name. "This is an old one, but . . . well, you decide for yourselves if it's any good."

The cheesy organ lead-in makes me first think that he's going to sing a Doors song, but then I realize it's "House of the Rising Sun." My first reaction is fear . . . for Dylan. Experienced singers know that there are certain songs you don't cover because they're so identified with the original. That's why no one with half a brain tries to sing anything from Queen.

But my concern vanishes the moment he utters the first lyric. He's . . . dominating. That's the word that comes to mind. *Dominating.* Eric Burdon has nothing on him. Dylan surveys the audience as he sings, and when his eyes return to mine, as they do every few seconds, I feel myself flush.

Even before he's finished, the crowd has drowned him out. So completely, in fact, that I can't hear my own screaming voice.

"Thank you," he says, and then I see an almost imperceptible chuckle. Like he's surprised he's done as well as he has. It makes me fall for him that much more.

"I'm allowed to do one more song," he says. "I hope you like this one. It's also a throwback. From Queen."

When the bass starts, it sounds like that Vanilla Ice song, but then I realize it's "Under Pressure." The crowd is ahead of me, and they're even louder than before.

When he's done, Dylan literally jumps off the stage, without any of the basking that some people do. I say a silent prayer of thanks that I'm not following him. In fact, I pity whoever has to live up to that performance.

He returns to the bar stool, glistening in sweat. I have no idea what comes over me—the whiskey or my Cassidy persona taking over—but I immediately pull him into me and plant my lips on his. At first he seems surprised by my aggressiveness, but it isn't long into the kiss before I feel him taking control.

We make out for the better part of the next few sets. Like teenagers at the drive-in, but with the promise of more to follow. I've forgotten all about the stage, when my name—or rather Cassidy's—is called.

He breaks our embrace. "That's you," he says.

A moment later, I'm peering down at the crowd. When I catch Dylan's eye, he winks.

"I'm going to do a Donna Summer song," I say. "Hope you like it."

I shut my eyes, and in the darkness I'm alone. This is the moment I try to hold on to. After the first note, it all becomes a blur. Right before, when the entire room is silent for just a moment, it's pure bliss. That's the high I'm chasing every time I become Cassidy.

Twenty minutes later, after I've done "Bad Girls," followed by two up-tempo Blondie numbers—"Call Me" and "One Way or Another," which I probably wouldn't have even attempted but for Dylan's show of courage covering Queen—I close with "Love to Love You, Baby," which I sex up with utter abandon, even for Cassidy.

The crowd is roaring as loud as they were for Dylan, which is as loud as I've ever heard it at Lava. But the reviewer I most care about is sitting at the bar with a half-full glass of whiskey in front of him.

His critique comes in the form of a whisper in my ear.

"I need to be with you, right now," he says.

I'm not so drunk that I don't realize it's a line, but it hits the mark. I throw back the rest of his whiskey and say, "Let's go."

On the street, the air has a chill to it that I hadn't recalled from earlier. It feels exhilarating. We immediately resume our make-out session outside, interrupted only long enough for Dylan to flag down a cab. When we get in the back, I blurt out my address before Dylan can direct the driver to his place.

The cab ride is less than five minutes, during which our lips barely separate. We break the embrace long enough to make it into my building and up the stairs, but we go at it hot and heavy as soon as we get inside. I never even turn on the lights.

———

I fall asleep with Cassidy's reckless abandon, but awake a couple of hours later with Ella's thumping head and her dry throat. Dylan is already wearing his pants, tying his shoes, but is still bare-chested.

"Sorry I woke you," he says.

"Are you leaving?"

"Yeah. Unfortunately, I have early rounds."

"Okay," I say, trying to sound cool. Cassidy should be experienced with casual hookups, even if I'm not.

After he's dressed, Dylan leans over me as I lie in bed and kisses me good-bye. It brings back the rush I felt the night before, and as I watch him leave, I feel a dull ache inside. There's nothing I want more right then than for him to return to my bed.

After I hear my apartment door slam shut, I realize that my fantasy is not going to come true, at least not right now. I reach for my phone to check the time. I assume from the early light that it's barely six o'clock.

Even before verifying the hour, I feel dread.

My phone shows three missed calls from Zach.

I blink.

Charlotte's Zach.

There's no reason Charlotte's boyfriend would call me even once unless something was wrong. Three times can only mean catastrophe.

And then I remember that I haven't spoken to, or even heard from, Charlotte since we met at Tom's. That was more than thirty-six hours ago—too long a silence. Much too long.

I can't tell when Zach first began calling because my phone only registers the last of his calls. It came in at 4:15 a.m., at which time he left a voice mail message.

I hit the "Play" button.

"Sorry to bother you, Ella, but I'm not sure where Charlotte is and it's not like her to be out so late without telling me. If she's with you, or if you know where she is, can you ask her to call me? I don't care what time."

His last contact was at 4:52 a.m. A text:

Call me anytime. Important. Zach.

I call Charlotte. She might be screening Zach, but she'll pick up for me.

Only she doesn't. I hang up and call again. When the call goes to voice mail for the second time, I leave a message.

"Char, it's me. Zach called and said you didn't come home last night. Is anything wrong? I'm worried because I haven't heard from you since Tuesday. As soon as you get this message, call me. I don't care what time." I take a beat. "I love you, Char-bar."

I debate waiting for Charlotte to call back before returning Zach's call, but I already fear the worst. Besides, Zach sounded like he needed to hear from me. So after hanging up with Charlotte's voice mail, I call Zach.

He answers on the first ring.

"Ella," he says breathlessly. "Is Charlotte with you?"

"No. Did you guys have a fight or something?"

"No." Then he repeats it. "No."

"And you have no idea where she is?"

"No. And she's not answering her phone or texts."

"Are you sure she didn't say anything to you about where she was going tonight?"

"No," he says for the fourth time. "I expected her home for dinner. It's not like her to be out all night, and certainly not without telling me."

"Did you call the school?"

I already know the answer. Zach must have tried every possible place he could imagine Charlotte being before involving me.

"They didn't have any information and suggested I call the police."

"Did you? Call the police, I mean."

"Yeah. They told me I had to wait forty-eight hours."

"When did you last see her?"

He doesn't answer, at least not fast enough for my liking. It's incomprehensible to me that he doesn't know the exact moment he last saw his girlfriend, especially if he's supposedly been sitting up worrying about her.

Finally he says, "It was this morning. I mean, yesterday morning. *Wednesday* morning. I'm sorry, but I've been up all night. I left early for an audition yesterday morning, and she was still in bed."

"What about her friends? Did they see her yesterday?"

"I called Julia and Brooke. That was . . . I don't know, around midnight. They said that they hadn't seen her all day, but would ask around and call me back if anyone else had. That's the last I heard from them."

For a brief moment I consider involving my father, but he's the last person Charlotte would go to with a personal issue. He's also the last person I want to tell that she's missing.

"I'm sure she went out with someone, lost track of the time, and just decided to crash at their place," I say.

"Yeah, I guess that's right," says Zach.

———

Once, when Charlotte was little, maybe three or four, I convinced her that I could read her mind. I told her it was a power that all older sisters possessed. I had her going for a day before she figured out that I had no such ability.

How I wish I had it now.

In need of something to calm me, I put on a kettle of water. I know peppermint tea isn't the answer, but I pour myself a cup nonetheless.

And then I wait. For Charlotte to call and tell me she'd just come home and was fine. False alarm. She was out with a friend and decided to stay over. She'd told Zach, but like the idiot he was, he'd forgotten.

But deep down I know that's not going to happen.

DAY THREE

THURSDAY

7.

From my days in the District Attorney's office, I know that a large percentage of missing-persons cases involve children abducted by a noncustodial parent, and they're usually found unharmed. It's difficult to know how many of those cases factor into the overall stats in order to make a reasoned analysis concerning the likelihood that a twenty-five-year-old woman who vanishes without a trace will come home safe and sound.

The Internet adds nothing I didn't already know, and greatly increases my already-through-the-roof anxiety. The one constant in the online stories is the unwavering belief that the first hours are the most critical.

The cops may have told Zach that forty-eight hours have to pass before an investigation can begin, but Zach isn't a former Assistant District Attorney. I decide not to wait another minute more.

Despite the early hour, I call Lauren Wright on her cell.

Lauren is more than just my ex-boss, or even a mentor. She's the closest thing I have to a mother figure in my life. I met her just as I was beginning my professional career, and she took me under her wing from day one. I've always considered myself extremely fortunate in that regard, and right now it's an absolute godsend. There's no better friend to have when your sister's missing than the head of the DA office's Special Victim's Bureau.

Lauren answers on the fourth ring with a quizzical "Ella?"

It sounds as if I've woken her. But even groggy, Lauren knows that I'm not calling her at sunrise to make lunch plans.

"I'm sorry to call so early, but I'm afraid I need your help," I say. "And not just yours, but all the favors you can pull in for me." I realize as I'm saying it that she might think I'm calling about a case, so I quickly disabuse her of that notion. "My sister's missing. She's twenty-five and a student at NYU, in the MFA program for writers."

Aside from my father, Lauren is the smartest person I know. She's also a methodical thinker, unwilling to draw any conclusions while key facts remain unknown. Her hesitancy to indict sometimes made me crazy, but it had also prevented at least two innocent people from going to jail.

"How long has she been missing?" Lauren asks.

"All day and all night."

This is met with silence. I know what Lauren is thinking: that Charlotte hooked up with some guy and she'll stagger home any minute now.

"Believe me—I wouldn't have called you if I didn't think something was seriously wrong. My sister lives with her boyfriend and Charlotte just isn't the type to stay out all night without telling someone. Her boyfriend says he saw her yesterday morning, but I haven't heard from her since Tuesday afternoon. So that's almost forty-eight hours. I've left her several urgent messages and she hasn't responded. That's just not like her. We usually text constantly. She'd never go two days without contacting me unless she was physically unable to do so."

For the second time, dead air fills the phone. Now it's as troubling as anything Lauren could say. She's not the kind to tell me that everything's going to be fine when she sees evidence piling up on the other side of the scale.

"Please, Lauren. I'm begging you," I say, although I assume my desperation has already come through loud and clear.

"No need to beg, Ella. You know I'll do anything for you. As soon as I get off the phone, I'll start making some calls. Someone will get in touch directly with you within an hour or two. If they don't, call me back and I'll get the DA involved."

"Thank you so much. I can't even begin to tell you how appreciative I am."

"Let's just hope that my help isn't needed."

———

My father prides himself on being the first person at the office. He usually comes in before seven, even though the firm officially doesn't start its day until nine. His first secretary, Robin, arrives at seven, at which time he's already working, coffee cup in need of refilling beside him. His second secretary, LeeAnn, works the three-to-ten swing shift.

Today he answers his own phone even though it's a quarter past seven. Robin must be running late this morning, or fetching his coffee refill.

"Dad, it's me. I have some troubling news. Zach called me and said that Charlotte didn't come home last night and he's worried about her. I haven't heard from her in more than a day, and that's not like her. Have you spoken to her?"

Silence on the other end of the line. My father is many things, but contemplative is not one of them.

"Dad? Are you there?"

"Yeah . . . I'm here. Just trying to think. No, I haven't spoken to Charlotte since . . . I don't know, to tell you the truth. Certainly not yesterday. When did you say someone last spoke with her?"

"I had lunch with her on Tuesday. We usually speak at least once a day. It's now been two nights since I last heard from her."

"When did Zach last see her?"

"He said he saw her early yesterday morning."

"You say it like you don't believe him."

"I'm not sure that I do."

My disclosure is met with another long silence. Yesterday he suggested Jennifer Barnett might well be safe and sound even though she'd been missing for four days, but I'm certain that now he fears the worst has happened to Charlotte after less than two. But isn't that always the way it works? A thousand planes take off and land every day without incident, and yet the moment you're aboard, the risk of a crash hardly seems remote.

"I reached out to my old boss at the DA's office," I tell him. "She said she'd contact the proper person at the NYPD and try to get them to open an investigation."

I'm brought back more than a decade, to the aftermath of my mother's death. The feeling that I needed to care for him, to keep my father from being overwhelmed by grief.

"I'm sure it's going to be okay, Dad."

"Okay," he says. "Tell me as soon as you hear anything."

His voice has dropped an octave.

He clearly doesn't believe anything is ever going to be okay again.

——

Shortly before 9:00 a.m., the phone rings. My first thought is that maybe it's Charlotte, even though the caller ID flashes a number I don't recognize.

"Hello?" I say.

"Is this Ella Broden?" a man's voice asks.

"Yes."

"Hello, Ella. This is Gabriel Velasquez. Lauren Wright reached out and asked me to call you about your sister."

I owe Lauren a big thank-you. If I had my choice of everyone in the NYPD to handle the search for Charlotte, I would have selected

Gabriel Velasquez. And I say that notwithstanding our personal history. Five years ago—before Jeffrey—Gabriel and I went on a couple of dates, the last of which ended with a particularly good make-out session. But then I never returned any of his subsequent calls.

Gabriel and I have since overlapped on a few cases, and our interactions have always been strictly professional. He never referenced our past or asked why I blew him off. I've always assumed that was because he was more than smart enough to figure out that I had passed up something real with him because I was a snob who couldn't see myself ending up with a cop.

"I'm very sorry to hear about your situation," he continues. "I'm hopeful that this is a false alarm. But, as you know, the first hours are the most critical in any missing-persons case. So, just to be on the safe side, I don't want to waste another second. I'd like you and your sister's boyfriend to come down to One PP as soon as you can."

8.

One Police Plaza is a prime example of Brutalist architecture, a term I've always found ironic because the classification has nothing to do with its English meaning—it refers to the French word for concrete. This despite the truly "brutal" appearance of many such buildings. The police headquarters in New York City fits the English connotation to a T. It's like a fortress with windows punched into it, and is about as uninspiring as a public building could be.

"My name is Ella Broden and I'm here to see Gabriel Velasquez," I say to Ruth, the police receptionist.

She's a civilian, which means she's wearing regular street clothes. Ruth has got to be close to seventy, and I imagine she's been sitting behind that same table for more than half of her life. She looks at me without a hint of acknowledgment that I was once a fixture on the floor. Even my name doesn't seem to register.

"Please have a seat," she says. "Someone will be out to get you soon."

"Is Zachary Rawls here?"

"Who?"

"Zachary, or Zach, Rawls. I'm supposed to meet him here."

"Nobody else is here. Have a seat and someone will be out shortly."

The only place to have a seat is on one of two unpadded wooden chairs set out in the hallway. I do as directed and wait for Gabriel to appear.

As a prosecutor, you spend a lot of time dealing with cops. And while I'm rather outspoken on the topic that the way attorneys are portrayed on television is nothing like real life, cop shows are even worse. For starters, people with 150 IQs or photographic memories rarely choose a career in law enforcement. Another thing is that real-life detectives don't look like movie stars. By and large, they're middle-aged men who haven't seen the inside of a gym in some time.

The one exception that I've encountered to that latter rule is Gabriel Velasquez. The female DAs call him "TDH"—tall, dark, and handsome. Gabriel—no one ever called him Gabe—is not only easy on the eyes, but also sharp as a tack. Many of the cops I worked with had street smarts, but most of them lack the candlepower to become lawyers or college professors. Gabriel undoubtedly had those types of choices, and I suspect he went into law enforcement because he sincerely thought it was the place where he could make the biggest difference.

We worked together on my first murder case, which, as it happened, was also the first case where he was lead detective. It was hardly a whodunit. A rich doctor beat his wife to death with a golf club and then claimed self-defense, putting a kitchen knife in her hand hours after she'd been killed. The husband stuck to that story on the stand—despite the fact that the ME testified that rigor mortis had already begun to set in when the wife's fingers were folded over the knife's handle—and the defense couldn't find an expert to testify to the contrary even though price was no object. The jury deliberated for less than an hour before coming back with a guilty verdict. Five minutes after that, Gabriel asked me out.

He looks even better today than I remember. In addition to all his easy-on-the-eyes physical attributes, Gabriel is also a good dresser. Not flashy, but stylish. More like an architect than a cop, usually favoring monochromatic combinations. Today, he's attired in gray slacks and a slightly darker gray button-down shirt. His badge hangs on a chain around his neck. Lots of cops wear their shields that way, but I always thought Gabriel did it with greater flair.

After we shake hands, Gabriel says that it's good to see me again and once again apologizes for the circumstances. When he asks me to follow him back to his office, I try not to show too much surprise at the fact that he even has an office. The plaque on his door indicates that he's been promoted since we last worked together. It's Lieutenant Velasquez now.

"I know that even though you've seen this process from the law enforcement side, it's not the same as when it's family," Gabriel says as he closes the door. He then takes a seat behind the desk and gestures for me to sit as well. "So I'm going to treat you as if you aren't my favorite former ADA, but the sister of a woman who's gone missing and fears the worst. Okay?"

I smile at his compliment. Anybody else might hold our past against me, but Gabriel is above that. It further proves just how much of an idiot I was five years ago for not returning his calls.

"That's what I want too."

"Good," he says with a smile of his own. "Obviously, we all hope that this is a case where your sister went home with someone, maybe had a little too much to drink, and is now sleeping it off. I know you're worried that it's something else, and so for purposes of the investigation I'm going to assume that as well. That means we're going to treat this as a missing-persons case from the get-go, so as not to lose any time. The first order of business is for me to learn everything I can about your sister. And it's got to be warts and all, because it's the warts that are going to help us find her."

I had been thinking about how to answer this very question on my cab ride over to One PP. What would they need to know? How could I distill Charlotte's essence into words?

"Charlotte's twenty-five and a graduate student in creative writing at NYU," I begin. "She lives uptown, at One Hundred and Eighth and Riverside. She has a boyfriend named Zach. Zachary Rawls. They've been living together for a year, probably a little less than that. He's an actor. Of course, that really means he's unemployed. The last time my sister and I discussed Zach, which was a few weeks ago, she said she was thinking about ending things with him, but I don't know if she ever said anything to him about that. I guess I should say that my sister and I are very close. Even though she's six years younger, we're really best friends. We talk or text multiple times a day, every day. The last time I saw her was Tuesday. We had lunch at Tom's Diner, at One-Twelfth and Broadway. Actually, that's not right. We met to have lunch, but I got called back to the office before our food arrived. The reason she wanted to meet was because she had this exciting news—that her first novel was going to be published and she wanted me to be the first person she told. I normally would have heard from her that night, but I didn't. Then the next day I got caught up in something and didn't focus on the fact that I hadn't spoken to her all day. That was yesterday. I spoke to Zach this morning, at around six. That's when he told me Charlotte didn't come home last night."

Gabriel nods as I give him this download, careful not to interrupt. Standard police intake procedure.

"Okay," he says when I come up for air. "It's good that you're close with your sister; that will help us. And that's important information about the boyfriend too. Let me start with the obvious question. Did she have any enemies? Anyone who might want to hurt her?"

"No. Everyone loved her." He smiles, and although I'm sure he didn't mean for me to take it this way, it strikes me that he doesn't believe me. "Seriously. Ask anyone."

"I believe you, Ella. So, if there weren't any enemies, what about other men aside from the boyfriend?"

"No one," I say with conviction, but as the words come out, I realize that I might not know if she was cheating on Zach. After all, I wasn't going to share with her my night with Dylan Perry, although in that case it wasn't because I was embarrassed, but so as to not reveal my life as Cassidy. But perhaps the point is still the same. No matter how close Charlotte and I were . . . are . . . we still probably keep secrets from each other.

"You know, I don't think there was anyone else, but who really knows what people choose to tell you about themselves? Especially family. I guess it's possible she'd keep that kind of thing to herself."

"Fair enough," he says. "Any exes that I should be aware of?"

"No. I mean, she had boyfriends from time to time, but she's been with Zach for more than a year, and she was single when they met. So I can't imagine anyone from her past coming back now to harm her."

In a matter of seconds, I've ruled out everyone but Zach. Could he have hurt Charlotte? She had shared with me that Zach had a hair-trigger temper, but she'd never even hinted that he'd gotten physical with her. Although, now in hindsight, maybe her reference to his volatility was that hint and I didn't pick up on it.

"Now you said it's been *two* nights since you've heard from your sister?"

"Yeah, but Zach—her boyfriend—didn't call me until early this morning."

"I know, but you think it's odd you didn't hear from her all day yesterday, right?"

Gabriel has latched on to my suspicion that Zach might not be an ally in the search for Charlotte. The boyfriend is always the first suspect, so I'm sure he was heading there even without my help. Still, I'm glad we're on the same page.

"Yeah. And I didn't speak to her the night before that either. Our last conversation was in person, on Tuesday. Two-fifteen or so. Usually we communicate every day. Multiple times. Without fail."

"So the fact that she didn't reach out to you Tuesday night could mean she was involved in something intense, and that could be relevant to her disappearance."

The phone rings. Gabriel answers by barking his last name into the receiver. Then, "Yeah, I'll be right out to get him."

"Zachary's here," he says to me in a softer tone than he'd used on the phone. "It's best if I talk to him alone. Then I'll ask him to step out, and I'll fill you in about the next steps. Sound good?"

"Sure," I say, although nothing sounds good right now.

———

Zach is sitting in the same wooden chair in the hallway outside of Gabriel's office that I'd previously occupied. When I approach, he stands and embraces me—which has to be the first time he's ever done that.

Standing behind me, Gabriel extends his hand to Zach.

"Mr. Rawls, I'm Gabriel Velasquez. I'm very sorry we have to meet like this, but I greatly appreciate you coming in. I've already spoken to Ella, so why don't you and I spend a little time together?"

I look for some tell of surprise from Gabriel that Zach is African American. If Zach's race was not what Gabriel was expecting, he doesn't show it.

Gabriel leads Zach back down the hallway, and I replace Zach in the wooden chair. As soon as they retreat into Gabriel's office, I begin to cry.

———

Zach's with Gabriel for an hour. When the office door finally swings open, Zach exits and then proceeds to walk right by me. No hug. Not even a good-bye. He wants to get out of the building as fast as possible.

Gabriel is a step behind him. "Come in," he says to me.

I'm literally shaking, holding my hands together so as not to show it, as I wait for Gabriel to tell me what Zach had said. I knew he hadn't confessed because if he had, they would have arrested him. But something must have happened, or Zach wouldn't have fled the building like it was on fire.

The time it takes to reenter Gabriel's office is less than thirty seconds, but feels interminable. Fortunately, he gets to the point right away.

"The interview did not go well," Gabriel says. "Zach's scared, which is understandable. I mean, everyone knows that the boyfriend is the first and sometimes only suspect in these types of things. Most people in his position, if they've got half a brain, shut us down. But I got the distinct impression that he's hiding something, and that means we'll be focusing a lot of attention in his direction."

"What did he say?"

"It's more what he *didn't* say. It started off fine. He said everything was good between him and your sister. No recent fights. No talk of breakup. The last time he saw your sister was yesterday morning. He claimed she was still asleep when he left for the day, and places the time at around eight thirty a.m. But when I asked him to account for his whereabouts on Tuesday, he started getting cagey. So I asked if he'd be willing to take a polygraph. He said something about how he thought they were unreliable. I told him that they were inadmissible in court but that as a law-enforcement technique we find them useful because if he passes, we'd know not to question anything he's telling us."

"He refused to take the polygraph?" I ask.

"Not exactly. He said he wanted to think about it. He said the same thing with regard to whether he'd consent to a search of their home."

"He's on his way home now to scrub the place clean, that asshole."

"Maybe. On the other hand, he's been in the apartment alone for enough time already that if there was something incriminating there, I'm relatively certain he's smart enough to have gotten rid of it by now."

"Why do you even need his consent? My father bought the apartment for my sister. Zach's name isn't on any lease. It's her apartment, not his."

Gabriel smiles at me. "Assistant District Attorney Ella Broden would rip me a new one if I searched someone's home without a warrant on the technicality that his name wasn't on a lease. It's Zach's home too, right? He doesn't live anywhere else? That means we can't go in without a warrant."

I'm thinking like a family member. Gabriel's right: there's no way to get a warrant to search through Zach's belongings based on the present facts. One night missing doesn't even create the probability of a crime, and a boyfriend's refusal to take a poly or consent to a home search doesn't even come close to meeting the probable-cause standard necessary for the issuance of a warrant. Plenty of innocent people don't like being hooked up to a machine and asked personal questions about their relationships, or to have the police rummage through their underwear drawers.

"Just because we can't search her home doesn't mean we're stuck," Gabriel continues. "I may be able to convince a judge to issue a warrant for your sister's e-mails and cell phone. That might help us trace her movements."

"Okay," I say. "Please tell me if that leads you to anything."

"I will," Gabriel says.

———

Gabriel walks me back to the elevator. I'm able to maintain a veneer of calm, but inside I realize that a seismic shift has occurred. I arrived thinking that the police might be able to find Charlotte and bring her back to us. Nothing Gabriel said indicated otherwise, but I could see it in his eyes. A happy ending is very unlikely.

9.

Standing out in the plaza in front of One PP, amid a throng of pedestrians, I begin to break down again. I don't even try to stanch the flow of tears. Instead I let the emotion crash over me like ocean waves in the surf. I imagine them just like that, considering the relief that would follow if I succumbed to the grief and let the water sweep me out to sea.

My father's call wakes me from this escapist fantasy. I pull myself together as best I can before answering.

"Hi, Dad."

"Hi, sweetheart. Everything going okay down there?"

"I just met with the detective running the investigation. I know him and he's really the best they have, so that's good."

I'm about to explain to him that Zach isn't cooperating when he interrupts me.

"I had a thought and I wanted to raise it with you because . . . well, my whole strategy with Garkov for these past few years has been to delay so he can continue living under house arrest in that palace of his. And now with Charlotte missing, the trial will have to be delayed, despite Judge Koletsky's dictate that we pick a jury next week. Garkov couldn't have asked for a better gift."

That, in a nutshell, is the problem with representing sociopaths. They'll do anything to protect themselves, including turning on their lawyers. I know from my father, and from the press coverage, that

Garkov had already blackmailed his prior lawyer and the original judge presiding over his case. So kidnapping his current lawyer's daughter to gain another year's delay would be consistent with his modus operandi.

"I don't think we're in a position to rule anything out, Dad. I'll mention to Lieutenant Velasquez that he should talk to Garkov too."

"Don't do that," my father says quickly.

He's using his lawyer voice, assertive and confident. I haven't heard it since I told him about Charlotte's disappearance.

"I'm still Garkov's lawyer, and . . . as crazy as this sounds, I'd never let him talk to the police about the disappearance of a young woman. Besides, even if I told him to do it now, he's got a dozen other lawyers who will tell him not to. The better way is for me to talk to him. On second thought, you should come too. I'll tell him that the conversation will still be subject to the attorney–client privilege so we can't share it with anyone."

I'm certain my father knows that the privilege permits disclosing attorney–client communications to prevent the commission of a violent crime. Hopefully Garkov isn't so informed.

———

One of the advantages of having a client under house arrest is that he's always available to meet with you. As a result, less than an hour after I get off the phone with my father, the two of us are met at the door of Garkov's apartment by a butler wearing a morning suit. He leads us to what he refers to as the *formal* living room, allowing for the fact that there are others that are less grand.

Nicolai Garkov is already standing when we enter, and the scene reminds me a little bit of when Anthony Hopkins first met Jodie Foster in *Silence of the Lambs*—how he seemed to sense our presence. I thought I was prepared for meeting Garkov because I'd seen him in photographs and knew he was a freakishly tall, blond Russian terrorist. Nonetheless, experiencing him was much different than reading about him.

His hair is yellow straw, and his eyes are an almost iridescent blue. He's so tall that my father and I look like children beside him, barely coming up to his waist. And he's clad in a purple velvet bathrobe that falls to midknee, channeling Hugh Hefner in his heyday.

The room we're in is indeed formal. It's at least thirty feet long, with views on all sides that rival those from our office. Six armchairs in an embroidered red-and-gold jacquard float on an enormous Persian rug, and every fixture is gilded.

"Welcome," Garkov says. "Please, sit."

He has only the subtlest trace of an accent, but what comes through most in his first words is that Nicolai Garkov is ice cold. It's as if he has read about human emotions but never experienced one firsthand.

If my father thinks that Nicolai Garkov is behind the disappearance of his youngest daughter, he doesn't betray it. He looks like I've seen him countless times, the very picture of learned legal counsel.

"Nicolai, this is my eldest daughter, Ella," he says. "I believe I've mentioned that she recently joined my firm."

"Yes. So nice to meet you, Ella. Your father has spoken about you so often I feel like we've already met."

My father continues. "The reason I'm here is to let you know that I'm going to ask Judge Koletsky for an adjournment of the trial."

My eyes are fixed on Garkov, looking for some evidence that he already knew his trial would be postponed. He gives me nothing. Not a twitch or even a blink.

My preoccupation with reading Garkov has caused me to ignore my father's distress. He has begun to choke up, although I don't realize it until it occurs to me that he hasn't yet explained to Garkov *why* he needs to postpone the trial. When I finally turn to my father, he's cradling his head.

I reach over to take my father's hand. He makes contact with me but doesn't allow me to get a grip. Instead he straightens, ready to take charge of the meeting again.

"Nicolai, I have something very serious to discuss with you," he says, his voice now trembling. "We've known each other a very long time, and I think you know all that I've done for you. Now I'm asking for a favor from you."

"Of course," Garkov says. "Anything."

"My youngest daughter, Charlotte, has gone missing. She's twenty-five years old and was last seen yesterday morning. The police are now investigating. As you can imagine, I'm currently in no mental state to begin a trial."

"My . . . I'm sorry, sometimes my English fails me. *Condolences* is not the proper word . . . so let me say that I pray for you, Clint, that your daughter returns unharmed."

"Yes. Thank you, Nicolai. We are praying for that too. But my daughter . . . she's the kindest person on this earth. It is hard to fathom that anyone would benefit in the least by harming her. But it did occur to me that you were hoping very much for a further delay of your trial, and now, because of this tragedy in my family, you're going to get it."

Nicolai Garkov remains a study in repose. He has just been accused of kidnapping—or murdering—his lawyer's daughter for no other purpose than to delay the inevitable, yet he hasn't flinched.

"Mr. Garkov," I say, "because I'm a partner at the law firm, my father has filled me in about your case, all of it of course subject to the attorney–client privilege. I'm also aware of the issues that caused your prior counsel to withdraw, and so I know that you'll go to extremes to get what you want."

He doesn't offer a word of protest. Nor does his expression change in the least. It's as if he's confirming what I've just said.

"Given that, I'm sure you can appreciate why it has occurred to us that *you* might be involved in Charlotte's disappearance. And if you are—I know I speak for my father, when I say that the only thing we care about is getting my sister back home. So please tell us. There will be no repercussions to you. My father will request the continuance either way, and we'd be disbarred if we ever revealed what you tell us. We just need to get Charlotte back."

My father's eyes start to moisten again. He wipes at them with the back of his hand.

"As one father to another," my father says slowly, "I'm begging you, Nicolai. All I care about is my daughter's safety. If you have anything to do with this, please, for the love of God, tell me. It won't leave this room. I swear it."

Garkov still doesn't outwardly display any reaction. He looks at me impassively before turning back to my father. Then, in a measured tone, he says, "I understand how this type of uncertainty can make you desperate, which is why I am not in the least offended by the accusation. But I swear to you, on the lives of my own children, I do not know anything about the disappearance of your daughter. If I did, I'd not only tell you, but I'd make it my business to make whoever was responsible pay, and pay dearly, for hurting your family."

My father looks at me. His eyes are still watery, and it triggers a similar response in me. He's silently asking whether I believe Garkov.

In truth, I don't so much believe that Garkov isn't behind Charlotte's disappearance as I am convinced that we'll never find out if he is. Given that the purpose of this meeting was to beg Garkov to return Charlotte, it's now clear to me that our pilgrimage was a waste of time. Nothing is gained by making an emotional appeal to a man who lacks a soul.

"Thank you, Mr. Garkov," I say. "As my father said, we're going to seek an adjournment of your trial. If you'd prefer to retain someone else, we would understand."

For the first time, Nicolai Garkov changes his expression. A thin smile now comes across his lips.

"Not at all. I'm willing to wait for Clint to be ready. No matter how long that takes."

———

At least during the day I had distractions. Back in my apartment that evening, I'm alone. After my mother died, my father immediately left for this big trial out in Dallas, and at the time I was furious at him for not postponing it. But now I understand. He needed to focus his mind on something else.

God, how I miss Charlotte. I'd give anything to talk to her.

Then I remember. Even if I can't talk to her, she can still talk to me. Clad in my pajamas, I go to my bag, pull out the loose-leaf binder containing her half-completed manuscript, and settle into the sofa to read.

DEAD CERTAIN

A NOVEL

BY

CHARLOTTE BRODEN

For my sister, Ella, because . . . because

CHAPTER ONE

Even in the beginning, I wondered about the end. I could envision only two outcomes, with nothing in between: happily-ever-after with a man I love, or my entire world blown to hell.

I've had half a dozen relationships that have lasted more than a handful of dates, and until recently I never found being monogamous to be any great feat. But in the last few months, I've had to compartmentalize my love life. Marco, an artist, is my boyfriend; Jason, a student in the musical-theater class for which I serve as a teaching assistant, loves me with the reckless abandon of someone who has never had his heart broken; and I've fallen head over heels for Matthew, a banker, who is married and but for that small detail would be reason enough for me to jettison the others.

As lovers, my three men could not be more different. Marco has the same selfishness in bed that he carries with him in everyday life. I dare say the loneliest I ever feel is when Marco's inside me. It's as if I don't matter at all as he grunts toward his own pleasure.

Jason wants to learn, and so he follows my lead in all ways. I can envision some woman in the future thanking me for making Jason the lover he will become, but I don't see myself ever saying that. He's a work in progress and won't be completed until well after we're over.

Matthew's a perfectionist in all things. I imagine he's dedicated himself to his sexual technique the same way he told me how he worked on his golf swing or his Mandarin. As with everything else he's attempted, Matthew is a master of his craft.

Like owning two dogs, two affairs aren't much more trouble than one. In my case, juggling three men wasn't difficult at all. All it took to keep Marco in the dark was to tell him that I was in rehearsal. He knows from prior times when I actually was prepping for a performance that it requires me to be at school until the early hours and unreachable, which means I can be anywhere, at any time, without giving rise to suspicion. And the truth is that MFA vocal students are always in rehearsal, but rarely do we perform for the public, so it's a perfect alibi.

Jason doesn't know there's anyone else in my life. I told him that I needed to keep our relationship a secret because it violates the school's policies, which prohibit sexual relations between students and teaching assistants. That was good enough for him.

Matthew knows about Marco, but he's hardly in any position to complain that I share my bed with another man, given that he's married. He doesn't know about Jason, however. He likes the idea of cuckolding Marco, but if he knew I was comparing his sexual prowess to a twenty-one-year-old's, I suspect that would be a different kettle of fish.

My venture, as the Eagles so aptly put it, to the cheating side of town, began in, of all places, a museum. I was at one of these benefits for the arts that the university makes grad students attend, staring at an out-of-focus photo of a topless woman, when Matthew walked up beside me and cocked his head at the blurry picture.

"I couldn't already be this drunk, could I?" he said.

He was wearing torn jeans and a sweater with a leather jacket over it—and sporting a few days of scruff. I thought he might be an associate professor in the theater department, as he had that leading-man, "alpha" vibe about him. He was very handsome. Tall, sharp-featured, with a Roman nose and dark, curly hair.

"I think it's the photographer who had a little too much," I said.

"*Good. For a minute, I thought I might be having a seizure. My name is Matthew.*"

His stare froze me in his orbit. So intense that it blocked out everything else in my line of vision.

"*Clare,*" *I said.*

"*So, are you an artist?*" *he asked.*

"*A singer, actually. And you?*"

"*Oh no.*" *He chuckled. "My only connection to the arts is as a lover of great beauty . . ."*

Afterward, I told myself that it was just one of those things that happen, but I knew from the first words out of Matthew's mouth that his goal was to get me into bed. When I chose to keep talking to him about the photo, it was because that's what I wanted too, which explains how we ended up at the Four Seasons hotel later that night.

Of course, I knew that his taking me to a hotel meant he was, at the very least, in a relationship. During our second rendezvous, which took place a few days later, I learned he was married. At a different point in my life, that would have been a deal-breaker, but at the time, I found it something of a selling point. After all, I had a live-in boyfriend, and Matthew's being attached meant the boundary lines of our relationship would be clearly demarcated.

Our normal routine is to meet on Tuesdays, a day that Matthew chose. I don't know why he favors it. Probably because his wife is out that night, although he's never said that to me. I imagine she takes a class. French cooking, maybe. Or a foreign language. Italian, if I had to guess.

Our sessions are normally three-act affairs. Then, as if he has an internal clock, at eleven he leans over to the nightstand to check his watch. It's a Patek Philippe chronograph, because of course Matthew wears a $50,000 timepiece. Then he showers and is usually out the door by 11:15, 11:30 at the latest. I assume that's because he has a midnight curfew. He always suggests that I stay the night and order room service for breakfast, even though he knows full well that someone is waiting for me at home too. The moment Matthew leaves, I shower and am back in my apartment by midnight.

Sometimes I add up the hours Matthew and I have been together. Six hours a week, four weeks. Twenty-four hours. Less time than Marco and I spend together every weekend, and yet the two time spans bear no similarity beyond the quantitative.

Matthew and I are completely consumed with each other during every second we're together. We're either having sex or talking after sex, which is just as intimate an activity. Sometimes we talk about our lives, the meaning of love, mistakes we wish we could correct. But other times it's light—movies, television, music, and books. It's not uncommon for him to have read something I've mentioned from the week before. Or he'll binge-watch some television show I was already midway through so we can discuss the most recent episode.

As much as I acknowledge that I'm a romantic, I'm not totally without self-awareness. I know Matthew and I exist outside the rules of the real world, where the monotony of daily existence can overwhelm even the strongest relationships. But I liken our affair to being on vacation. You might laugh a little more and have better sex than you do when you're home, but if all you do is have great sex and laugh, that's got to bode well for your life back in reality too.

If I were halfway normal, I would find one affair—with my soul mate—to be enough complication in my life. But two months ago, Jason appeared during my office hours to discuss the progress he was making on a term paper. I hadn't really noticed him in class up to that point. He's attractive enough, tall and lanky, with sandy hair, a pleasant smile, and kind eyes, but nothing about him—looks or personality—is particularly memorable. He's the very epitome of the kind of guy who blends into the background.

He was my last appointment of the day, and I surprised myself when I suggested that we continue our discussion about the finer points of Rodgers and Hammerstein at the Starbucks on MacDougal. After coffee came dinner at some taco place, with a pitcher of frozen margaritas that reminded me of my own undergraduate days. Two hours later, we were back at his place.

Jason is in love. And not just a little bit either. It's the whole "I worship the ground you walk on; I'll die if I'm without you" kind of love. It's sweet, but also sad. It can only end badly for him. In fact, if he weren't so far gone, I would have ended things after the second or third encounter.

I haven't only because it's easier to continue seeing him than to have to deal with the fallout of a messy breakup. Besides his tears, I fear the possibility of my expulsion from the university if he tells anyone about our affair—a sexual relationship between a teaching assistant and a student is strictly prohibited.

Finally, there's Marco, my boyfriend as far as the world is concerned. He's an artist and a painter, but not the starving type. His relationship with me sees to that, as I'm the youngest daughter of a very successful criminal-defense attorney.

When we met, Marco seemed larger than life to me. He overflowed with confidence at a time when I didn't think I did anything right, and when he declared that we were meant for each other, I was in no position to disagree.

Back then, he lived with his girlfriend, Belinda. She was about as different from me as I could have imagined—a mousy Latina who worked as a waitress. But she had an apartment, which in hindsight must have been what attracted Marco to her. Marco and I were seeing each other on the sly for about two months when Belinda caught wind of Marco's cheating, and that's when he showed up on my doorstep with all his worldly possessions in a beat-up duffel bag.

In the time we've been together, I've had cause to wonder whether anything Marco ever says to me is true. Starting at the beginning. I don't even know whether Belinda actually found out about us and threw him out, or Marco decided to trade up in terms of living space and played on my guilt. I do remember that he originally said the move would be for a few weeks only, but he never lifted a finger to find a new place.

It hasn't been all bad, of course. I've learned from Marco about passion for your craft, and at his best he can be thoughtful and sometimes even kind.

But at other times he can be cruel and unforgiving. In those moments, the danger I'm courting comes to the forefront.

As I said, there was a time when I was consumed with wondering how this melodrama I'd written for myself would conclude. The only silver lining in all that has happened is that I no longer obsess about that.

I know how it ends.

It concludes with my death. A particularly gruesome murder, I'm afraid.

DAY FOUR

FRIDAY

10.

News of my sister's disappearance broke at two yesterday. I was determined to avoid the media onslaught, which required that I spend the rest of the day inside and away from my computer, social media, and the television.

Nearly every day the front pages of the tabloids blare with a horrific headline. A toddler killed by a ricochet, a fire that takes the lives of multiple people, an elderly woman raped and beaten for her social-security check. I rarely give those stories a second thought, never considering the lives of the families that have been forever altered or the tragedy of the victims' lives being cut short.

Today it's Charlotte's photograph on the front page. My father and I are the people whose lives have been forever altered. Hers is the life tragically left unfinished.

I flag a taxi and tell the driver that I'm going to One Police Plaza. As we start to move, I turn off the taxi TV to insulate myself from the media. My plan is thwarted because the driver is listening to the all-news radio station.

"Can you turn that off?" I request. "Or put on some music?"

He nods. "Very upsetting. That poor girl."

———

The police have scheduled a press conference for noon. The idea is to bring the public into the search for Charlotte.

I arrive at One PP at eleven. It's immediately apparent that something is happening. There's a frenzy of activity, with people running through the halls and yelling out short phrases to one another. "I'm on it!" or "Not yet!" or "Let's hope!"

My stomach tightens. The one thing I can discern from the commotion is that whatever has occurred, it isn't good.

"What's going on?" I ask Ruth the receptionist.

"I'm not at liberty to say," she says without making eye contact.

I wait in the wooden chair for Gabriel for the next five minutes, convinced that the delay is because he's thinking of a way to tell me that they've found Charlotte's body. Why else would he make me wait?

He's smiling when he approaches, however. I take that as a good sign, but just as quickly convince myself that this could be Gabriel's demeanor when breaking bad news.

"Come. Let's talk in my office," he says.

My legs are wobbly as I follow him down the hall. Inside his office, I take a seat in his guest chair. He shuts the door behind me and then assumes his position behind the desk. I can feel my heart beat so loudly that I fear it might break out of my chest if he doesn't just tell me already.

He doesn't say anything, however. It's as if he's searching for the words.

I can't wait any longer. "Is there any news about Charlotte?"

"No," he says, looking confused. "I would have told you if there had been any developments. You asked for this meeting, Ella. I thought *you* had something to tell me."

I'm such an idiot. I did ask to see him in advance of the press conference. His silence wasn't about working up the courage to share tragic news—he was waiting for me to get to the point.

"Right. The reason I wanted to see you is because when I last saw Charlotte, she told me that she'd just sold her first novel." I reach down into my briefcase to pull out the loose-leaf binder. "She gave it to me last Tuesday, and I finally read it last night. I don't know how much of it is truly fiction and how much is based on her own life, but the main character is named Clare, which is Charlotte's middle name, and she's a graduate student studying music, which isn't that much of a stretch from Charlotte's actual life as a graduate student studying creative writing. And in the book, she's murdered."

Gabriel sits up straighter and then reaches across his desk to take the binder out of my hand. When it's within his grasp, he skims the pages. "Who's the killer?"

"It's . . . it's frankly unclear in the book. She's written only the first half or so, and it ends in a bit of a cliff-hanger. But in addition to the character who's a stand-in for my sister, there's one pretty clearly based on Charlotte's boyfriend, Zach. He's called Marco in the book, and she paints a picture of the relationship that's abusive. There are also two other men that Charlotte's character—Clare—is involved with. The first is a Wall Street banker she calls Matthew. The second is an undergraduate student named Jason, who's in a class that Clare TA's. I don't know if either of those people existed in Charlotte's real life, but she was the teaching assistant in some creative writing class at NYU. Did you find anything in her phone messages or e-mails that's consistent with her being involved with other men? Specifically a student or a banker?"

He gets up from his chair and pulls a banker's box off the floor, then drops it on the desk between us. After flipping through the manila folders, he yanks out a file toward the back.

"These are her phone records," Gabriel says. "We've been through them, cross-referencing to people." He turns a few pages before stopping at what I assume is a summary, based on the fact that it appears to be some type of chart. "There are a bunch of phone calls to and from what we think are prepaid phones. Your sister's a student, and that's not uncommon in their world. We've called the numbers, but no one's answering. That could just mean that the minutes were exhausted."

"In the book, the Wall Streeter, the guy Charlotte calls Matthew, he uses a burner phone to communicate with her because he's married," I say.

Gabriel nods. "That's another big market for prepaid phones. We call the users PMS—poor, married, or students."

I'd done enough burner-phone cases to know that the incoming calls to Charlotte were going to wind up being a dead end. People use burners precisely because they're untraceable. Sometimes you get lucky and the phone is activated where it was purchased, but cheating husbands always pay in cash, so there's never a credit card connected to the purchase. Then you're left flashing photos at the store owner in the hope that he can remember the customer. In this case, even that wouldn't help because we didn't have anyone's picture to flash besides Zach's—and there was no reason for him to call Charlotte from a prepaid phone.

"What about texts or e-mails?" I ask.

"Without having the phone—which we don't, and Zach is claiming that it's not in the apartment—we can't get texts. The iPhone finder shows the phone isn't on, which means all we have to go on is the list of incoming and outgoing calls. And as for e-mails, it's just school-related stuff. Certainly nothing that indicated a romantic relationship or threats or anything of that nature."

This was even worse than I'd expected. Roadblocks at every turn.

"Do you mind if I take a look? I may recognize some of the numbers."

He hands me the folder. The dates are from this month. My number appears by far the most frequently—almost half of the calls Charlotte made and received. The others I don't recognize at all, except for Zach's. He called infrequently. Even on Tuesday night into Wednesday morning—when he was supposedly frantic because Charlotte wasn't home—his phone number appears a grand total of three times. In other words, he called just enough to *look* like he was worried. And on the day before, Monday, not even once.

"Were you able to get the search warrant for the apartment?" I ask.

I know that's going to be another dead end. If Gabriel had searched the place, he would have told me that by now.

"We tried, but no dice. We told the judge that the family is worried, and dropped yours and your father's names. I think that's the only reason we got access to the e-mails and phone records, to be honest with you. Unfortunately, the judge drew the line at letting us rifle through Zach's stuff or his phone or computer without more proof that a crime has actually occurred. The more time that goes by, the more compelling our argument is that your sister is a victim of foul play. We'll get the warrant eventually."

Time. The one thing we didn't have.

I'm quickly losing any hope of a happy ending. Charlotte must be dead . . . or worse, being held captive somewhere. That's the only explanation.

As if he can sense my despair, Gabriel says, "Stay positive, okay? This is very important stuff you're telling me about the book, and it's going to be a big help in finding your sister. We'll take a look at the students in the class, and also keep an eye out for anyone in her life that seems to be a banker type. For the time being, though, let's keep the manuscript between us, okay? I don't want anyone else knowing it exists."

I'm about to ask him why when our meeting is interrupted by a knock at the door. The man who opens it is another detective wearing his badge on a chain around his neck. He has the look of a retired football player. Beefy and not too bright.

"Hey, Jim, you remember Ella Broden, don't you?" Gabriel says.

He looks at me with a hint of recognition, but not much more. I can't place his face at all.

"Hi," he says, and extends his hand. "Jim McCorry. Nice to meet you." Then he looks back to Gabriel. "Can I talk to you for a second?"

"I can step out," I say.

"No, you stay," Gabriel answers, already getting up. "I won't be long."

I'm only by myself for a few minutes, but it feels like hours. In my head, Jim McCorry is telling Gabriel my worst fears about Charlotte have been realized.

"It wasn't about your sister," Gabriel says as soon as he returns to the office. "I feel like I need to say that every time I see you or you're going to jump out of your skin."

"Sorry. But that *was* what I was thinking."

"There was a break in the Jennifer Barnett case," he says.

I'm careful not to reveal that we have a client involved in the Barnett investigation. Not only because such a disclosure would be a violation of the attorney–client privilege, but because I'm ashamed that we're representing Paul. Here I am begging Gabriel to find Charlotte while at the same time I'm ready, willing, and able to do what I can to thwart him from finding Jennifer Barnett if it's in my client's interest.

"Do you think that the Jennifer Barnett case is connected to my sister's?"

His expression makes clear that he's been expecting this question.

"We haven't seen any evidence that Jennifer Barnett knew your sister or that they had any friends, or even acquaintances, in common. But it's quite the anomaly. Two young, white women of means being abducted in Manhattan within days of each other. It goes without saying that we're not making any public statement about the possibility that they're linked. The very last thing we want is a panic that twenty-something women are at risk of being abducted. So at the press conference I'm just going to say that we have no reason to believe that there's any connection. And that's the truth. But as you're not just a family member, but also someone who knows how things are in the real world, I want you to know that we're looking into that possibility."

I say a silent prayer that Jennifer Barnett's disappearance is not related to Charlotte's, and that, like Gabriel said, it is just a horrible coincidence. The only alternative is that the same man did this—a man who likely had no connection to either of them. That would almost certainly mean they're both dead.

11.

My father unabashedly tries his cases in the press. So much so that he often claims his best opening statements have been made on the courthouse steps. The impromptu press conferences he holds there are designed to win over the jury, even when they won't actually be selected for another year or more. His hope is that by the time they are actually seated in the jury box, he's already won their hearts and minds through the media. Prosecutors play that game too, but according to my father they're pikers compared to him. He says their press conferences lack the pizzazz of a catchy sound bite, and so even when they make the news, no one remembers a word that was said the next day—much less months later when the trial begins.

In the DA press conferences I used to attend, I would stand off to the side, usually just out of the camera's lens. The speaking was handled by the DA himself, or Lauren Wright, in the rare instance that the DA decided someone who actually knew something about the case was better able to provide information to the press. My one and only star turn occurred when Lauren got a question she couldn't answer and she called on me to respond. I stepped up to the microphone and said, "At this time, we have no evidence supporting that theory."

For the press conference about my sister's disappearance, more than a hundred reporters are in attendance. That's more than sat through the last briefing about Jennifer Barnett. An ordinary missing-persons case might only attract four or five, if that many, and that assumes the police even hold a press conference.

My father and I wait in a small conference room at One PP for Gabriel to arrive. Then we'll all go to the press room together.

"There's something I need to talk to you about," I say, "and it may be a little difficult for you to hear, but I think it's important."

He looks at me with concern. Given how tragic his world has turned in the last forty-eight hours, I'm certain my father can't conceive of what I could say that would add to his pain.

"Charlotte wrote a novel. Or part of one. It's really good. In fact, it was going to be published. The last time I saw her, she told me the good news and gave me a copy. I think it might contain clues as to what actually happened to her. You know how Charlotte's stories always have real-life aspects to them?" He nods. "I think this one does too. It's about a woman named Clare who's an MFA student at NYU—so no mystery there. This Clare has a boyfriend who's a stand-in for Zach. And in the book, at least, the boyfriend is abusive and Clare's scared of him."

My father winces as if he's been struck. "Did Zach ever . . . hit Charlotte?"

"I don't know," I say, ashamed that I don't have the first clue whether my little sister was being abused by her boyfriend. "I can't imagine Charlotte putting up with something like that, but . . . the book has a lot of stuff that makes me wonder how well I actually knew her. This Clare character is also seeing two other men: a banker named Matthew and a student she calls Jason. The student's in a class that Clare TA's, and you know how Charlotte was a teaching assistant for an undergraduate class last semester? That makes me think that maybe this Jason character is real. And if he's real, maybe Matthew is too."

My father looks at me with a distant gaze. He obviously knows even less than I do about Charlotte's life.

"What's the book about?" he asks.

Damn. I buried the lede, and now I have to tell him the worst part.

I exhale deeply. "It's a . . . murder mystery. In it, I think Charlotte actually foresaw her own death. Her character in the book—Clare, the one based on her—gets murdered. Charlotte never reveals the killer because the manuscript she gave me was only half written. But the reader knows it's one of three men: Marco, the artist-boyfriend; Jason, the student; or Matthew, the banker."

———

Gabriel arrives a few minutes later. He introduces himself to my father and apologizes for making us wait.

"We only have a minute before this is going to begin, but I wanted to give you a sense of how it'll work," he says. "First I'm going to say a few words, mainly designed to disabuse the press of the idea that a serial killer is on the loose. After that, I'll answer half a dozen or so questions. Following the Q and A, I'm going to turn the microphone over to you, Mr. Broden. I think only one family member should speak—if that's okay with you, Ella?"

I nod. "Yeah. That's fine."

"Okay," Gabriel says. "Any questions for me?"

"No," my father and I say in unison.

He checks his watch. "Let's do this, then."

Gabriel leads us through the door of the waiting room and into the police department's press space. The lighting is too harsh, and I shield my eyes slightly with my hand. Gabriel doesn't flinch, however. He's done this before. In fact, he did it just last week regarding Jennifer Barnett.

Once behind the lectern, in a strong, confident voice, Gabriel says, "My name is Lieutenant Gabriel Velasquez. I'm going to make a brief statement, and then I'll take some questions. Charlotte Broden, a twenty-five-year-old graduate student at New York University, has been missing since Wednesday morning. Although it's early in the investigation, we've already developed a short list of people of interest in the disappearance. Let me say at the outset that we have absolutely no reason to believe that there is any connection whatsoever between Ms. Broden's disappearance and the previously reported disappearance of Jennifer Barnett. Now, I know that some of the more irresponsible members of the press have raised the possibility that someone might be targeting young women in our city. There is absolutely no evidence to support that conjecture. Obviously, I cannot share with you the leads we have uncovered in either investigation, but I will tell you that at the present time we have a limited number of suspects in both matters, and I can further state that there is no overlap between the two suspect lists. Now I'll take a few questions."

Virtually every hand in the press gallery shoots up. They look like third-graders with the right math answer.

Gabriel points to an older man sitting in the first row. I recognize him from television.

"Jack, why don't you start it off?"

"Thank you," Jack says, coming to his feet. "Should the public be concerned about a possible serial killer? Are there any patterns that people should be cognizant about? Like with Son of Sam in the 1970s, when it was known he was looking for couples parked in cars?"

Gabriel takes a deep breath. "As I said just a moment ago, there is nothing for the public to fear because there is no evidence of any link between these two disappearances. It is extremely irresponsible to claim otherwise, as your question implies."

Gabriel next selects a younger woman in glasses sitting in the middle of the press pack. "Is the police department considering imposing a curfew?"

"No. Next question."

This time an African American woman is chosen. "Can you identify the person or persons of interest in the Broden case?"

"No. Not at this time."

"What can you tell us about the suspects, then?" the same reporter follows up.

"I can tell you that there are a limited number of people who are our primary focus. And I can say that each one was personally acquainted with Charlotte Broden."

"Is that also true with regard to the Barnett investigation?" another reporter blurts out without being called on.

"Yes," Gabriel says. "The suspects in the Barnett case all knew Ms. Barnett, and the suspects in the Broden investigation all knew Ms. Broden. There is no overlap between the suspect lists."

He points toward the back row. An Asian woman stands.

"Is Nicolai Garkov a person of interest in this investigation? Or anyone related to Garkov or the Russian mafia?"

I lean closer to my father, squeeze his arm at the elbow. A sign of support that I don't want the press to witness.

Gabriel is quick to answer. "At this point we have no basis to believe that Ms. Broden's disappearance has anything to do with that. Margaret?"

A small woman in the second row with curly gray hair rises. She's so short her head is barely visible behind the man seated in front of her.

"Do you believe Ms. Broden is still alive?"

My gaze swings toward Gabriel. Would he tell the press anything different than he told me?

"We pray that she is," he says. "We have no reason to believe that she's not."

Gabriel nods in our direction. Apparently he views the question about Charlotte being alive as a good segue to my father.

"Now I would like to turn the microphone over to Charlotte Broden's father, F. Clinton Broden, to say a few words."

My father takes his cue and moves closer to the microphone. "Thank you, Lieutenant."

His voice is a hoarse whisper, barely audible. I know at once that he's not going to be able to say another word.

I take the microphone out of his hand and place my other hand on his shoulder.

"My name is Ella Broden. Charlotte Broden is my sister. My father is obviously overcome with emotion, as we all are. We miss Charlotte so much. On behalf of our family, I want to thank the NYPD for all the work they're doing to find my sister. I also want to announce that tomorrow we will be holding a search for Charlotte at Riverside Park. It's open to the public, so please join us. We will be meeting at Ninety-Sixth Street and Riverside Drive at noon. Our family has also established a reward of one hundred thousand dollars for any information leading to Charlotte's safe return."

I stop, trying to hold it together myself. It's time to go for that sound bite. The clip that will play on the news tonight.

"If anyone knows anything about my sister's whereabouts, or has any information at all, please call the police . . ." I wait a beat and then say, "And if you're out there, if you can hear me, Charlotte, please know that we love you . . . that *I* love you, Char-bar."

Gabriel thanks the press for coming and the reporters begin to depart. My father and I follow him out of the press room. Almost as soon as we step away, I feel my phone vibrate.

It's Paul Michelson.

"Hello," I say in a whisper, cupping my hand over the phone.

"Sorry to bother you, Ella. I tried your father first, but I was told that he was in court."

My father is obviously not in court. He's standing right beside me. But that's what my father likes clients to be told when he isn't in the office.

I find it hard to believe that Paul hasn't heard about Charlotte yet. Her disappearance is all over the media. Then again, maybe it just seems that way to me and Paul is one of those guys who follow only sports and business news.

"I don't know if you've heard, but my sister is missing. I'm at the police station now."

"Oh my God. I hadn't . . . I'm . . . I don't know what to say. I'm so sorry, Ella. Since when?"

It's another one of my father's rules about criminal defense, to make the client think that his lawyer has no problems, no concerns, no life outside of zealously representing clients. Clients never want to hear that their lawyer is focused on anything else—another case, a pending divorce, money problems, or the possible abduction and murder of her baby sister.

"It's only been a day, and I'm sure that . . ." I can't even articulate the lie that everything is going to be fine. "What's going on?"

"I just got off the phone with the police. They want me to meet with them."

I look around the room. I'm literally behind enemy lines. Not the best place to discuss the status of the investigation with my client.

"Who called you?"

"A guy named Jim McGary."

"McCorry," I correct.

"Yeah, maybe."

"I met him today," I say, using my grown-up-in-the-room-who-needs-to-make-the-client-feel-protected voice. "What did you say to him?"

"Nothing. I told him that I needed to get back to him."

"I have a meeting I'm heading to now, but let's meet back at my office at three. Until then, don't say anything to anyone."

12.

The doormen in Charlotte's building never stop me when I enter, even though they stand beside a sign that says **ALL VISITORS MUST BE ANNOUNCED**. I normally don't show up in the middle of a workday, however, so the man on duty now isn't someone I recognize. I stride by him with a sense of purpose, avoiding eye contact to give the impression that I'm a resident in a hurry to get home. Nevertheless, I half expect him to ask me to stop. But either Zach hasn't put the word out that I'm to be denied entry or this guy hasn't seen the memo because he lets me pass without comment.

In the elevator, I reach for the key to Charlotte's apartment that she gave me to use in case of emergency. I can't imagine a greater need than this. If Zach isn't home, I'm going to let myself in and conduct my own search. Sisters don't need warrants, after all.

I knock on the door. Hard.

"Who is it?" he says.

"It's me, Zach. Ella. Open up. We need to talk."

I'm prepared for him to tell me to go away, in which case I'm also prepared to use the key. To my surprise, he opens the door.

He looks absolutely terrible. Clad in sweatpants and a white T-shirt that likely also serves as his pajamas. He clearly hasn't showered or shaved today, and maybe not since I last saw him at One PP.

The apartment looks even worse. A pizza box with the remnants of last night's dinner sits open on the dining-room table, with a single glass, half-filled with some brown liquid—maybe Coke, maybe bourbon—beside it.

Zach doesn't say anything to me after opening the door. Instead, he retreats back to the living room and drops himself onto one end of the sofa.

I follow him inside. Taking the seat opposite him, I scan the room more thoroughly. He hasn't scrubbed the place clean; that's for sure.

Before saying anything, I take a moment to calm myself. I don't want to come on too strong. I'll lose him right off the bat.

"I know Charlotte's disappearance has been tough on you. For me too, of course. The reason I'm here is because you and me, Zach, we're the people who know Charlotte best. We need to work together to help find her. And that means you need to cooperate fully with the police."

He isn't making eye contact with me as I tell him this. Instead, he stares at the floor.

"Zach, look at me," I say, using a sterner voice.

This causes him to raise his head. His gaze is unsteady. Alternating between my eyes and my shoes.

"Are you wearing a wire?" he finally says.

"What?"

"Are you tape-recording this?"

"No. God, no. Zach, I'm here to talk to you. To convince you to help the police. Every hour that you don't is another hour that Charlotte's in danger."

Zach exhales loudly and then focuses on me with much more conviction than he had a moment ago. "I didn't kill her. I swear to God I didn't."

"I know you didn't," I say, hoping I sound convincing. "You loved Charlotte, and she loved you. That's why I know that you want to help the police find who did this. If you do that, there's a good chance that Charlotte's going to come home safe."

"You never thought I was good enough for Charlotte."

"No," I lie. "All I ever wanted was for Charlotte to be happy, and you made her happy. And I also know that you always wanted the best for her. Don't you still want that?"

"Of course. I love her."

His use of the present tense is a hopeful admission. Then again, Zach is too smart to be tripped up by wordplay.

"Then why won't you talk to the police?"

"They think I killed her. And I didn't. But they think I did."

He says this with an accusatory tone. As if *he's* the victim with whom I should sympathize.

"No, they don't," I say softly, as if talking to a child. "I've known Lieutenant Velasquez a long time. He may come on strong, but he's always been honest with me. He would have told me if he suspected you of anything. The truth is the opposite, in fact. He told me there's evidence pointing to other people. It's your refusal to cooperate that's raising suspicions. Until you told him that you wouldn't cooperate, he'd assumed you'd be just like me—willing to do anything to help them find Charlotte."

"That's bullshit and you know it!"

I'm shocked by Zach's sudden flash of anger. It reminds me of Charlotte's description of the fictional Marco—how his rage could be triggered as easily as flipping a light switch.

"I'm her boyfriend, not her sister," Zach says. "And I'm a god-damn black man! The police were looking to put the blame on me from day one, and they're not going to look anywhere else if they can pin it on me."

He's right. He knows it, and he knows that I know it too. Nevertheless, I try to convince him that he couldn't be more off base.

"The only thing that I can think of worse than Charlotte being gone is the wrong person being accused of it. And look, Zach, I'm not going to lie to you. Like I said, I've always liked you, and I liked you with Charlotte because she was happy with you. But Charlotte is my family. If you guys broke up, you and me, we'd probably never talk again. But I don't want the police falsely accusing you any more than you do. If they did that, we wouldn't be any closer to getting Charlotte back."

"The difference is that *I* know I didn't hurt her, but you don't know that," he says, calmer now. "And so if the police tell you that I did it, you're going to believe them. But I *didn't* do it, Ella. I swear to God I didn't."

One of the occupational hazards of being a prosecutor—or a defense lawyer, for that matter—is that people lie to your face every single day. I can't even begin to count the number of suspects who've made the exact same pronouncement as Zach. They'll swear their innocence to God, on their children's eyes, on all that's holy, and yet they're still as guilty as sin.

Despite my training, I still can't get my head around the idea that Zach killed Charlotte. There's something he's hiding—that I can feel in my bones—but I don't believe it's that he murdered her. Perhaps that's only because I want to believe—hope—that *no one* murdered Charlotte.

I stop, and quiet fills the room. My father preaches that silence is the best interrogator. "I learn more about the other side's evidence by letting them talk than by asking pointed questions," he told me once. "You'd be surprised what people will reveal if you give them the chance to do it."

This silence is not an ally in the interrogation, however, but a wall between us. Zach isn't going to budge. I decide to change tack. Perhaps I can get something out of him about whether Matthew or Jason exist outside the pages of Charlotte's manuscript.

"Did you read Charlotte's book?" I ask.

Even though Gabriel asked me not to disclose the manuscript's existence, I assume that Zach already knows about it. He and Charlotte were living together, after all. I can't imagine she could keep such an extensive project from him, even if she had been so inclined.

"What book?" he says, indicating my assumption is incorrect.

"She wrote a novel. A romance." Far better that he not know Charlotte's novel involved a murder. "Some of the characters are based on people in her life. For example, there's a boyfriend who seems to be loosely based on you. She calls him Marco. He's someone she loves and who is very talented, although she made you a painter in the book."

Zach stares at me, stone-faced. It occurs to me a beat too late that Charlotte might actually be having an affair with a painter named Marco.

"And there's a character based on me too," I continue quickly. "The protagonist's older sister is named Emily, which is my middle name. And she's a lawyer. Among the other characters . . . one is a banker and the other is a student at NYU. The banker she calls Matthew and the student is named Jason. I know this is an awkward thing for me to ask, but . . . was there anyone like either of them in Charlotte's life? Past or present?"

"I don't know," Zach says, but his voice clearly belies his claim. He knows things. Things he isn't sharing.

"Zach . . . please. I'm begging you. Help me."

More silence. Then he says, "I have a friend over at the law school, and she told me that the smartest thing for me to do is keep my mouth shut. Maybe I should call her now."

He's lawyering up. The piece of shit.

In a police interrogation, when the suspect asks for a lawyer all questions must cease. The police are precluded from trying to talk someone out of invoking his right to counsel. If they do, anything that's said after the request for counsel is inadmissible at trial.

But this isn't a police interrogation.

"She's giving you terrible legal advice, Zach. Trust me, I'm not some first-year law student trying to impress you. I was a prosecutor for a long time, and I've seen a lot of people dig deep holes for themselves by keeping their mouths shut. But I'll say this: if you *did* kill Charlotte, then your friend is absolutely right. One hundred percent. But if you didn't, then all lawyering up does is cause reasonable people to conclude that you're guilty. Because why else wouldn't you cooperate? So, which one is it? Did you kill her? Because if you did, you should definitely tell me to leave. But if you've got nothing to hide, then all you're doing by staying silent is making me think you murdered my baby sister. And if I think that, you bet your ass that I'm going to make it my mission in life to make you pay. So, which is it, Zach?"

He shakes his head. I can't tell if it's because he disagrees with my analysis or if it's just his way of telling me he's sorry.

"*Please*, Zach. For the love of God, please help me and the police find Charlotte."

"I need to think about things, Ella," he says softly. "I'm not saying I won't help the police, but right this moment I can't say I will either."

He walks to the front door. I'm certain he expects me to follow him, but after he opens the door and looks back, he sees me still in the living room.

"Please, Ella," he says. "Don't make me call the police to get you to leave. That won't be good for anyone."

He's right about that. In fact, it's the first thing he's said that makes any sense to me.

CHAPTER FOUR

"Clare, goddamn it, you have to stay still!"

For the last forty minutes I've been frozen like a statue, clad in nothing but a bra. Nevertheless, Marco's voice is full of contempt, as if my need to scratch my nose is a deliberate attempt to sabotage his work.

He's wearing boxers and a T-shirt, his painting garb. The canvas he's working on is large, not quite the size of a movie poster, but at least the size of our television turned vertical. I haven't seen a brushstroke of his masterpiece yet, even though this is the third day I've sat for him.

"I'm tired," I say back, knowing full well that I sound whiny. What my older sister Emily calls my baby-of-the-family voice. "Can't we take a break?"

"Soon," he snaps without making eye contact, or at least not with the me that is flesh and blood. He might be staring right at the eyes of the painting of me for all I know.

"You said that twenty minutes ago."

"It was true then, and it's true now. Soon doesn't mean now. Someone should have told you that before."

It's a common refrain of Marco's to remind me that I'm spoiled. I've long been inured to that criticism, but I'm always on the lookout for some sign that he's self-aware of its hypocrisy, given that he also reaps the rewards of my father's indulgence. I haven't seen it yet.

"I don't understand why I'm not allowed to move. Your paintings never look like me anyway, so what difference does it make?"

This stops him in his tracks. I knew it would, and that it would give me the opportunity to pee.

"Go!" he shouts. "Take your fucking break. You obviously don't value what I'm doing here anyway."

I immediately grab the robe lying on the sofa. It's a bit of affect I adopt when serving as Marco's model because I walk naked in front of him all the time in our day-to-day existence. He turns the canvas so it faces the wall, to prevent me from sneaking a peek, and then heads out to the terrace to smoke.

After I return from the bathroom, I continue to let him stew a little on the balcony, but not for so long that his anger will bake in. I've seen Marco angry, and it's something to be avoided at all costs.

When I step onto the terrace, the breeze off the river is cool. I breathe it in, enjoying a moment for myself before I must focus on Marco's enormous, eggshell-fragile ego.

"Are you happy with it?" I ask.

"I'd be happy if my model and, I dare say, my muse, was a little more interested," he says back, without making eye contact.

"I'm committed. But I'm also human. And standing there naked without moving for hours at a time is not my idea of a good time."

Now he looks at me. A cold stare.

"It's not supposed to be a good time. It's art. There's got to be some pain involved."

"I thought the artist was supposed to suffer. Not his subject."

"Everyone suffers in the making of true art. If you understood that better, you'd be more successful."

He shakes his head, once again denoting that this is all my fault. Then he takes a long drag on his cigarette and blows the smoke away from me.

"What's going on with you?" he asks.

"What?"

"You heard me. It's like . . . I don't know who you are anymore. Something's going on with you."

My heart rate involuntarily spikes. I've wondered for some time if Marco has any inkling of what is actually going on with me. I had assuaged myself with the belief that he's sufficiently self-absorbed not to notice anything other than himself.

"Jesus, Marco. Nothing's going on."

He turns to me, looking almost menacing. It's a look I've seen before. It frightens me enough that I tighten my grip on the terrace's railing.

"You really think I'm stupid, don't you?"

"No. Why would you even say that?"

"Little rich girl shacking up with your Mexican painter boy."

This is another running theme for Marco. It fits in with the tortured artist thing for him to also identify himself as a member of a marginalized ethnic group. His father is a doctor and his mother a college professor in Mexico City, but to hear Marco tell it he came to this country in a banana boat, not on JetBlue.

"Please," I say.

"Tell me it's not true."

"It's not true."

"Fuck you, Clare."

And with that, he walks away.

———

As I watch Marco stomp around our living room, I realize I can no longer push my fears to the recesses of my subconscious. The honest truth is that I'm afraid of him. In the past weeks, his mood swings have been wilder. Sweetly affectionate one day and a raging lunatic the next.

I come in from the terrace. Without saying a word to Marco, I head toward the bedroom.

"Where in the hell do you think you're going?" he barks.

"*To take a shower.*"

"*Not when we still have work to do, you're not. I'm going to lose the light in an hour.*"

"*I assumed that when you said 'Fuck you, Clare' and then walked away, that meant you were done with me for the day.*"

"*Done talking to you. Not done painting you.*"

I find myself at a decision point: submit or defy.

"*Maybe I'm done with* you *for the day. Ever think of that?*"

He rushes forward, coming so quickly that I freeze in place. I can see the rage in his eyes. Marco has never hit me, but he's the first person I've ever been with who I could see someday crossing that line. There's anger boiling within him that I know he can't control. Whenever I've tried to talk to him about his temper, he brushes it off as passion.

He doesn't touch me, but he stands right in front of my face. With the snarl of an animal he says, "Take your fucking robe off and get over there."

I follow his command, hating myself every second of the next two hours that I stand naked before him. My only solace is fantasizing about my revenge.

———

Not two minutes after Marco vacates the apartment, I'm sending a text to the burner phone that Matthew uses only with me.

Want you. Now!!

The response is immediate and expresses equal urgency.

Four Seasons. ASAP

Less than half an hour later, Matthew opens the door to his hotel room wearing nothing but a robe. From our first kiss, I can feel him hard against my leg. His body is the way a man's should be. Neither too muscular nor so slight you can feel his bones. And he has the exact right amount of chest hair. He reminds me in both respects of a young Sean Connery—maybe of Goldfinger *vintage.*

I trace my tongue around his nipples and then along the soft hairline that dissects his chest. I always stop just below his hip, running my hands across the scar in the shape of an M.

When I first happened upon it, I asked him how he received it. He told me a cock-and-bull story about a fight he had in college with a guy who pulled a knife. A month or so later, when I told him that the scar's smooth edges didn't look to be the result of a stabbing, he confided that he'd actually fallen on the sharp-cornered edge of a metal box.

Finally my mouth arrives at where he's been aching for it to go. Like everything else about Matthew, I find this part of him to also be pure perfection. To change any of it—length, girth, texture, smell even—would be to lessen it.

He often tells me that I possess extraordinary oral skills. It's a compliment I've heard before, and I've always just assumed that men are so thankful to receive it that they'll say anything to keep it going. Still, Matthew usually has a frenetic energy about him, but when he's in my mouth I can feel that he's completely in another world, oblivious to everything. Much the way I am when the roles are reversed.

He pulls himself away and brings his mouth to mine. His hands on my breasts, his tongue everywhere—my earlobe, running down my neck, caressing my nipples. When he traces his mouth down the center of my body, I begin to tremble with the anticipation of what's to come. I have no doubt that he knows how close I am by the way he holds back just as I'm about to hit the point of no return, only to resume again and bring me right to the edge without allowing me to cross over.

When he finally enters me, I'm more than ready to explode. He goes faster in response to my demand, trying to keep up with my pace. It doesn't take more than a few strokes before I've reached the summit.

I have to confess that I'm never happier than I am with Matthew. And not just in bed, although that's truly magical, but simply in his company. It's the only time I feel like I'm really me, as corny as that sounds. Even with my sister, who is the closest I've ever come to this sense of true actualization, I sometimes feel like I'm playing a part. The little sister. The artist. The free spirit. With Matthew I'm allowed to be more complex, permitted to show the contradictions that define me on a daily basis, to express my insecurities without concern that I'm whining for no purpose, to dream about a future with him in which I'm happy.

In a word, I'm in love with him. Truly.

13.

I return to the office a few minutes before my 3:00 p.m. appointment with Paul Michelson. Stopping at the reception desk, I ask Ashleigh if my father is in.

"He's in court," she says.

"No, really, Ashleigh. Where is he? I'm not a client."

She laughs. "No, he really is in court. Garkov."

Right . . . the adjournment.

"Any news about your sister?"

"No."

"Your father is . . . he's taking this hard, I think."

Ashleigh is a few years younger than me, closer to Charlotte's age, I'd guess, but the four-decade age gap between her and my father doesn't necessarily mean that they couldn't be romantically involved. That would certainly explain why she considers it appropriate to opine about the mental state of the head of the firm. I don't want to engage her about my father, however, so I switch to business.

"Paul Michelson will be here any minute now. Please preclear him through security downstairs and put him in the conference room when he gets here."

I'm sitting in my office for less than five minutes before Ashleigh calls to tell me that Paul has arrived. In that time, I've done some cyber-searching and found the press release issued this morning by the DA's office about Jennifer Barnett.

It's not good news for Paul. The police conducted a search of Jennifer Barnett's apartment and found DNA and fingerprint evidence. As a banker with licenses to sell securities to the public, Paul's finger-prints are on file with the Securities and Exchange Commission, and that means they now have proof that Paul's been in Jennifer Barnett's apartment. Not the most incriminating thing in the world, but when a male boss visits the home of his beautiful, twenty-two-year-old subordi-nate, most people reach a common conclusion as to why he was there.

When I arrive at the conference room, I see Paul sitting in the same seat as he did the last time we met. Like then, his back is to me. This time he quickly rises when I enter.

He kisses me as if we were old friends greeting each other at a party instead of a lawyer meeting with her client because he's a person of interest in a potential murder. Being in Zach's company has stripped me of whatever vestige of goodwill I previously had toward Paul. I now feel repulsed by the sight of him.

"Thanks for seeing me on such short notice," Paul says as I take the seat at the table's head, the one my father occupied at our first meeting. "Given the situation with your sister, are you sure you want to do this?"

I have little doubt that his question is motivated more by his con-cern about our ability to represent him than for my well-being. That said, I can't hold his self-interest against him too much. I wouldn't want a brain surgeon to operate on me while her sister or daughter was missing either.

"My father and I discussed it, and we believe that we're more than able to give you one hundred percent of our effort. If that changes, we'll tell you. And, of course, if you want to move on from us, that's understandable too."

He doesn't hesitate. "No. You're my lawyers until you tell me you can't do the job."

With that out of the way, I get down to it. "The police searched Jennifer's apartment and found some fingerprints and DNA. My guess is that they reached out to you because you're a match."

"How'd they get a set of my prints and my DNA?"

His question tells me two things. First, he has definitely been in her apartment. He isn't going to claim there must be some mistake. And second, he doesn't have an innocent explanation as to why he's been there.

"You have a series seven, right?" I say, referring to the license to sell securities to the public.

"Yes, and a sixty-three."

"Well, that's how they have your prints. It's part of the background check for getting your securities license, if you recall. On the bright side, they probably don't have your DNA on file—unless you've previously been arrested for a sex crime."

Paul isn't the kind of guy to panic. In college, he played on the tennis team and often told me that he was at his best when he was down a set. Met with the disclosure that the police are going to be able to place him at what is very likely a murder scene, he doesn't display anything but cool-as-can-be confidence.

"Where does the fingerprint thing leave us?"

"Well, I think it's a safe bet that the police have evidence that you've been in Jennifer Barnett's home."

We stare at each other for a few seconds. I wonder if Paul understands that I want him to confess. To tell me that he can't take it anymore and blurt out that he killed her. To be a good person and do the right thing.

When the quiet passes long enough that I know he's actually waiting for *me* to say something, I ask him, "So what do you want to do? About the police's invitation to submit to an interview, I mean."

"I was hoping you'd tell me," he says.

I think about how I want to answer, actually running the response through my head before committing to it. I can't imagine my father offering the advice I'm about to give, but I convince myself that I'm providing it for Paul's benefit and not to further my own sense of justice.

"The conventional wisdom is definitely what my father advised when we last met—hunker down. Talking to cops now will lock you into a story, and if new evidence subsequently refreshes your recollection about something down the road, it will look like you lied. Here's just one example. If you'd talked to the police before we were retained, you might have denied ever being in her apartment. Now that we know your prints are likely there, I can ask you to search your memory as to why that would be. So, for the sake of argument, maybe now you remember being there for some perfectly innocent reason. Maybe you now remember that you'd visited once to drop something off or to attend a party. If you tell the police one thing and then your memory gets 'refreshed,' they view that as a lie when the reality is that you just forgot. Also, cooperation's like being pregnant, as they say. There's no halfway. If you agree to an interview then they're going to ask you to take a polygraph. They're not admissible in court, but if you decline—or worse, fail—then they'll think they've got their man. Same thing with their requesting to search your place. Right now, they probably don't have enough to get a warrant, so they'll ask for your permission. If you say no, then they again think it's because you've got something to hide."

I can tell just from the way he looks at me that he isn't going to cooperate. And not because of my bullshit refreshed-recollection scenario. He's hiding something.

"You've more than convinced me, Ella. Tell them thanks but no thanks."

I've done my job the way my father taught me. But I'm not willing to let Paul off the hook just yet. I need to know just how deep in the muck he is.

"There's a second option. And it's an important one for you to consider."

I look at him with my most no-nonsense stare. I clearly have his attention.

"If you were involved *in any way* in Jennifer Barnett's disappearance, you should tell me. Telling me doesn't mean we're going to change our approach, but it allows us to better evaluate the risks. That's because if you *were* involved, there's a pretty strong likelihood that the police will ultimately be able to prove that. By contrast, if you weren't, then cooperating has far fewer downsides and much greater rewards."

My proposal is met with a stony silence. I knew even while I was speaking that there was no way that Paul Michelson was going to confess, even just to me. He doesn't seem to be built that way.

"I didn't do it, Ella. Please believe that. I know we haven't spoken in more than ten years, but . . . you're not just my lawyer, you're someone who knows me. You know I couldn't have hurt this girl."

His use of the phrase *this girl* doesn't help his cause. I would have found Paul slightly more believable if he had referred to Jennifer Barnett by name, or at least recognized she was a woman, not a girl.

"But I also don't see any reason why I should help them out," he adds.

I let the words settle before responding. The echoes of Zach's self-interested response are almost more than I can bear.

"In that case, we follow my father's script. I'll call Detective McCorry and tell him that we're representing you and that, for the moment, you're going to decline their offer to submit to an interview."

———

In different circumstances, I might have waited for my father to return from court so I could run the decision by him to tell the police to pound sand with regard to Paul Michelson. But Paul was unequivocal, and this was my father's standard operating procedure, so I figured I might as well just get it over with.

He answers on the first ring. A gruff sounding, "McCorry."

"This is Ella Broden. We met earlier today, when I was with Gabriel Velasquez."

"I remember. Do you need me to get Gabriel?"

"No. I was calling to speak to you. It's about Paul Michelson. He's a client of my law firm. I practice with my father, Clint Broden. Paul said that you reached out to him and expressed interest in an interview. I'm calling to inform you that he's going to decline that offer at this time."

"Really?"

The question throws me a bit. I was prepared for him to tell me the usual cop line—that my client was making a huge mistake by refusing to cooperate—but not to suggest that I might be joking.

"Yes, really," I say. "I find it hard to believe that you've never had an innocent man turn down an invite to chat with the police. I don't think my father has ever—and I mean *ever*—brought someone in for a voluntary interview."

I surprise myself at how easily I flip into defense-lawyer mode. Paul might very well be a murderer and here I am, claiming the moral high ground for his refusal to cooperate with the police.

"No . . . not on the cooperation," Detective McCorry says. "I'm surprised that you're representing Paul Michelson. It just seems . . . odd, given what's going on with your sister."

It's more than a fair point, so I drop the attitude. I could explain that Paul retained us before my sister went missing, but that would violate the attorney–client privilege.

"The two really have nothing to do with each other, Detective. Paul is innocent."

"Okay," he says with the same tone as if I'd told him that I think Santa is real. "I know you know this, but we focus hard on anyone who won't cooperate with us. So if Mr. Michelson isn't the guy, the best thing is for him to just tell us that."

"Thanks for the advice. I can tell you that he's *not* the guy, and we're going to have to leave it at that for the moment. He's now going to go about his life. He and I are both confident that, if something did happen to Ms. Barnett, your investigative skills will be good enough to find the person responsible."

Less than a minute after I hang up with McCorry, my phone rings. The call is from the same number I had just dialed—the main line at One PP.

"Did you forget something, Detective McCorry?" I ask without so much as saying hello first.

"It's Gabriel. Jim just filled me in."

"Oh," I say.

"Yeah. Oh. Look, I know everybody's got to make a living, and the way of the world is that the toughest ADAs sell their souls for big money, so I'm not complaining about that. But you don't want to represent Paul Michelson. Not now. Not on this."

This doesn't sound like the normal police posturing. Gabriel has taken on the tone of a friend staging an intervention.

"Care to share why not?"

"You playing coy, or do you really not know?"

"Why don't we pretend that my father follows a policy that it's not our job to prove our client's innocence but to rebut evidence that you come up with indicating otherwise. There was no reason for us to ask Mr. Michelson anything about his relationship with Jennifer Barnett or the circumstances behind her disappearance."

"Hell of a way to earn a buck, Ella."

I let the comment go without response. He's right, but so is my father.

"Let's just say that you should probably talk to your client about the affair he was having with Ms. Barnett. While you're at it, ask him if the muckety-mucks at Maeve Grant heard that he was diddling a research analyst on his desk, whether that'd be the end of his seven-figure bonuses."

"What evidence do you have about the affair?"

"She kept a diary," he says.

———

My father returns to the office an hour later. He looks like a beaten man, which is the last thing I'd normally say about my father, especially when he returns from court.

"How'd it go with Judge Koletsky?" I ask.

"Fine. I got the adjournment. He said he had no problem with an open-ended continuance—as a courtesy to me. The prosecution cried bloody murder, of course, and so he ended up cutting the baby in half. He granted the continuance but said we have to come back next month and tell him if conditions concerning Charlotte's disappearance have changed. As if he lives under a rock and wouldn't find out on his own."

"Garkov must be happy."

"I haven't told him yet. But I'm sure this isn't going to disappoint him."

"There's news about Paul Michelson," I say.

"Ashleigh told me that he called. What's going on?"

"A lot. The police likely have a match of Paul's prints at Jennifer Barnett's apartment, and they've invited him to come down and chat. I met with him and gave him the pros and cons—"

"Emphasis on the cons, I hope."

"Yeah, don't worry. He was con all the way. So I called over to One PP and told the lead detective no. And then, like two minutes after I told Detective McCorry that Paul wasn't cooperating, Gabriel called me. He said that Jennifer Barnett kept a diary and it leaves no doubt that she was having an affair with Paul."

"So? If he said it was an *affair*, doesn't that, by definition, mean it was consensual? Why would he need to kill her when he can just break it off? Paul's not married, right?"

"No, he's not married. But it's still the twenty-first century, Dad. Maeve Grant's policies prohibit superior-subordinate relationships. Big firms have cracked down on that sort of thing. If Jennifer Barnett were to claim sexual harassment—which she could just by virtue of Paul being her boss—Maeve Grant might well fire Paul."

"So you're saying that Paul has a decent motive."

"That's what I'm saying."

My father doesn't look the least bit fazed about the possibility that we're representing a murderer. I'm not at all surprised. He's represented them in the past and swears that they have been some of his nicest clients.

"All the more reason to hunker down," he says.

14.

I come home on the early side and order my favorite pad thai for dinner. My original plan was to watch a movie, but all the titles on pay-per-view remind me of Charlotte in one way or another. I give some fleeting thought to heading over to Lava, just to drink surrounded by people rather than drinking alone. I decide against it and open a bottle of chardonnay waiting in the fridge.

The thought of Lava makes me think of Dylan. I figure that now is as good a time as any to do some cyber-snooping about my one-night stand. Unfortunately, I don't know anything about him beyond his name and that he's a doctor of some type temporarily living in Brooklyn.

I type "Dylan Perry" into Google. The first hit is the Wikipedia page for the character on *Beverly Hills, 90210*—Dylan McKay, who was played by Luke Perry. I refine my search to focus on Brooklyn. That turns up some real people—a seventy-year-old lawyer, the Facebook profile of someone who looks like a science teacher I had in middle school, the LinkedIn page for a banker at Citibank who's bald as a cue ball. None of them is my Dylan.

I click on to Lava's website, but Dylan doesn't have a profile there. Next I check my own profile to see if he's left me a message, but my inbox contains nothing but spam.

I'm considering what other searches might bear fruit when my cell phone rings. As has been my Pavlovian response whenever I've received a call over the last two days, my entire body clenches, preparing itself for the call I've been dreading. The fact that the caller ID reveals it's from One PP makes that likelihood all the greater.

"Hello?" I say, tentatively.

"It's Gabriel. I've called to share some good news. We found the student your sister was involved with."

"Jason?" I say, and immediately realize that isn't his real name.

"His name is Josh. Josh Walden."

The name means nothing. I'm quite sure that Charlotte had never mentioned a Josh Walden to me before.

"Have you spoken to him?"

"He's sitting in our interrogation room as we speak."

For the first time, I actually feel as if there's a ray of hope. I'm afraid to ask Gabriel what Josh said, for fear that he'll dash it.

Gabriel offers it up without my prompt. "He admitted to the affair, but says he had no idea what happened to your sister. In fact, he claims he didn't even know she was missing."

"Do you believe him?"

"I don't believe anyone. You know that."

"Can I see him?"

"That's why I called you. You should get down here as fast as you can."

Detectives work in two shifts. The first team starts the day at 8:00 a.m. and goes home at 4:00 p.m. The second team arrives at 4:00 p.m. and stays until 1:00 a.m. For my sister's case, and Jennifer Barnett's too, for that matter, everyone is pulling doubles.

That means that the squad room at One PP is fully staffed even though it's near midnight by the time I arrive. Jim McCorry is tasked with retrieving me from the security guard downstairs. Meant as a tacit reminder, perhaps, about Paul's lack of cooperation regarding Jennifer Barnett.

"It's an all-hands situation upstairs," Detective McCorry says. "Not only are all of our guys here, but we've pulled a team from Domestic Violence and Homicide. Also, two detectives from BRAM."

I speak most of the police lingo, but BRAM is a new one. "What's that?"

"BRAM? Oh, Burglary, Robbery, Apprehension Module. There are two more detectives working who are pitching in on your sister's case that are also on the Barnett investigation. The last thing anyone here wants is for either case to go to Missing Persons."

In New York City, a missing-persons case is handled by the local precinct for the first seven days. If you've got a little more pull—as my father and I do, and apparently Jennifer Barnett's family as well—you get a top team like Gabriel's to handle it, with the local precinct providing backup. It doesn't go to Missing Persons until seven days have been exhausted, at which time it's generally considered unsolvable.

Detective McCorry brings me into Gabriel's office. To my surprise, it's empty.

"Where's Gabriel?" I ask.

"He's in with the witness."

"He wanted me to join him."

"No. He wanted you to watch. He told me to tell you that he'll be in shortly to discuss the interrogation with you."

Of course, that was right. I'm no longer an ADA. I'm the victim's sister. I'm not going to get within twenty feet of Josh Walden while he's in police custody.

Detective McCorry leans over to the computer terminal on Gabriel's desk and turns the monitor so it faces me. A few keystrokes later, I have a window into the interrogation room.

The picture is hardly high definition, but it's in color at least. The camera is overhead, making the angle of the shot downward.

My first reaction to seeing Josh Walden is that he does not remotely look like Charlotte's type. I always go for the straight arrows but she has a thing for the bad boys, forever drawn to dark souls in the unyielding belief that her light can save them. But Josh makes even the guys I dated look like rebels. He couldn't be more vanilla if he tried.

He's rail thin, as if he still hasn't finished filling out yet. His hair is sandy brown, short, neatly parted on the side. Even though it's near midnight, he doesn't appear to have the slightest stubble on his chin. His eyes are blue, and he's dressed in a white polo shirt and khakis, like he's just stepped out of the J. Crew catalog.

His leg bounces up and down with nervous energy. But he doesn't have any of the shifty-eyed look of the liars I've seen. Then again, the best liars betray no tells.

Gabriel must have received some notification that we were listening in, because he says, "Let's recap where we are here, Mr. Walden. Tell me if I have any of this wrong, because it's very important to me that I understand exactly what you're telling me. First, you admit that you had a relationship with Charlotte Broden."

Gabriel stops, obviously expecting Josh to confirm this part. Josh, however, looks at him like a deer caught in headlights.

"That's right, isn't it? For the last two months, you've been having a sexual relationship with Charlotte Broden?"

"Yes," Josh says.

His voice is squeaky. Yet another reason for me to wonder how Charlotte ended up in bed with this guy.

"And you had no knowledge that Charlotte was seeing other people. Is that also correct?"

"I still don't," he says. "I just know you told me she had a boyfriend. I thought *I* was her boyfriend."

At least to my ear, it doesn't sound like backtalk. Josh Walden actually believes that Charlotte has been faithful to him and that the police investigating her disappearance are lying when they tell him otherwise. I could see the fictional Jason reacting the exact same way.

"And the last time you saw Charlotte was on Monday of this week . . . four days ago?"

"Right. Monday night."

"And that was also the last time you spoke with her?"

Josh nods.

"Please answer audibly, Mr. Walden."

"Yes. I sent her some texts after that and tried her cell two or three times, but she didn't respond."

"And you have absolutely no idea what happened to her?"

"None."

Gabriel stands and walks to the corner of the room. Then he looks directly into the camera. It's as if he's asking me, *What do you think?*

The truth is that I don't know what to think. None of it makes any sense. If Josh doesn't much look like the kind of guy Charlotte would have sex with, he *certainly* doesn't give off the vibe of being the kind of guy who would kill her and then dispose of her body. But looks are a notoriously fallible indicator of guilt. Everyone said Jeffrey Dahmer seemed mild-mannered too.

Gabriel resumes his seat, this time turning the chair so he's facing the back, sitting in the wrong direction, but staring right at Josh. It looks to me like Gabriel isn't buying anything Josh is selling.

"Here's the thing. I believe you," Gabriel says, as sincere as I've heard those words sound. "I really do. But it's department protocol that we can't clear a suspect unless we check off some boxes. That includes getting your permission to allow us to fingerprint you, and for you to give us a swab of DNA. We'd also like to search your apartment, examine your computer and your phone, and administer a polygraph. We can do it all within the hour. If it all checks out, you're in the clear."

This is the moment of truth. Will Josh decline, showing that he probably has something to hide, or continue to be an open book?

15.

The NYPD's polygraph administrator, a guy named David Samuels, doesn't answer his phone. That isn't too surprising given the late hour.

"I'm not going to wait until tomorrow to do this on the off chance that Josh finds a defense lawyer between now and then," Gabriel says to no one in particular, but I take the comment to be a not-too-thinly veiled reference to my work for Paul Michelson. "Nardello!" he calls out to a uniform cop loitering in the hallway. "Send a squad car over to Samuels's house in Queens, roust him out of bed, and drag him down here."

Samuels arrives at One PP at a little after 1:00 a.m. A short, fat man, with a thick black beard, he looks like he's literally been dragged down from Queens. He's wearing sweatpants and a New York Mets T-shirt and sporting quite the bed head—at least concerning the hair he still has on his head, which for the most part is sticking straight up or to the side.

Gabriel handles the introductions. "This is Ella Broden, she's a former ADA in Special Vics and the sister of the missing woman, Charlotte Broden."

Samuels shakes my hand but keeps his focus on Gabriel. "What's the story?"

"The short version is that Charlotte Broden is a twenty-five-year-old woman who was last seen on Wednesday at around eight thirty a.m. After that . . . nothing. She lives with her boyfriend, a guy named Zachary Rawls, who was the last to see her. He isn't cooperating with us, so he's still in the mix. But the guy we got in here is Josh Walden. He's a college student at NYU who was in a class that Charlotte was teaching over there, and he's admitted to us that they have been having a sexual relationship for the last two months. He said he hasn't seen her since Monday, and claimed not to know anything about her having a live-in boyfriend or even that she was missing."

Gabriel looks over at me. "Anything else?"

"Charlotte wrote a novel—or at least half of one," I say. "It's loosely based on her life. That's how we discovered that she might be involved with one of her students. In the book, the narrator's a TA having a fling with one of her students. Josh is that student. In the story, she's also involved with another man, a Wall Street banker. His character is named Matthew, but I'm sure that's not actually his name."

"Okay," Samuels says. "So three men. Boyfriend . . . what's his name again?"

"Zach," I say.

"Zachary Rawls," Gabriel adds.

"And this here is the student, Josh. And there's a Wall Street banker type who probably isn't named Matthew."

"Right," I say.

"Any last name on the banker?" Samuels asks. "In the book, I mean."

Gabriel looks to me. "Harrison," I say. "Matthew Harrison."

"Okay, I think I got the lay of the land," Samuels says. "Give me ten minutes to prep, and then I'll be good to go."

———

The word *polygraph* literally means "many writings." It doesn't portend to ascertain the truth, but to give the examiner a set of data from which he or she can interpret whether the subject is being deceptive. There are many who distrust the machine, as false positives and inconclusive results are not unheard of—which is why polygraph results are generally not admissible at trial. I've never met anyone in law enforcement, however, who didn't believe in the device's infallibility in detecting a liar.

Gabriel has joined me in his office, as Samuels emphasized that it was important that he be the only person in the room during the examination. We watch on the computer screen as Samuels arranges the band around Josh's chest and places the rubber tubes on his fingers.

Josh looks more relaxed than he did during Gabriel's questioning. His knee has stopped bouncing.

"Are you comfortable?" Samuels asks.

Josh shrugs. "Yeah, fine."

Samuels looks directly into the camera and then nods, apparently to communicate to us that he's about to begin.

"Mr. Walden, my name is David Samuels. I am a licensed administrator of the polygraph device and I work for the New York City Police Department. Before we begin the actual test, I'm willing to answer whatever questions you might have about the process, and I also want to tell you a little bit about how it works. Okay?"

Josh nods. "Sure."

"Good. When we officially begin, I will ask you a series of questions. Some of them I already know the answer to. I'm asking those questions merely to establish certain baselines. The machine records various physiological factors such as your heart rate, blood pressure, even sweat, all of which will read differently when a person is lying. After the test, I will examine the results and then provide the police with my findings as to which answers indicate deception, if any."

"Okay," Josh says.

For the first time since he's been hooked up, Josh's knee begins to bounce. It's subtle, but I can see it. I wonder whether Gabriel notices it too.

"Now, for the machine to work accurately, I need to establish a few things. These are not part of the actual test, but I still need you to answer them truthfully. Okay?"

"I'm going to answer everything truthfully," Josh says.

"Good. Are you currently on any medication?"

"No."

"Are you under the influence of any drug or narcotic?"

"No."

"Have you had any alcohol in the last twenty-four hours?"

Josh hesitates. "I had a beer with dinner."

"That's fine. Was that around six o'clock tonight?"

"A little later. Maybe seven or seven thirty."

"Okay. That won't affect the results. Now, do you have any questions for me?"

"Just one. Are these things really accurate? Because I know you can't use them in court, so I'm just wondering."

"Yes. They are highly accurate. And the idea that you can't use them in court is not true. Many courts permit their usage."

My stomach drops with the fear that Josh will get up and leave. Besides which, what Samuels said isn't entirely true. While some courts do permit the introduction of polygraphs, they only do so under highly controlled circumstances, requiring, for example, when both sides agree to their admission, or for sentencing purposes only.

"Why'd he say that?" I ask Gabriel.

"We find it helps the results if the subject believes the test works and will be used against him if he lies. Remember, it's not measuring truth telling, but anxiety. We want him to be afraid that his false answers will hurt him because that ratchets up the anxiety level."

"Any other questions?" Samuels asks Josh.

"No."

"Then let's get started."

Samuels flips the switches on the machine, which looks like one of the old-time computer printers. Then he takes a black Sharpie out of his breast shirt pocket and makes some type of notation on the printer paper.

"Is your name Josh Walden?"

"Yes."

"Is it Monday?"

"No."

"Are you in a police station?"

"Yes."

"Are you in Canada?"

"No."

The knee-thumping has gotten progressively worse with each question. By the Canada query, Josh's hands are also trembling, to the point that he looks like he's suffering from Parkinson's disease.

"Do you see that?" I say to Gabriel. "His hands."

Gabriel leans closer to the screen. "Yeah. He did the same thing during the interrogation. He's a nervous kid, that's for sure."

"Do you know Charlotte Broden?"

"Yes."

"Were you engaged in a sexual relationship with her?"

"A romantic relationship," Josh says.

"It was a sexual relationship too, correct?"

"Yes."

Samuels marks the computer printout. I wonder if that last answer is significant for some reason, although I can't imagine why it would be. Josh wouldn't be falsely claiming that he had sex with Charlotte.

"Do you know whether Charlotte has a boyfriend?"

"I thought I was her boyfriend."

"But you now know that she has another boyfriend?"

"That's what the police told me."

"Prior to the police telling you that Charlotte has a boyfriend, did you know that there was another man she was involved with romantically?"

"No."

He marks the printout again. Josh's knee keeps bouncing. It's now as high as it's been so far.

"Have you ever heard the name Zachary or Zach Rawls?"

"No."

"Was the last time you saw Charlotte on Monday of this week?"

This time Josh's slower to answer, as if he's counting off the days in his head.

"Yes."

"Was the last time you saw Charlotte yesterday?"

"No."

"Was the last time you saw Charlotte on Tuesday?"

"No."

"Was Charlotte having a sexual relationship with a banker?"

Josh looks oddly amused, as if this question strikes him as ludicrous.

"No."

"Prior to today, did you think Charlotte was having a sexual relationship with anyone besides you?"

"No," he says, sounding uncertain.

His knee continues to pop up and down. It feels almost like he's mocking me, as if it's a wink directed at me to indicate he's beating the machine.

"He's lying," I say to Gabriel. "You can see it."

"We'll know for sure in a few minutes," Gabriel replies.

Samuels grimaces slightly, and I wonder if that's because the machine confirms what I'm witnessing—that Josh is lying through his teeth.

"Do you know where Charlotte is now?"

"No."

"Did you and Charlotte break up?"

"No."

"Have you ever driven a car above the speed limit?"

"Yes."

"Do you know if Charlotte is alive?"

Josh uses his hand to wipe a trickle of sweat from his forehead. Samuels reaches across the table, pulling Josh's hand away.

"Please, Mr. Walden, leave your hands on the table."

"Okay," Josh says.

"Let me ask that last question again. Do you know if Charlotte is alive?"

"No. I don't."

"Was your relationship with Charlotte a violation of university rules?"

"I think so."

"Have you ever told a lie?"

"Um . . . yes."

"Did you ever strike Charlotte?"

"Never."

"Are you aware of anyone who would want to harm Charlotte?"

"No."

"Is my shirt blue?"

"Yes."

"Is your shirt blue?"

"No."

"Thank you, Mr. Walden."

Samuels unhooks the apparatus from Josh, carefully placing the tubing and the other sensors back in their box. After everything is meticulously put away, Samuels tears the paper off the printer.

My eyes are glued on Josh. He looks relieved to have it over. The knee thumping has stopped. His hands are steady again.

"I'm going to take a few moments to review your answers and the readouts from the machine," Samuels says. "Then I'm sure that Lieutenant Velasquez will share the results with you."

Samuels stands to leave and seems surprised when Josh offers him his hand. "Thanks," Josh says.

———

"The kid's like Mount Vesuvius," Samuels says when he joins us in Gabriel's office. "All over the place. I couldn't get a decent reading on anything. I mean, even his answers to the calibration questions indicate deception."

"Doesn't that mean he's lying?" I say. "He certainly *looked* like he was lying."

"It could," Samuels said, "but I can't certify that the results to any particular question indicated deception because his answer to *every* question—I mean, even his name—indicated deception. All I can say is that the results are inconclusive. How long has he been here?"

"A few hours," Gabriel said.

"That could skew the results too. It's late, he's obviously tired, he just found out that his girlfriend is missing, and he knows he's a suspect. He's also just been told that she wasn't exclusively his girlfriend. Who wouldn't be anxious under those conditions?"

My heart sinks. All of this seems to have been a colossal waste of time.

"Can we try again tomorrow?" I ask. "Maybe after he's rested it'll be different."

"That's up to the lieutenant," Samuels says. "But I doubt very much we're going to get a different result. What a lot of people don't know is that it's awfully hard to beat the poly, but much less so to make it useless. Mr. Walden has done the latter with great expertise."

CHAPTER SEVEN

"I know this sounds stupid, Clare, but I'd really like to go to a movie with you. Or just out to dinner."

It does sound stupid, and yet the worst part of all is how far off the mark Jason is about why it's so preposterous. He actually thinks that we can be one of those couples holding hands at the movies or sitting side by side drinking sangria at some outdoor café.

We're at his place, which looks like every boy's dorm room I've ever been in. It's barely large enough to fit his futon, which is pushed up against one wall. A fifty-inch television is the only thing hanging on any of the walls.

"It's not stupid, Jason. It's sweet," I say. "But you know why we can't do that. Not this semester, at least. Next year will be different."

He looks at me with stars in his eyes. "I love you so much, Clare."

Jason is a junior and just turned twenty-one. He reminds me of the boys I knew in high school. Insecure, unsure of what to do next, uncertain about who they are. Yet it's the very fact that he's so unformed that draws me to him. He has no hidden agenda and plays no games. I truly believe that all he desires in life is to be with me.

We decide to watch a movie. He picks a romantic comedy, which doesn't surprise me in the least. When the closing credits roll, I kiss him. More often than not, it falls to me to make the first move to initiate sex.

Jason told me that he had two sexual partners before me. His first was a virgin too, and so it was one of those blind-leading-the-blind situations.

He said his second had some experience, but the relationship didn't last long enough for him to profit from it.

I've taught Jason the things he has to know. The importance of kissing. How to use his hands. Timing and tempo. He hasn't mastered any of it yet, but he's showing steady improvement.

Tonight I can tell that he's not going to last very long. His hands are actually trembling as they touch my breasts. I decide that rather than have this end badly, I'll move things along more quickly.

"Don't," he says, as I move slowly down his hairless torso.

"Just relax," I tell him. "Let me do this for you, and then we can talk about what you can do for me."

His head lolls back and his body relaxes. I take him into my mouth just a little, but that's all it takes to bring him over the edge. His body clenches and he pushes himself farther into me. I stay with him until his body goes limp again, and then I put my head on his chest, listening to his rapid heartbeat begin to slow.

"My God, Clare," he says. "That was unbelievable."

"Shhhh," I say. "Don't speak. Just be."

He falls asleep shortly thereafter. Marco isn't expecting me home for a few hours, so I crawl off Jason's futon and make us both grilled-cheese sandwiches because all he has in his mini fridge, aside from Coca-Cola and beer, is Wonder Bread and Kraft American cheese singles. Either the crackling or the smell wakes him, because Jason wakes up just as I'm flipping the sandwiches over.

"I'm sorry," he says.

"For what?"

"That was a bit selfish of me."

I laugh. "Don't worry. You'll make it up to me later."

"And not only do I get"—and he nods toward the bed rather than say the word blowjob—"but grilled cheese too?"

"My cooking options were somewhat limited. Why don't you keep any food in here?"

"Because I'm on the partial meal plan and there's a pizza place downstairs and a McDonald's across the street."

"What am I going to do with you, Jason? You're a child."

"Then you need to make a man of me," he says.

———

Jason did make it up to me. After dinner we got back into bed, and he tried his very best to bring me to a climax with his mouth. Matthew is able to do it every time and Marco's an even-money bet, but it just wasn't going to happen with Jason. So I suggested he try it the old-fashioned way. I go through my usual routine—screaming out his name, telling him how big he is, the whole nine yards, but even with that encouragement, I need to help it along with my own hand.

When I start dressing, Jason gently pulls me back to the futon. "Stay," he says.

"I'm sorry, sweetheart. But you know I can only fall asleep in my own bed."

"I know, but it would be so nice to sleep together. I mean actually sleep together. Can't we do it just this one night?"

I laugh. "Jason, I'm not sleeping on a futon."

"We could go to your place."

"We've already talked about this," I say with my butter-wouldn't-melt-in-my-mouth voice. "I'd love to do that, but it's too risky. The associate dean lives in my building."

Jason looks at me with his puppy-dog eyes. The associate dean doesn't live in my building, but there's no way that Jason would know where he lives—or even where I live, for that matter.

He walks me to the door. Before I open it to leave, we kiss again. He pulls me tightly against him so I know he's ready, willing, and able to go another round. But I have no desire for any more. Besides, if I'm out much later, Marco will become suspicious.

"Good night," I say.

"You know, Clare, someday I'm going to follow you home and come upstairs to your apartment."

I'm sure he knows that was the wrong thing to say by the daggers my eyes shoot at him. "Don't even joke about that," I say.

He backtracks immediately. "Sorry. I wouldn't do that. It's just . . ."

I don't give Jason an inch. I want him to understand that he's crossed a very serious line.

"If I thought you were considering doing anything like that, I'd stop seeing you right now. Do you understand?"

He looks more like a child than usual, which stands to reason because I've cast myself in the role of the disappointed mother. His eyes are glued to the floor.

"Look at me," I say, and I actually grab his chin between my thumb and forefinger to lift his gaze so that it meets my eyes. "I need you to look at me and tell me that you understand. If you care about me . . . If you care about our relationship, you'll promise me that you're never going to do anything that would hurt me."

"I'm sorry," he says again, looking as if he's trying to fight back tears. "I would never. I swear."

"Okay," I say.

I kiss him quickly and leave. As I'm walking toward his elevator, I tell myself that I need to end things with Jason before he does something from which there will be no coming back.

DAY FIVE

SATURDAY

16.

Gabriel calls me at a little before eight. His first words are to apologize for waking me. Needless to say, I have already been awake for two hours.

"Is there any news?" I ask breathlessly, already thinking the worst.

"I'm not calling about your sister. But Jennifer Barnett's body's been found."

It takes a moment for this to register. For some reason, I just assumed that "missing" would be Jennifer Barnett's permanent state.

"She's dead?"

"Yes. Died the day she disappeared, we assume. She was found in a landfill over on Staten Island."

That's his way to indicate it wasn't a suicide or an accident. Jennifer Barnett was murdered.

I had been praying that Jennifer Barnett was alive because, in my mind, that would somehow increase the chance of Charlotte's safe return. Of course, one thing really had nothing to do with the other; it's like thinking the odds of a coin turning up heads will be improved if the three previous flips are tails.

But now that Jennifer Barnett is dead, the two *do* seem connected. One maniac is responsible for both, which means the odds are very good that Charlotte is also buried beneath a pile of garbage. The very thought makes my stomach lurch.

"Ella, you still there?" Gabriel says.

I hadn't realized how long the silence must have been. "Yeah. I'm . . . just trying to process, I guess."

"Jennifer Barnett notwithstanding, you've got to stay positive. Being optimistic costs the same as losing hope."

I appreciate the pep talk, but it doesn't change my outlook. I know in my heart that, like Jennifer Barnett, Charlotte's corpse is awaiting discovery too.

———

After getting off the phone with Gabriel, I go online to see for myself the media circus surrounding the confirmation of Jennifer Barnett's death. A banner headline on CNN shouts SHE'S DEAD, and beside it is the same photograph of a smiling and beautiful Jennifer Barnett I've seen for the past week. Among the subheadings are two related to my sister. One is the basic story they've been running since her disappearance was announced: a short biography of Charlotte with a direct segue to my father's representation of Nicolai Garkov. The second article is new, quoting sources "close to the investigation" as saying that it is extremely unlikely that Charlotte's still alive.

Having learned all I can from the Internet, I call Paul to share the grim news about Jennifer Barnett.

He sounds as if I've awakened him. Paul obviously wasn't losing sleep over her disappearance.

"Hey, Ella," he says.

"I'm sorry to have to tell you this, but Jennifer Barnett's body was found this morning. In a landfill on Staten Island."

"Jesus," is all he says next.

"Yeah," I confirm. "We need to strategize. Now that they have a body, it's definitely a murder investigation, and they're going to be looking hard at you."

He initially doesn't offer any response. Then he says, "Why do you say that? The looking at me part, I mean."

The question at first confuses me. How could he be so obtuse? Then I remember that he doesn't know about the diary.

"The police found her diary," I say flatly.

More silence. I wonder if he's still going to deny the affair, but instead he says, "Okay. I guess we need to talk, then."

"I'm busy during the day today, but we can meet later tonight. Does seven o'clock work for you?"

I don't tell him that I'll be engaging in a search for my sister's body this afternoon, adhering to my father's commandment about not sharing anything personal with the client.

"That's fine, but if it's all right with you, I'd rather not be going to your office after hours on the weekend. How about if I buy you dinner?"

Normally alarm bells sound when male clients want to meet with me outside the office. In my three months at the firm, I've had half a dozen overtures to meet in hotel bars—or worse, hotel rooms. But Paul's right. Our building makes everyone sign in and indicate who they're visiting, and I'd rather not leave a paper trail showing that the same day Jennifer Barnett was found dead Paul Michelson showed up for a late-night, weekend strategy session with his lawyer.

"Okay," I say. "Somewhere quiet, though."

"How about we meet at Mas? I know the owner, and he'll give us a table in the back."

17.

The weather is absolutely beautiful. Eighty degrees, no humidity, not a cloud in the sky. A perfect day for a stroll in the park—if only our purpose wasn't to find my sister's corpse.

My father picks me up at my apartment with his car and driver. We arrive at Riverside and Ninety-Sixth Street, where my father's PR guy, Phillip Lashley, is waiting.

I have never before met Phillip in person, but he fits the image I've had of him, and PR guys in general. Sharp featured, tall and trim, and well dressed. For our day in the park, he's wearing a blue blazer and cream-colored pants—what someone else might don to attend a country-club dinner.

"Clint," he says as my father alights from the back of the car. "It's all set up. The local TV news, the *Times*, and the tabloids have all agreed to cover it. I even got some network interest. George Stephanopoulos's kid goes to school with my kid, and I asked for the favor. No promises, but my guess is that today's event gets national exposure."

Phillip seems very pleased with himself. For an instant it bothers me that he's living off someone else's misery, but then I realize that's also what I do for a living. Of the two of us, he likely has the nobler calling.

"We've plastered Charlotte's picture and the notice for the hundred-thousand-dollar reward everywhere in the city," Phillip continues. "You'll see the pink fliers throughout the park. I think we're going to have more than five hundred people here today, and we'll tell the press we got twice as many. A lot are volunteers, but some are the people we go to when clients need to fill a room for an event or something, and those we pay. It doesn't cost very much, and it's well worth it because it makes for a good shot on the news to see a high-volume search going on. The way it's going to work is that half of the volunteers will walk down from Ninety-Sixth to Seventy-Second, and the other half will go north to One Hundred and Sixteenth. We're giving out these silver wristbands so the volunteers can identify one another, and we're encouraging everyone to keep them on until Charlotte comes home. We're also going to be distributing them throughout the city."

He hands me one. It's rubber, like the yellow bracelets everyone once wore to support Lance Armstrong's cancer foundation. I slide it around my wrist, and then my father does likewise.

Phillip keeps on talking. "We've set up a podium. I think you should say a few words, Clint. Ella, you can too if you want. Be brief, because we want to be able to control the message. I recommend you don't say anything about Jennifer Barnett. Stick to Charlotte. Something along the lines of thanking the volunteers for coming and then a word or two about what a wonderful person Charlotte . . . is. I've taken the liberty of jotting down some talking points, but I know, Clint, that you prefer to speak off the cuff, so just use them for guidance."

He thrusts an index card at my father, who scans it, then hands it to me. The card contains five bullet points that recite what Phillip just said. He has actually written the words, "We love Charlotte."

I put the card in my pocket. Like my father, I don't need a PR flack to tell me how wonderful my sister is.

In the distance, the flashing of police lights comes into view. A black SUV with four squad cars behind it pulls up along Riverside Drive. Gabriel is the first one to get out of the SUV.

"Please excuse me," I say. "That's the lieutenant in charge of the investigation."

Despite the summerlike weather, Gabriel is in all black, wearing a long-sleeve Henley and flat-front slacks. He has on what look like designer sunglasses, not the standard aviator ones most cops wear. As usual, his badge is on a chain around his neck.

He looks over at the crowd. "It looks like you've got a very good turnout."

"Something like five hundred people," I say. "But . . . I know this is going to sound strange because we scheduled the event, but I feel really odd about doing it. I mean, the last thing I want is for someone to find Charlotte's body, and here we're essentially asking people to give up their Saturday to look."

"I get it. You want closure, but only if it's the good kind. That's perfectly understandable. If it takes some concern away from you, your sister isn't here. We've already been through the park with cadaver dogs."

Cadaver. The word jolts me as if it were a racial slur, taking away Charlotte's humanity. To those dogs she's nothing but rotting flesh, a scent.

He obviously reads my discomfort with the thought. "The search is still a good idea," he says. "It will generate a lot of media coverage and that's always helpful. Someone hears about it on the news and it jogs a memory . . . or you pull on some heartstrings and someone turns in a brother or something. That's the way these cases get solved a lot of the time. We instructed your father's PR guy to make sure everyone signs in and provides some contact information. We'll cross-reference the names and phone numbers to see if they have any connection to Charlotte we didn't already know about. I'm not saying that the criminal always returns to the scene of the crime, but it's a cliché for a reason."

It is true, although I've never understood why people are so stupid. A shrink or criminal profiler might say it's all about power. There's some psychosis in the perp—he or she is convinced of their superiority, and seeing the cops fumble around reinforces it. Others get off on the chaos and pain they're inflicting on the family, a way to commit the killing all over again. And still others find it's a way to shadow the investigation. Coming to these types of things allows them to see the evidence the cops are uncovering in real time, so they can figure out if they're at any risk of getting caught.

None of the psychology behind it matters to me in the least, of course. All I care about is that, if it's true, my sister's killer might show up.

———

Phillip strategically places my father in front of the flower garden on Ninety-Sixth, so that the plantings are in the foreground. After my father gets into position, Phillip hands him the microphone.

My father squints in the bright sun. Then he turns to me and tries to force out a smile. After my father's inability to speak at the police press conference, I stand close by, ready to step in if needed even though I doubt my father will falter again.

"Thank you all for coming today," he begins. "I can't tell you how touched I am by the outpouring of love for Charlotte. Of course, it doesn't surprise me. Everyone who met Charlotte instantly fell in love with her. So thank you. Thank you all from the bottom of my heart."

He hands the microphone to Phillip. "Everyone," Phillip says, "you were each given numbers when you arrived. On the back is the location where you should check in. Go to that spot, and your group leader will be waiting with further instructions. Once again, on behalf of the Broden family, thank you all very much."

A few of the faces in the crowd I recognize as Charlotte's friends. Brooke actually gives me a cheerful wave before she realizes it's inappropriate for the setting. Josh and Zach are on opposite ends of the crowd, and I can't help but wonder whether it's intentional on their parts to stay as far away from each other as possible, but realize that it must be a coincidence because they've never met. I wonder too if either is really here because they're murdering sociopaths and want to watch the police fumble around and witness my father and me suffer, or to stay abreast of the investigation.

———

For the next two hours, we all parade up and down Riverside Park, searching for something no one wants to find. Rows of people walking straight lines, like some grim military exercise.

Every so often, the shrill sound of a whistle rings out, the signal that someone has found something that requires further attention. Despite Gabriel's confidence that no one will discover Charlotte, my heart stops with each blare. But then I hear the two rapid-fire whistles declaring the first interruption to be a false alarm.

In the end, no one locates Charlotte or anything belonging to her. I take the failure as good news, but can't deny a part of me wants this to be over. It has been more than three days now. Surely, Charlotte is dead.

———

Everyone meets back at Ninety-Sixth Street for refreshments. Phillip tells me to stand in front of the tent, to welcome each volunteer with a smile and a thank you. While I'm waiting for the last of them to report, I see a familiar face approach.

I'm beyond shocked. It's Dylan Perry, my one-night stand from Lava.

"Dylan?"

"Hello . . . *Ella*," he says.

I can feel my cheeks flush. I've finally been outed by someone who knows that Cassidy is actually Ella Broden. At the same time, I'm pleased that if anyone's going to crack my secret identity, it's Dylan. I've definitely wanted to see him again, but hadn't realized just how much until this moment.

"I wanted to get in touch with you," he says, "but I'm such an idiot. I never got your number the other night, and you never gave me your last name—and, as I since learned, *Cassidy* is a stage name. I thought about dropping by your apartment building, but that seemed kind of stalkerish. I was just about to leave you a note at Lava when I saw you on the news and decided that I'd come here to see you. I hope that was okay."

"Yes. I'm really glad you came, Dylan."

"I'm so sorry about your sister," he says. "I can't imagine what a nightmare this must be."

"Thank you," I say. "It's been really awful."

"I know this is going to sound odd because we don't really know each other at all, but if there's anything I can do, please just ask. Even if it's just to talk."

"That's very sweet. Thank you. I appreciate your coming out today, and wearing the bracelet."

He lifts his arm up to show off the accessory. "Normally I'd ask for your number, but I don't want to reach out to you until you're ready, so why don't I give you my number instead? That way, you can call me whenever you want. No pressure, though."

He smiles at me, and I'm instantly jolted the same way I was at Lava.

I take out my cell phone. "Ready."

He recites the numbers, and I punch them into my phone. When I'm finished, I hit "Dial."

His ringtone is "Under Pressure"—the same song he sang at Lava.

"No pressure, huh?" I say, laughing.

It's the first time I've laughed in days.

CHAPTER ELEVEN

My sister Emily is many things that I'm not. All of them good. She's honest, loyal, and cares about other people more than herself. She's also brilliant and beautiful. The apple of our father's eye, and our mother's favorite too, while she was alive.

I know that comes across like I'm jealous, but I'm not. If I were our parents, I'd favor Emily over me too. When our mother was diagnosed with cancer, Emily stepped up and took care of me and, truth be told, our father too. In many ways, it's Emily who actually reared me. She's the voice in my head—not my mother, whose voice I sometimes have trouble even remembering, or my father—who expresses the profound disappointment in the person I've become.

Not that Emily knows the depths to which I've sunk. I keep my issues secret from her due to my own shortcomings, not hers. I'm certain that if I confided in her, she'd provide me with good counsel. The reason I don't talk to her about it is that I'm even more certain that I'd reject her advice.

My sister is an Assistant District Attorney, and her office is a block from the courthouses in Lower Manhattan. I almost never venture that far downtown, as my usual southern boundary is Tribeca, but figure it's the least I can do for Emily, given that she has a full-time job and I don't have any commitments today. Aside from the commute, another reason I hate the courthouse area is that there are very few places to eat unless you venture into Chinatown, and I'm not a big fan of Chinese food. At least Emily has selected a diner where we can meet.

People have long commented that we look like sisters, but I truthfully don't see it. I possess my father's features, which gives my appearance a slightly masculine bent, or so I've been told by casting directors. Emily, on the other hand, is the spitting image of our mother—so much so that if it weren't for the fact that photos of our mother are actually prints, and not in the cloud, I might mistake them for selfies of Emily.

I'm slightly taller than my older sister. Not by much, half an inch, at most, but as anyone who's grown up as the baby in the family will tell you, it's enough that it matters to me. I take every opportunity possible to point out that although I may be younger, she's shorter. In this case, that amounts to me standing when Emily approaches, and going on my tiptoes to do my best to kiss her on the top of her head as we embrace.

"I only have forty-five minutes," Emily announces when we're both on our sides of the booth. She raises her hand to attract the waiter's attention.

"Relax, Em. The city will be safe if you take an hour for lunch."

The waiter asks if we'd like anything to drink, but Emily tells him that we're ready to order. Then she lets me go first.

"I'll have . . . I don't know, grilled cheese, with Swiss and a tomato, on rye. With a . . . coffee, I guess. Oh, and a side of french fries."

Emily orders a chef's salad, balsamic vinegar on the side, and a Diet Coke.

I smile when the waiter walks away.

"What?" she says.

"I can't remember the last time I was in a diner with you when you didn't order a chef's salad, balsamic vinegar on the side, and a Diet Coke."

"I like it," she says, defensively. "Besides, we're all not in our midtwenties anymore, my dear. French fries are only for stealing off other people's plates when you cross the big three-oh. But, enough about my figure. What's going on with you?"

What's going on with me? If ever there were a loaded question, that's it.

I want to come clean. To tell Emily the truth about myself. But something inside me overrules my best intention.

"You know me. I'm rehearsing all the time."

I sing a lyric from the show I'm rehearsing—Into the Woods. It's appropriately titled "I Know Things Now."

Emily smiles. She always likes to hear me sing and often complains that I don't do it enough in front of her. There's a reason I don't: she's the one with the talent in the family. My efforts, I fear, are a pale imitation. No matter how good I get or how far my career takes me, I'll always feel like an imposter next to her.

She offers up the key lyric, about being prepared.

In our little duet, she's hit the nail right on the head. I'm not prepared, and she knows it.

"I'm thinking of ending things with Marco," I finally admit. "He's . . . not going to change."

She nods thoughtfully. If this is a surprise, she doesn't betray it. Then again, she's seen Marco and me together, so I'm sure she must have thought my seeming epiphany about him has been a long time coming.

"You approve?"

Emily nods emphatically. "You deserve to be with someone who appreciates how amazing you are, Clare. I've never thought that was Marco. I get that he thinks he's amazing, but that's hardly the same thing."

"He's not so bad," I defend. A reflex that's highly attuned in me.

"That's not what I want you saying about the man you're living with. I want you to say, "He makes me a better person." And in your case, that's a very tall order for any man. Way too tall for the likes of Marco."

"What if I told you that there's a man . . . who might fit that bill?"

"I'd ask you why you weren't living with him."

"And if the answer was that he's married?"

"Oh," my sister says.

"Are you disappointed in me?"

She shakes her head in protest, and I know I'm being too hard on my sister. I don't need a shrink to tell me that I'm projecting. I'm disappointed in myself.

"I have no judgment when it comes to you," says Emily. "But I do know that being involved with a married man normally leads to heartache for everyone . . . except for the man."

18.

I arrive at Mas a few minutes before seven. The hostess tells me that Paul has already been seated, and then she leads me through the restaurant. I follow her between two rows of seating, tables for two against one wall and a communal table that runs the restaurant's length along the other, and around the wall of wine encased in glass, until we enter the back room. A giant etching of a blue fish dominates the main wall.

Paul is sitting alone at one of the pair of tables for two directly under the fish. The other table in the space is empty.

He stands as I approach and kisses me on the cheek. "I hope this is quiet enough," he says. "Galen was able to give us the entire back room."

Galen is Galen Zamarra, one of New York City's celebrity chefs. I wonder if Paul really knows him, or just paid for the other table too.

The waiter, a young man clad in all black, approaches with a bottle of wine. He uncorks it, and pours a taste for Paul.

Paul swirls the white wine in his glass and then takes a sip. "Yes, that's excellent," he says to the waiter. Then to me, "I took the liberty of ordering a bottle of chardonnay. This is a Château Génot-Boulanger 2009, and it's truly excellent."

The waiter fills my wineglass. I don't swirl it, but take a small sip. It's good, but tastes like any other white wine to my primitive palate.

Paul orders our appetizers, but allows me to order my own main course. As soon as the waiter leaves us alone, I tell Paul, "We need to talk a little business."

"If we must," he says with a sigh.

"As I told you over the phone, the police detective running the investigation told me that they found Jennifer's diary. Obviously, I haven't seen it, but he said it left no doubt that you and she were lovers."

"Would that be a problem?"

He says this with a smile that I bet he thinks is sexy as hell. I'm in no mood to play his game, however.

"I'm your lawyer, Paul. No need to charm me. And what you tell me is privileged. So it's now truth time. Yes or no. Were you?"

He doesn't answer right away, which is always a bad sign.

"Let's assume, for the sake of this discussion, that's a yes. Where would that leave us?"

For Paul, the truth is obviously beside the point. He doesn't want to commit to a story, even with me.

"Anybody else in her life, as far as you know?"

"No. Could be, though. It's not like . . . well, assuming we were involved, you can also assume it was casual and didn't go on for very long."

Of course it didn't go on for very long. That poor girl was only employed at Maeve Grant for three months. Paul must have pounced on her like a lion devouring fresh meat. A little initiation ritual to which he undoubtedly subjects all the attractive newbies.

"As I'm sure you know from your television viewing, the first suspect is always the boyfriend. And no matter how casual you claim it was between you and Jennifer, if there was no one else in her life, you're the boyfriend in the eyes of law enforcement."

He grimaces. I suspect Paul has tried for most of his adult life not to be the boyfriend.

"What's my motive?"

"Only you know that. But it doesn't matter. Motive isn't an element of the crime for which the prosecution bears the burden of proof. And that's because it could be a million things that they could never, ever prove. She could have threatened to break it off, so you killed her in a rage. You could have found out she was cheating on you, so you killed her in a rage. She could have burned dinner, so you killed her in a rage. Or she could have threatened to go to Maeve Grant and sue for sexual harassment, so you killed her in a rage."

My words hang in the air as the first of our courses arrives via two waiters, each holding a plate of something I can't identify, with froth around it. Our main server, the man who took our order, announces, "Fluke tartare with pomegranate marmalade."

The waiter leaves us with a "*buon appetito*," at which time Paul says, "So, tactics-wise, now what?"

"That's up to you. My father will likely advise that the diary proves his point that hunkering down is always the best play in the early stages of any investigation. He'd say that it's still possible the prosecution won't be able to prove the affair, and so it's a good thing you haven't admitted it. We could fight the diary's admission on hearsay grounds. And if you're very lucky, you didn't leave semen or a pubic hair in her place. Then we claim that the presence of your fingerprints might just be the result of a one-time visit for some totally innocent reason."

He smiles, obviously pleased with what he's hearing. It's a smug look, and I decide to slap it off his face.

"Don't celebrate quite yet, though. The truth of the matter is that, no matter how careful you think you were, the odds are very good that they're going to be able to prove the affair. Texts or phone messages are usually what clinches it."

"There's nothing in our communications to suggest a sexual relationship," he says with confidence, as if he always knew to be careful whenever he talked with Jennifer, just in case he later found himself in exactly this situation.

"The frequency is sometimes enough all by itself. Bosses don't call their employees multiple times on the weekends."

"We usually work weekends. And our phone frequency is not going to appear obsessive. A few times a week, tops."

"Trust me, if push comes to shove and someday you're before a jury on this, by the time the prosecution is finished, every one of those jurors will believe you were sleeping with her. She probably told a friend or a family member. Even if she didn't, and even if you think you were incredibly discreet, coworkers always know when the boss is involved with an underling, and one of them will testify to something you didn't think had been observed. You calling her 'sweetheart' or just a vibe, even. Or a neighbor will say that she saw Jennifer leaving your building early in the morning. Or they trace your credit cards to a romantic restaurant and the waiter ID's Jennifer's photo. Or worse, testifies that the two of you were holding hands or kissing."

The waiters arrive again en masse, removing our first course and simultaneously delivering our entrées. For Paul, that's Long Island duck breast with parsnip puree, while I opted for the wild striped bass with a leek fondue and carrot-turnip stew.

As soon as they walk away, Paul says, "I think I'm going to continue following your father's sage legal counsel and hunker down."

I knew that would be his decision.

"Any news about your sister?" Paul asks, changing the subject from his own legal problems.

My fork has just stabbed some bass, but I put it back down on the plate. I don't want to engage him about my sister's plight—seeing that he's a suspect in Jennifer Barnett's disappearance. But he asked, so I have to say something. I decide to conjure a happy memory of my sister to share.

"Remember when Charlotte came to visit me during spring semester of our senior year?" I say. "She was . . . what? Fifteen, I guess? Anyway, we all went to that party at that frat house. You gave her some grain alcohol mixed with Kool-Aid, and I thought she was going to go blind."

"I do remember that," he says, smiling at the memory. "Did Charlotte ever tell you that I saw her a few months ago?"

The moment's levity shatters. My guard immediately springs up.

"No. When?"

"Earlier this year. No, that's not right. It was late last year. Christmastime, because the museum still had its Christmas decorations up."

"You saw her at a museum?"

"Yeah, at MoMA. It was some benefit type of thing for NYU. I bought a table on behalf of Maeve Grant and before the dinner there was a cocktail party honoring some photographer. So there I was, staring at this out-of-focus photograph, when who sidles up next to me but your sister."

My jaw must have hit the ground. It's the exact same scenario as when Clare met Matthew the banker in Charlotte's book.

Why is Paul telling me this? If he was in any way, shape, or form involved in Charlotte's disappearance, he's certainly smart enough to know not to share with me that he'd recently seen her. But maybe it's like Gabriel said—classic sociopath behavior—and Paul's version of returning to the scene of the crime is telling me about him and Charlotte.

"Did you see her after that?"

"After that night, or later on during the dinner?"

"Um . . . either I guess."

"I said good night to her when I left. She said something about having to stay later, and I had a dinner meeting, if memory serves. And I'm almost certain I told her to give you my regards, which I gather she never did."

"No . . . she didn't say anything about it."

"I'm sure she just forgot. In fact, she probably never gave me a second thought. I was actually hoping at the time that she would tell you about our chance meeting and it would cause you to reach out to me. I figured when I never heard from you that it just meant you weren't interested."

I can't process what I'm hearing. I feel as though I'm literally going to fall out of my chair.

"I think I need to go home."

"I'm sorry, Ella. I didn't mean to upset you by talking about your sister."

"No. It's not that. I just . . . I just hit the wall. I haven't been sleeping much lately and today was a long, emotional day. I didn't mention it earlier, but we held a search for Charlotte in Riverside Park. Obviously, we didn't find her there, but . . . you know, just going through the ritual was draining."

I don't know if he buys it or is just being polite, but after he pays the check Paul walks me home. Neither of us say much as we travel the few blocks. There's an awkward moment in front of my building, when I can tell he's deciding how to say good-bye, and then he leans down to kiss me on the cheek.

DAY SIX

SUNDAY

19.

I used to love Sundays. I'd wake up whenever and go to the Koffee Klatch around the corner. I could spend hours sitting on one of the outdoor benches, drinking my large skim latte with a double shot and people-watching.

Today, however, all I can think about is Charlotte. Where is she? Will I ever see her smile again?

Still, I try to hew to my routine. I go to the Koffee Klatch and sip my coffee on the bench. A woman with a schnauzer sits beside me, but I can't summon the energy to pet her dog. The rest of the passersby go about their day, blissfully unaware that somewhere out there Charlotte Broden is being held against her will, or that her lifeless body is waiting to be found.

———

My childhood home was a limestone-facade townhouse just east of Park Avenue. When Charlotte left for college, my father moved into a classic six—New York real estate jargon for a two-bedroom apartment with a formal dining room and a maid's quarters—with a view of Central Park, in one of those snooty co-op buildings on Fifth Avenue. The white-gloved doormen always smile when I visit and call me by name, as Ramon, the man on duty today, does when I appear.

"Sorry about your sister," Ramon says.

He looks sincerely distressed. I wonder if Ramon has children of his own and is projecting. Then again, maybe even his limited encounters with Charlotte were enough to make him feel like they had a real connection.

"Thank you."

"Your father said you should go right on up," he says.

My father opens the door wearing a pained smile. His eyes look even worse. Bloodshot, with dark circles under them. He obviously hasn't been sleeping. I know the feeling, as sleep and I haven't been on good terms as of late either.

I follow him to the living room. It's a space I've always enjoyed being in. It reminds me of what New York City apartments look like in the movies: high ceilings, intricate decorative moldings, a working wood-burning fireplace, oil paintings covering the walls, and a large Bokhara rug on the hardwood floor.

He lowers himself into a corner of the sofa. Rather than take a seat in one of the armchairs, as I would normally do, I sit beside him so that I can place my arm around his shoulder. I squeeze him into me in a hug and see what appears to be an effort at a smile.

I decline the offer of coffee, telling him I'm already fully caffeinated. He declares that he'll make us some eggs.

"You don't have to, Dad."

"Don't be silly. I'm going to make you the candy eggs, like you like."

I follow him into the kitchen. He's already prechopped the ingredients for the dish—so named by Charlotte because there's a sweet taste to them. In fact, they're just made with caramelized onions and tomatoes.

"How you holding up?" he says as he stirs the onions, the scent taking over the kitchen.

"About as good as you, it seems."

"I was thinking about your mother."

"Yeah, I've been thinking about Mom a lot too lately."

"Even though I miss your mother more now than ever, there's a part of me that, for the first time, is a little happy that she's not here. Is that a terrible thing for me to say?"

"No, I know exactly what you mean. I'm glad Mom didn't have to go through this. Sometimes when it all gets too hard for me, I think that, if the worst has happened, then at least Charlotte and Mom are together, and that makes me feel better."

My reference that Charlotte might be dead is too much for him, and I see a tear break free and roll down his cheek. I kiss him on the forehead, the way he did when I was younger and needed to be comforted.

A few minutes later, we're situated in his dining room. Even though my father lives alone, his dining table seats twelve. He takes the chair at the head and puts my plate of eggs kitty-corner to him.

"What's going on with Paul Michelson?" he says, taking a forkful of his creation.

It's a ham-handed effort to move the conversation to safe ground. A topic he thinks—wrongly, as it turns out—has nothing to do with Charlotte.

"I had dinner with him last night," I say.

"Really?"

I can't tell if my father is surprised or being judgmental.

"Did you know he ran into Charlotte last Christmas?"

"Paul Michelson?"

"Yeah."

My father shakes his head. "I didn't."

"Remember I told you that Charlotte's book had a main character involved with three different men?"

He nods in a way that says, *How could I forget?*

"The student turns out to have been real. The police found him and questioned him. He said he didn't know Charlotte was even missing, but he failed the polygraph."

My father looks as if he's about to say something, but I don't give him the chance. I want to keep moving and focus him on the part that worries me.

"And, of course, the artist we *know* is real, because it's Zach. That leaves the banker, as the third of Charlotte's potential lovers in real life. In the book, the character based on Charlotte meets the banker at a museum benefit. She's staring at an out-of-focus photograph when the Matthew character approaches her, and they end up having an affair. He's the character in the book that the protagonist—Clare—truly loves. But he's also one of the possible murderers."

My father doesn't say anything. He's waiting for me to get to the point.

"Paul told me that he met Charlotte the same way. They were at a museum, staring at an out-of-focus photograph."

Neither of us says anything for a good ten seconds. Me because I'm waiting for him; my father's silence is likely because he's trying to process that his client might have murdered his daughter.

I'm expecting him to react with rage. Instead, when he resigns himself to what I've told him, he looks frightened.

"You know Paul much better than I do, obviously," he finally says, "but I know you. I know how badly you want to fix this—to solve the mystery, to punish whoever did this to Charlotte. But I need you to promise me something. If you think that there's even a remote possibility that Paul might be involved in Charlotte's disappearance in any way, tell the police and then let them do their job." My father begins to choke up, but still manages to complete his thought. "Ella, I can't . . . I just can't risk anything happening to you too."

"Okay," I say. "I promise."

As soon as I say it, the guilt hits me, as it always does whenever I lie to my father.

———

After I leave my father's apartment, I reach out to Gabriel. I've always hated when victims—or clients—called me on the weekend. I have little doubt that Gabriel feels the same way. I am prepared to leave a message on his work voice mail, but it turns out that he's at the office, so at least I'm not intruding on his R & R.

"I'm sorry to bother you," I say, "but there was something I wanted to talk to you about. Not over the phone, though. Could we meet for lunch? My treat."

"No need to apologize. Sure. Lunch sounds good. Two conditions, though. We go somewhere near One PP, and you let me pay my own way."

Of course. Even a sandwich would be considered a bribe. I never let citizens pay for my lunch back when I was on the public payroll either.

"Okay, Dutch treat it is."

"How about Bubby's at one o'clock?"

I refrain from using my usual closing—"It's a date." Instead I say, "See you there."

20.

Bubby's conjures the sense of comfort food from the moment you walk inside. There's hardly anything on the menu that doesn't include melted cheese on top.

"This a regular haunt of yours?" I ask Gabriel.

"Yes, even cops get out from time to time."

"I should have known. Given the pie selection," I say with a wink.

We both order the grilled cheese. He asks for a cup of coffee and declines the offer of French fries for only two dollars more. I pair mine with seltzer and take the fries.

"I'll share," I say. "I mean, if that won't compromise you ethically."

He smiles. A very nice smile.

"Just don't tell IA, and we're good."

After the waitress leaves, Gabriel asks, "So, what was so important that you were afraid to say it over the phone?"

"It'll be a week on Wednesday," I say. "I know that's still seventy-two hours from now, but . . . she's dead, isn't she?"

I trust Gabriel to give it to me straight. It's actually that fear that has caused me not to previously pose the question.

"Ella . . . I wish I could tell you that it's going to be fine, but I know you know, at this point, the odds of that aren't good. But that's not a reason to give up hope. I haven't. And while there's even a sliver of hope that she's alive, I'm going to do everything I can to find her. That's why

I'm not turning it over to Missing Persons on Wednesday. I got our captain to allow us to work it for another week, at least."

"Thank you," I say. "Anything new with Zach?"

He shakes his head. "Radio silence."

"What do you think about my father throwing him out of the apartment? Maybe the thought of becoming homeless will get him to talk."

"I got no problem with that. But I know that's not why you asked to meet me for lunch. So, tell me. What's on your mind?"

He sits up straighter, ready to receive my not-to-be-shared-on-the-phone information. Unfortunately, the waitress takes this opportunity to tell us that our food will be right out, and to ask Gabriel if he'd like her to freshen up his coffee.

"No thanks," he says, and she smiles at him in a come-hither way. When she's out of earshot, he says, "You were about to say . . ."

"You remember that in Charlotte's manuscript she met the banker character at a museum?"

"Okay . . . ," he says, making it clear he hadn't remembered that tidbit.

"I had dinner with Paul Michelson last night. I guess I didn't tell you before, but I dated Paul in college. That's how we came to represent him."

"Small world," Gabriel says with a wan smile.

"Yeah, about to get much smaller when I tell you why this is important. He told me that he had seen Charlotte recently, when he met her at *a museum*. And he described their meeting *exactly* the way she wrote about the Matthew character meeting the Clare character in the book. They were both staring at an out-of-focus photograph."

"And Paul Michelson is a banker," Gabriel says.

"And he's a banker."

Gabriel takes a mouthful of air into his lungs. "When did he retain you?"

I put my lawyer hat back on. When Paul retained us is subject to the attorney–client privilege, and therefore off-limits for me to disclose. It'll reveal that he obtained counsel *before* the police requested a formal interview about Jennifer Barnett, and that always suggests guilt, despite what my father thinks. None of that matters to me in the least, however. I'd gladly be disbarred to get Charlotte back.

"It was . . ." I count back the days. "Wednesday."

Now it's Gabriel's turn to count backward. "Jennifer Barnett went missing on . . . the prior Saturday. That means he waited . . ." Gabriel ticks the days off on his fingers. "One, two, three, four days to retain counsel. And your sister was last seen on Wednesday morning by Zach. Same day. What time of day did you meet with Paul?"

"First thing in the morning," I say.

"So the timeline doesn't work out exactly," Gabriel says. "Meeting with your father first and then killing the man's daughter. Why would he do that?"

"But if Paul is a sociopathic killer, then normal human emotions—like shame or whatever stops someone from retaining the father of someone you're going to murder—don't apply to him. Maybe he thought that first hiring my father and then killing Charlotte would give him exactly the kind of alibi you're suggesting, and that's why he did it in that order."

"Okay . . . so what's his motive?"

"I've been thinking about this a lot," I say. "You guys are convinced Paul was seeing Jennifer Barnett, right?"

"Diaries don't lie. Not usually, anyway."

"What if he was also seeing Charlotte?"

"What if he was? I still don't see a motive for him to kill your sister. Jennifer Barnett could bring a sexual harassment claim, but your sister couldn't."

I spell it out for him. At least as far as I could take it.

"Remember, in Charlotte's book, Matthew the banker is married. But Paul isn't. If the diary is correct, however, Paul had a girlfriend . . .

Jennifer Barnett. That's the kind of small change that Charlotte might make so that her book was, you know, fiction. To protect the innocent, as it were. With me so far?"

Gabriel nods. "Yep."

"Maybe Jennifer found out about Charlotte. If that happened, she'd probably threaten Paul. Woman scorned and all. Then Jennifer goes missing. Maybe Charlotte knew about Paul and Jennifer. In that case, Charlotte would have known it was Paul who killed her. Charlotte probably confronted Paul about it, and Paul killed her too. That would explain the time gap. He could have met with my father and me *after* he killed Jennifer, but before he realized that Charlotte knew about it. Or maybe he already was planning on killing Charlotte when he retained us, and he did it for the classic sociopath reason—to get inside information about the case. What better way than to be in an attorney–client relationship with the victim's father?"

Gabriel doesn't say anything at first, but I can tell from his eyes that he's intrigued. "I'm not saying there's not some stuff there that we need to investigate more fully, but that's a lot of maybes. Also, I just want to draw you back to what we know is true, as opposed to the conjecture part of your theory. We don't have any evidence that Paul and your sister were even having an affair. And everything you just said flows from that."

He's right. But he's also wrong.

"Tell me, then, what are the odds that Paul Michelson, a banker, met Charlotte at a museum looking at an out-of-focus photograph, and it has no connection to Charlotte's protagonist meeting Matthew the banker in the same way?"

"Agreed that's not a coincidence. But all it really tells me is that Paul and your sister met that way, and then your sister used that in her book. It doesn't mean that everything else about this Matthew character is true—or that it's really Paul."

"What about showing his picture around the Four Seasons hotel? In the book, that's where he took Charlotte."

"We've already been through the hotel's video surveillance. Charlotte never shows up on it. We'll go back and see if Paul's credit card is on file and flash his photo, but given that we didn't see Charlotte there, it's pretty much a wasted exercise."

I sigh to signify my displeasure. He catches my drift immediately.

"Hey, I'm more than happy to pick Paul up and question him about this, but . . ."

"But what?"

"But I already know that he's got a high-priced lawyer who's going to shut us down."

"I suppose I deserve that," I say.

He shakes his head. "No, you don't deserve any of this. I'm frustrated too. But you know as well as I do that if Paul Michelson lawyered up about Jennifer Barnett, you can be damn sure he's going that way regarding your sister's disappearance. On top of which, Paul Michelson's phone number doesn't show up on your sister's call log. Of course, that's not surprising because if the Matthew-is-Paul theory is right, that means Paul used a burner, and we know that your sister got calls from a burner. But the problem is that the burner phone is a dead end. We don't know where the phone was purchased, so we can't even show Paul's picture to a store clerk. And I know you know this too, but no judge on earth is going to issue a warrant to search Paul Michelson's home on what we have right now."

"Okay," I say. "I get it."

And I do. But what I really understand is that Gabriel's hands are tied and I need to get more information about Paul Michelson to untie them.

CHAPTER FOURTEEN

Our terrace is small. It's furnished with two chairs and a round table. When Marco first moved in with me, we'd often come out here to share a bottle of wine, but nowadays he usually occupies it alone—it's the only spot in the apartment where I allow him to smoke.

Today it's warm, above seventy degrees even at this early hour. As a result, when I awake, I'm not too surprised to see Marco sitting outside, a cup of coffee in one hand, a cigarette in the other.

"I'm out here," he shouts.

He sounds like he's in a good mood. I know better than to let that opportunity pass without taking full advantage. So after a quick stop to pour myself some coffee, I join him outside.

I have little doubt that his good spirits relate to tonight's art show. Marco's been a little vague about details, but the way he first explained it to me was that a Mexican painter of some renown named Juan Quinones Perez—who of course I'd never heard of, which Marco, for reasons I couldn't comprehend, found more insulting to him than to the Mexican artist—was going to be showing at a gallery in Chelsea. One of the conditions the artist imposed was that a small number of student artists of Mexican descent be allowed to show as well. Marco has been selected from many entries to be one of three student exhibitors.

To hear Marco tell it, this show will change his life. He's certain that his work will outshine the others'—not only his fellow students' art, but the main attraction as well—and he will instantly become the darling of the art world.

I'm pleased that he has such confidence, although I'm fearful of the crash that will undoubtedly follow. I've seen Marco deal with rejection, and to say it's not a pretty sight is like saying that the Taj Mahal is "fancy." The slightest criticism—a professor suggesting that he add more light or a gallery owner telling him that his work isn't quite what he's looking for—gives rise to weeks of brooding. Shows are particularly treacherous ground, as anything from the location of his pieces in the space to the font size of his name in the program can spark a rage.

"I take it that the gallery is pleased with the work?" I say, taking a seat beside him.

He takes a long drag on his cigarette and blows a smoke ring toward the river. "Very. Henry—he's the curator of the show—is pricing my piece of you at ten grand."

Marco has never sold a painting. Not one. In fact, he hasn't even been able to give them away, which he tried to do back when he actually had a landlord he wasn't sleeping with and didn't have the money to cover his rent. I doubt very much that anyone goes from zero to ten grand in one fell swoop, but I've never truly understood how the art world works. The one thing I do know is that I'm not going to be the one to bring Marco back down to reality.

"That's great. Which pieces did you finally select for the show?"

I've asked this before, and when I did, he acted as if maintaining the confidentiality of this information was a matter of national security. I am hoping that his good mood might make him more inclined to share.

"You'll see tonight."

Even his high spirits have their limits, apparently. At least he says it with a smile.

"Can I at least see the one you did of me?"

"You know that's bad luck."

"I think you mean seeing the bride before the wedding. I'm not aware of any similar superstitions concerning subjects and art."

"The answer is still no. You can see it at the show, like everyone else. And remember, it starts at seven."

"I know. But I told you, I have rehearsal today. I'm not sure when Tobias is going to let us go, but I've told him that I have to be in Chelsea by seven."

Marco looks at me suspiciously. I can't really blame him. Tobias is my director, and I often cite his demandingness as my alibi for the late nights I'm with Matthew or Jason.

"What play are you rehearsing for, again?"

I must have told him that I'm playing Little Red in "Into the Woods" at least half a dozen times.

"'Into the Woods.'"

"Right. How's it going?"

"Good. It's a hard part because I'm doing it in a character voice, playing a ten-year-old. I don't have the main song down exactly right yet. Sometimes it sounds like the character is singing and sometimes it sounds like my normal voice. Also, Matisse still isn't off book, which is a problem."

I'm quite sure that Marco doesn't know that Matisse is playing The Wolf, or what "off book" means, even though I've also told him both things numerous times. In fact, his stupid grin tells me he hasn't even been listening to me.

"You should get there about ten minutes early so I can introduce you to Juan."

He name-drops as if he and Juan Quinones Perez are besties. I'm quite sure they've never met or spoken.

"I'll try my best."

If Marco were in lesser spirits, he would have called me on my hedging. He's not above saying something like, "Don't try, just do it." But his faraway gaze at the river tells me that his mind has already moved on to something else.

"*This show's gonna be the break I've been working toward,*" he says. "*My work will finally get seen by people who can appreciate it. Let me amend that: people with money who can appreciate it. It wouldn't surprise me if I get a mention in the* Times. *I heard they're sending a reporter.*"

I smile, a look designed to tell him that I couldn't agree more. In reality, I'm far more certain that I'll never witness Marco this happy again. In my head, the chronology will be as follows: he won't sell anything in the show, and that will begin the downward spiral. Drinking at first, his chosen method of self-abuse, but not long after that, he'll start to take it out on me.

21.

I call Paul from the back of the cab on my way home from Bubby's.

"Hi, it's Ella," I say, trying to sound casual.

"Hey, you. So nice to hear the sweet sound of your voice."

Jesus. Do women really fall for this crap? I guess maybe twenty-two-year-olds like Jennifer Barnett. I'd like to think that Charlotte was too smart to be taken in by the likes of Paul Michelson.

"I wanted to apologize for the way things ended last night. The wine just really hit me all of a sudden. Can I make it up to you tonight?"

"Of course," he says, sounding positively wolfish. "How about . . . I don't know . . . have you ever been to Sant Ambroeus? It's on Madison and Seventy-Eighth."

Paul lives on Park and Seventy-Eighth. I'm not surprised that he suggests we have dinner around the corner from his apartment.

"Sounds perfect. Does seven work?"

"It does for me. Can't wait to see you, Ella."

"Me too," I say.

When I hang up the phone, I feel both dirty and empowered at the same time.

———

Sant Ambroeus is a favorite dining spot of the art crowd, being situated among various galleries a few blocks south of the Met. As we eat, I offer into the conversation tidbits about Charlotte, but Paul doesn't take the bait. He claims not to know that Charlotte is a writer, and that he's never been to a Four Seasons hotel in New York City. Why would he? he says. He lives here, after all.

If anything, he seems more interested in me than my sister. He asks if I like being a lawyer and why I left the DA's office to join up with my father. I answer with my usual talking points about how it was time for a new challenge and that I was eager to stop making public servant money.

"There was something I wanted to ask," he says, suddenly sounding very serious. "Something that's been bothering me since we graduated."

"Okay. What?"

"Why'd you go to law school?"

"What do you mean, why? Because it's a prerequisite for becoming a lawyer."

"C'mon, Ella. I knew you back then. The Ella Broden who was the star of Columbia's drama department. I was devastated when you said you were going to California for law school. You always told me that your post-graduation plan was to be a singer."

I have absolutely no remembrance of him caring one way or the other what I did after graduation. Certainly, I don't recall Paul Michelson being *devastated*. I was the one who cried every day that summer. He was off screwing Kelly Nelson in Paris.

He sees my confusion. "You don't remember, do you? I literally begged you to stay in New York. But you'd gone and applied to law school without even telling me and then sprung on me that you'd been accepted at Stanford and were going in the fall."

"I didn't want to be a singer anymore," I say as if it were the truth.

"Obviously. You found the bright lights of criminal-defense law so much more exciting."

"Prosecution, actually. And it was exciting."

"Hardly a passion, though."

"You're one to talk. I don't remember you being passionate about derivatives back in college."

"That's different. I didn't have a gift. My options were more limited in that regard. That wasn't your story. Look, I'm not trying to make you feel bad. It was a long time ago and you've done more than all right for yourself. I just always wondered how it all came about. Funny, right? I mean, I was there in the thick of things, and yet I still don't have the first idea."

Him and me both. I lived it, and it was a blur to me too.

I dissemble. "I just wanted a different kind of life, I guess."

His tight smile leaves no doubt that he's dissatisfied with my response. Yet he must also know that no amount of cross-examination is going to yield a more revealing explanation, because he lets it end there.

After he pays the check, Paul looks down at his watch. I do a double-take.

"That's a nice watch. What kind is it?" I ask, trying to sound calm.

"A Patek Philippe."

Son of a bitch. That's the same $50,000 watch Matthew the banker wore.

"I figure if I'm going to be the last person on earth who doesn't rely on his smartphone for the time," he says with a grin, "I might as well have something that's going to keep its value."

He looks at me with lust in his eyes. "I have a very nice bottle of Armagnac that I've been dying to crack open—just looking for the right special occasion."

I have no idea what Armagnac is, but I also couldn't care less. The evidence is beginning to mount that Paul Michelson was involved with my sister. Getting inside his apartment might just allow me to find the evidence Gabriel needs for a warrant.

But then I hear my father's warning in my head. In truth, I might have ignored it except for the fact that Charlotte's voice creeps in too, telling me not to be alone with Paul unless I have a plan—and a means to protect myself.

"That sounds lovely, Paul. But I need to take a rain check, I'm afraid."

He puts on a smile as phony as a bad toupee. He must have thought my agreeing to let him buy me dinner at a restaurant near his apartment was akin to executing a letter of intent for sex.

"Another time, then," he says.

———

At ten, back in my apartment and alone, I feel the need for interaction with a man who doesn't repulse me. So I begin to compose a text to Dylan.

Hey there. Wondering how you're doing.

I stare at it on my screen for a good ten seconds before I hit the "Send" button. Then I anxiously wait another ten, trying to will his reply. I'm about to put the phone down when I hear the ping.

I'm good. And you?

I'm actually better than I've been in a long time, considering the speed of his response. I'm not going to put myself that out there, however.

I've had a crappy day, to tell you the truth.

Sorry. Anything I can do?

I'm smiling ear to ear. My face is so out of practice that I actually feel the muscles move in an unfamiliar way.

I decide to bring our relationship to the next step and dial his phone. He answers immediately, and practically the first thing he says is that he was hoping that I would call.

"I have to be honest," I say, even though I wonder if honesty is the best policy when embarking on a new relationship, "I've been struggling with the whole can-I-meet-someone-new-while-my-sister-is-missing thing."

"I totally understand. Timing . . . couldn't be worse. But I'm a big believer that things happen for a reason . . . at least sometimes. We met, we really clicked, and then this terrible thing happened to your sister. I think . . . I don't want to get all higher-power on you because I'm not religious, but I do consider myself spiritual and, well, I think the universe does send us messages. And yes, I know that makes me sound like someone dressed in pajamas giving out daisies at the airport, but I believe it."

I truly don't know what to say to that. While I'm formulating a response in my head, he repeats the question he previously texted.

"Is there anything I can do? To make things easier on you, I mean."

I decide to let down my guard. Having a distraction—especially such a handsome one—would definitely improve my mental state.

"In fact, there is. Would you mind terribly keeping me company tomorrow night? I'm just going crazy here all alone and I don't want to do it again another night."

He asks if I have a favorite restaurant, but I don't want to be in public, so I invite him to my place for dinner. I'm tempted to suggest that he not expect anything, but I think that's implied. Another reason I don't say it is that I'm not certain it's true.

DAY SEVEN

MONDAY

22.

It takes every ounce of energy I have to get out of bed on Monday. I drag myself into the shower and then get ready for work as if my life hasn't been ripped apart. I'm buoyed only by the thought that after I get through the workday I'll see Dylan.

I make it to the office at 9:15. I'm nearly floored when Ashleigh says that my father hasn't yet arrived. In my three months at the firm, I've *never* gotten to work before him.

"Have you heard from him?" I ask.

"No. I guess with Garkov adjourned, he decided to sleep in."

Like my father, I also have no pressing work this morning. With Paul Michelson in hunker-down mode, there's nothing to do there, and while there are some smaller matters to which I could bill time—a Medicare fraud sentencing memorandum, an SEC inquiry into insider trading that's heading toward an on-the-record interview next month, a call I need to return to our expert witness in an art-forgery case—none of those things is time-sensitive.

So I stare at the blank walls of my office. Wondering when all of this will finally end, and what it'll look like when it does.

My father knocks on my office door a little after ten. He looks like something the cat dragged in. His tie, which is always perfectly knotted with a center dimple, hangs askew, and his complexion is the color of smoke.

"You look terrible," I say.

"Good morning to you too, dear," he says, trying but failing to smile.

He steps inside and closes the door behind him. His body crumples into my guest chair. He's completely and utterly bereft.

"She's dead, isn't she?" he says.

"I don't know, Dad. But what I am certain about is that we need to stay positive."

He puts his face in his hands. "I . . . don't know how I'm going to be able to go on if . . ."

I want to comfort him, but I feel the same way. How can I continue to live in a world without Charlotte?

My life has always been bisected by my mother's death. The before and the after. When my mother was alive, my father reminded me of an exotic bird that only appeared at certain times of the year. The two weeks before Labor Day, when he'd work from his home office in our East Hampton house, or the week of winter break when we all went to Aspen and he skied the double-black diamonds. At all other times, he was working. When I was little I thought my father must be a criminal himself because my mother was always telling me that he was "on trial."

It now seems as though my life will forever be cut into thirds. Before my mother died. Before Charlotte died. And after.

———

At noon, Gabriel calls. As is the case every time I see his number pop up on my caller ID, my heart stops.

"I have good news," he says, and for the briefest moment I allow myself to think the good news is that Charlotte has been found safe and sound. Then he crashes that fantasy. "Zach came down and agreed to cooperate with us."

Compared to what I had let myself imagine was his good news, this revelation was nothing of the sort. On top of which, I don't trust a word out of Zach's mouth.

"Did you hear me?" he says, a reaction to my silence.

"Yeah. So, what's Zach saying?"

"He came in here with a friend who's a first-year law student. Said that he'd thought about it, and because he hadn't done anything wrong, he wanted to help in any way he could. Turns out that the last time he saw your sister wasn't Wednesday morning like he's been claiming. He didn't see her at all on Wednesday. The last time he saw her was on *Tuesday* morning."

Damn him. We had the timeline wrong.

"Why did he lie about that?"

"He said that he didn't come home himself on Tuesday night. He was out with the law-school friend all night, and claims that when he finally came home—which he puts at a little after nine a.m. on Wednesday morning—Charlotte was already gone. He said that he knew she had an early class, so he didn't think twice about her not being home. Then, when she didn't come home that night, he figured she was out to get back at him. You know, he stayed out the night before and so she was staying the night somewhere else to give him a taste of his own medicine. But when it was getting close to daybreak, he started to worry. That's when he called you."

I honestly didn't know how to react. Should I be happy that we had more information? Or feel even more distress because Charlotte has now actually been missing six days, rather than five?

"What's to say he's not lying now?" I say. "Because his law-student girlfriend gives him an alibi for Tuesday night when he doesn't have one for Wednesday night?"

"Yeah, I thought of that too. But he passed the poly. She did too."

"On everything?" I ask.

"Like they're George and Martha Washington."

"Jesus."

"This is a good thing, Ella. Now we can rule Zach out, and we have the correct timeline. Wednesday-night alibis don't matter. It's Tuesday night that we need to focus on."

The last time I saw Zach, I didn't want to believe that he could have killed Charlotte, largely because I couldn't accept that she might be dead. Now I'm certain that she's gone, and I want Zach to pay for it. Even if he's not guilty of killing her, he still bears culpability for the crime.

"If Zach's so goddamn innocent, why'd he take so long to tell us this?"

"He told me what he told you. Everybody thinks it's the boyfriend. On top of that, there's the whole race thing. He's a black man dating a white woman, and he's cheating on her. And, needless to say, he knew he wouldn't pass the poly because he'd boxed himself into a lie about when he last saw her. He figured if all that came out, we'd just lock him up and throw away the key."

Zach wasn't wrong. If I were representing him, I would have told him the same thing. *Don't cooperate. The police will eat you alive with that story.*

"And so why the change of heart, then?"

"He said he thought we'd find the guy who did this without his help. When the weekend passed and we still didn't have someone in custody, his conscience got the better of him and he decided to help. At least, that's his story."

"And you believe that crock?"

"You know how it is. Nobody's ever totally cleared until we get the guy who did it. But, yeah, for the time being, we're focusing away from Zach. We might still throw an obstruction charge at him, but that would wind up being a sideshow, and I want to direct all our resources to finding your sister. Believe me, I would have loved it if the evidence took us right to Zach, but the fact is that all indications now are that your sister went missing Tuesday night, and Zach's got a solid alibi. Not just the law student's say-so, although like I said she passed the poly too, but her dorm has video surveillance. Zach comes in that night around a quarter of ten and doesn't leave until seven a.m. the next day."

"Yeah, but who's to say he didn't kill her before ten? Who's to say that the law student and Zach didn't do it together?"

"The timing is very tight. The law student claims that they were together all night on Tuesday. Charlotte left you at Tom's at about two, right?"

"I actually don't know how long she stayed after me, but I left at around two thirty. We ordered food but I didn't stay to eat, so it's possible she stayed a little later."

"When she left doesn't matter much because Zach didn't get out of rehearsal until four thirty. Then he's off the grid until he shows at Margarita Grill in the Village with the law-school friend. Now, we don't have a positive ID from the waiters or anyone in the restaurant yet, but the law student puts him there, and her credit-card receipt shows they left at eight forty-two."

Of course she paid, I think to myself.

"So, assuming dinner took an hour, he could have seen Charlotte between four thirty and seven forty-two, right?"

"Yes, that's the only window. But logistically, it doesn't work. His rehearsal was in the Village, and your sister was uptown. Now, it's possible she came to him and they met at exactly four thirty, but if he went to her, that's another thirty to forty-five minutes in which he couldn't have committed the crime. He's back downtown at around seven thirty, which eliminates another thirty to forty-five minutes. That's an hour to an hour and half when he couldn't have done it. So, at most, he would have had ninety minutes to commit the murder and get the body out of wherever he killed her. Aside from the timing being very tight, I don't see how he kills your sister in her apartment and leaves with her body—even if he has it hidden in something—without the doormen remembering that. And they don't remember your sister—or Zach—coming or going at all that day."

"Okay, but if she went downtown to him, then he's got three hours. That's enough time. And there's no doorman problem."

"It's enough time, but where and how does he do it? It's broad daylight in a densely populated part of the city. On top of which, he's perfectly put together—no ripped clothes or scratches or blood—when he sees the law student at seven thirty."

"So she says."

"So she says," he confirms.

Gabriel's right, though. It doesn't make sense for Zach to lure Charlotte to some public spot in the Village and kill her there.

"What about after dinner?" I ask.

"That's even less likely. Like I said, dinner was over at eight forty-two, and then there's a receipt at a gelato store about three or four blocks away from the restaurant at nine ten. They next show up on the dorm security camera at nine forty-nine, and not again until the following morning."

The facts indicate that Zach is a cheater, but not a murderer. Good news there. He and Charlotte were simply two people caught in a dysfunctional relationship. Period. End of story.

"Okay, so where does this leave us?"

"We have to redo a lot of our investigating now that the time of Charlotte's disappearance has moved up a day. We're going to start with Josh. He's agreed to come in and meet with us again. But given that he can't effectively be polygraphed, whatever he says to us is kind of meaningless."

"And what about my theory about Paul Michelson? The change to Tuesday makes it more likely he's the guy. It means he hired us *after* he killed Charlotte. To stay close to the investigation about Charlotte. Classic sociopathic behavior, right?"

"Yeah. It would certainly be that, Ella. I mean, if he's the guy."

CHAPTER FIFTEEN

Despite my best efforts, I'm delayed at rehearsal. That means there's going to be hell to pay with Marco for being late to his big night. Whether my tardiness is by ten minutes or two hours hardly matters. To him, my not showing up on time to "his" show means I do not respect his work—which is the same thing as not caring about him.

The gallery is on the fourth floor. A tiny elevator takes forever to climb the few stories. When the doors finally open, I literally run into the space.

I had assumed—wrongly, it turns out—that the art crowd would be fashionably late. Even though my iPhone tells me it's only 7:15, the space is already wall-to-wall with people.

A server wearing a tuxedo—sans jacket, but with a black tie and silver vest—offers me a glass of champagne from a tray. I take it and quickly look around for Marco. In the center of the room is a fifteen-foot-high minimalist, abstract sculpture entitled Infinity *that can only be intended to evoke the thought of a penis. From my quick glance at the rest of Quinones Perez's oeuvre, it seems phallus-shaped pieces are the common thread running through his work.*

I make my way through the room, assuming that Marco's pieces will be near the back, but there's no sign of him or his work. When I reach the far wall, I approach an elderly woman. She's accompanied by a much younger man, and they're holding hands.

"I heard that there were some student artists also showing," I say. "Any idea where that would be?"

"Yes," the woman says with a smile. "Go through those doors—it's down the hall a bit."

Marco has been relegated to the bullpen. Now I'm certain he'll be furious. The one bright spot of him being in Siberia is that at least I'll be able to claim that I arrived on time but couldn't find him.

I don't see anyone else in the hallway, so I fully expect Marco's room to be similarly uninhabited. But when I enter, he's talking to another man.

I'm anticipating being on the receiving end of some type of death stare from Marco, his way of making it clear to me that he's angry that I'm late. Instead, he greets me with a broad grin.

"Speak of the devil," Marco says.

The man who has held Marco's attention turns around.

It's Matthew. My Matthew.

I can't believe he had the nerve to show up at Marco's event. And worse, he's engaged him. I can only imagine the hell I'd have to pay if I pulled a similar stunt with Matthew's wife.

"Very nice to meet you," Matthew says. "Clare, is it?"

"Y-yes," I manage to say even though my jaw is so tight it could press a diamond from coal.

"Matthew here is interested in purchasing the piece I did of you," Marco says. "He said it held . . . what was your exact turn of phrase?"

"Transcendent beauty," Matthew says with a smile.

I can finally see Marco's portrait of me. It's propped up on an easel in the middle of the room. Me, in all my naked glory.

I'll give Marco this—the piece is magnificent. He's captured almost my fantasy of myself, and even though I'm wearing next to nothing it isn't prurient in the least.

Words escape me. After all, what can you say when your lover is catfishing your boyfriend? But then it occurs to me that Marco might be expecting me to suck up to his potential buyer.

"I couldn't agree more," is all I could come up with.

Matthew looks deeply into my eyes, as if I'm totally in on this joke. Then, turning to Marco, he says, "Do I really need to take up the business arrangements with the gallery? I can't just tell you to name your price for this piece and walk out with it?"

Marco laughs. "I wish, but it doesn't work that way. The gallery handles all sales for this show, but I can arrange a private showing of my work if you like. On those pieces, you can deal with me directly."

Marco reaches into his pocket and pulls out a scrap of paper. It looks like a receipt. On the side without the print, he scribbles his address and number. "Here you go," he says. "You can reach me on my mobile. Day or night."

The transaction seems as if it's unfolding in slow motion, the way you might witness a car accident. All I want is for the two of them to stop occupying the same space.

"Thank you," Matthew says, taking the scrap from Marco. "And now I better put in my claim on this beauty before someone else snatches it out from under me." He extends his hand to Marco and as they shake, Matthew says, "I'm so glad that I wandered out of the main room. You're very, very talented, Marco. I'm thrilled that I'll be getting in on the ground floor of what I have every expectation will be a long and prosperous career." He turns and smiles at me again. "And very nice meeting you too, Clare. I look forward to hours of staring at you . . . at least on canvas."

Marco waits for Matthew to leave. Then he gushes, "Can you believe that? 'Transcendent beauty.' You know, that's what I should have titled it. Well, at least I won't have to split the price with Henry when Mr. Wall Street buys my other pieces."

I know there'll be no other purchases. In fact, I consider it a fair possibility that Matthew won't even buy this one of me. And if that's the case, there truly will be hell to pay with Marco—even if he doesn't figure out that I'm in love with his would-be patron.

23.

When I arrive at Charlotte's apartment, there's a duffel bag in the living room.

"Going somewhere?" I ask Zach. "I would have thought you'd have no reason to run now."

"I have the definite feeling I've worn out my welcome here."

He's right about that. In fact, he's about a week late in coming to the conclusion.

"You can't blame us for that. Even if you didn't kill Charlotte—and I'm far from certain of that still—your courageous decision to mislead everyone as to when she went missing might very well have ended her life just the same."

He can't make eye contact, which pleases me. Even so, I'm certain he doesn't feel nearly bad enough for the havoc he's wreaked.

"When will you be out of here? The sight of you in my sister's apartment sickens me."

He doesn't rise to the bait. His self-control surprises me—a sign of just how much my understanding of Zach has merged with Marco the painter.

"Another hour or so," he says.

"Let me guess. You're taking up residence with your little law-school friend?"

This time he looks at me. I can see the anger just beneath the surface, even though Zach's trying mightily to suppress it.

"That's none of your business."

I laugh in the patronizing way I perfected back when I was an ADA and suspects thought they had the upper hand. It unequivocally told them that they had no idea how out of their depth they really were.

"Suit yourself. You won't be living with her long, anyway. Lying to the police makes you guilty of obstruction of justice. That's a class E felony in New York, punishable by three to five years in jail. I'm going to make sure you serve every day of it. A pretty boy like you . . . I'm quite confident you'll become the girlfriend of some animal at Rikers soon enough."

In reality, under New York law, obstruction of justice is a class A misdemeanor. Jail time is limited to one year by statute, and I'm not aware of any first-time offender going to prison for a misdemeanor infraction. Zach, of course, doesn't know the law. I'm hoping the specter of jail time will unnerve him.

But he doesn't show the slightest reaction. It's as if there's nothing I can say that matters to him any longer.

His nonchalant attitude pushes me over the edge. Even before I realize it's happening, I hear myself screaming.

"Get the fuck out of here right now, you fucking lowlife piece of shit!"

Next thing I know, my hands are around the handle of Zach's duffel bag and I'm running toward the door. I throw it into the hallway and am coming back to do the same to Zach when I see his palms in front of his chest. He's telling me to stop.

"Please," he says. "Sit down. I know we're likely not going to talk again after today, so we should talk now."

Still enraged, I follow Zach over to the sofa. If he has something to say, I'll hear it. But that's all the civility I'm prepared to provide him.

"Thank you," he says softly when I'm finally seated. "I know what you think about me, Ella. And I don't blame you for hating me. I hate myself for what I did. I know you don't believe me when I say this, but I truly loved Charlotte. And, I think, in her own way, she loved me too."

"She wouldn't love you now."

"Probably not. But I think she'd understand why I did what I did."

"Help me with that, Zach. Because to me, it seems like you didn't give a flying fuck about Charlotte. All you cared about—all you ever cared about—was Zach."

To my surprise, these words seem to sting him. His eyes begin to tear, and although my first instinct is to remind myself that he's a trained actor, I actually believe that his emotion is sincere.

"That's just not true. Your sister . . . she was the most amazing person I'd ever met . . . I mean, I don't have to tell you. I never could see what she saw in me. And part of me, I suppose, knew that she'd figure it out soon enough, and then it would be over. But I didn't care because every day I was in her company I was a better man for it."

"So you repaid her for making you such a good man by lying to the police so they couldn't find her?"

"No. No. No. That's not the way it happened at all."

"Then tell me. How did it happen?"

He sighs loudly and exhales a mouthful of air. Then he shakes his head, as if silently rejecting his own advice not to talk to me.

"I don't remember exactly when I first started to think about it, but around Christmas, I got the sense that something had changed. She was out a lot. Much more than usual. And then when I questioned her about it, she'd claim that she was at rehearsal until one or two in the morning, or something equally implausible. I understood what was going on. I knew there was someone else."

"So it's all Charlotte's fault. Is that what you're doing here? Blaming the victim?"

"No," he says with another shake of his head. "The motherfucker who did this to Charlotte . . . if I knew who he was, I'd fucking kill him myself. But what I'm trying to say is that your sister was out a lot over the past few months, and I decided that two could play that game, so I went to Carly's for the night. I didn't realize that Charlotte hadn't been home on Tuesday night because I was out all night. When she was out late the next night, I figured it was because she was pissed at me. That's why I wasn't worried. To be honest, I was sure she was safe and sound—in somebody else's bed. So of course I wasn't calling the police. But when none of her friends knew where she was, and I couldn't track her iPhone . . . that's when I called you."

I follow Zach's train of thought and know full well what dysfunctional relationships can make you do, but that doesn't mean I'm going to cut him any slack.

"I couldn't care less who you're fucking. I feel sorry for her. That's all. But you crossed a very serious line when you lied to the cops. That lie might have cost Charlotte her life. You're going to have to live with that, and I'm going to hate you forever for it."

"I know. And I . . . I can't even begin to understand what this has been like for you. But at the same time, I don't think you can begin to understand what it was like for me when she disappeared. I mean, I'm her boyfriend. I'm a black man. I'm cheating on her. I think she's cheating on me. And now she's missing? Who's going to believe that I didn't kill her?"

"You got that right."

"But I didn't. I swear to God, Ella. I didn't. I never would have hurt Charlotte."

"I know that's not true, Zach. You hurt her plenty."

24.

Dylan arrives at my place exactly at seven. He's clad in blue jeans with the kind of fade that only comes with years of ownership, and a dark, long-sleeved, collared shirt that's tight enough to remind me of what he looks like without it.

While getting ready, I briefly considered breaking into Cassidy's wardrobe for an outfit, but then I realized that he'd seen the real me at Riverside Park, which meant that I should stop pretending around him, especially given the circumstances. So I opted for something that was in keeping with Ella Broden's life—jeans and a loose-fitting top, although I did select my favorite of each.

Dylan hands me a bottle of wine. "I don't know much about wine," he says. "But the guy in the store said that this was good."

I can't help but contrast Dylan's unabashed ignorance about wine with Paul's flawless pronunciation of the fancy chardonnay we ordered at Mas. I much prefer Dylan's unpretentiousness.

"My motto is that every wine goes with Italian food," I say. "There's this great little place I always order in from. They have pastas and small pizzas, so I thought maybe we'd have a carbfest and do one of each."

"I'm in your hands," he says.

The wine turns out to be a rosé, which must have been refrigerated in the store because it is reasonably cold. Over dinner—pizza with prosciutto and figs, and penne alla vodka—Dylan Perry tells me his life story. He's thirty-nine but has no trepidation about turning forty and has never been married, although he lived with a girlfriend for three years in his early thirties, claiming, "It was fine, but I kind of knew all along that she wasn't the one." He was born in Wyoming, of all places, but spent most of his formative years in Manhattan, Kansas, where his father taught in the English department at the university. "So, I like to tell people that this is the second time I've lived in Manhattan, even though I actually live in Brooklyn." He attended college at Duke—"Go Blue Devils!"—and med school at Johns Hopkins, practicing for a few years in San Francisco before coming to New York to work with Doctors Without Borders. He's spent the last six months in Peru.

He asks about my time as a prosecutor. I answer the way I always do, telling him that the best part of the job was knowing you were making the city safer and delivering justice for the victim and her family.

It isn't until I've emptied the last of the bottle of wine into our respective glasses that he asks the question I can only assume he's been dying to pose since he learned my true identity: "What was a nice girl like you doing all vamped out under an alias at open-mic night at Lava?"

"I'm a cautionary tale," I begin. "I went to the high school for the performing arts here in New York City. You know, the one that the movie *Fame* was based on. College at Columbia, majoring in theater, with every intention of becoming a singer after graduation. Then my mother died the fall of my junior year, and . . . I guess it made me feel like I needed to do something more solid, more grown-up. I suppose a shrink might also surmise that I wanted to curry favor with my father. Anyway, I went off to law school. Fast-forward fifteen, sixteen years, and here I am, wishing I had made vastly different life choices."

I've never said it so forcefully before. But there it is. The tragic story of Ella Broden in less than a hundred words.

"And that's why you turn into Cassidy at Lava?"

"That's why. To live the life not taken. If only for one night a week."

Dylan smiles in a way that makes it impossible for me not to smile back. *It's okay,* he's saying. *We all feel that way.* Or at least that's how I choose to interpret it.

"So now it's your turn," I say. "How'd you end up at the Lava Lounge?"

"You mean how, of all the open-mic nights in the world, did I happen to walk into yours?"

"Yeah. Exactly."

"I've always enjoyed singing and was in a band in high school, but I never seriously considered that music could be a career for me. It was just a way to screw around with my friends and get girls. But there's something about living in a third-world country that makes you take stock. One of the things I decided was that when I came back home, I'd try to get back into singing. You know, let my creative side out a little. I saw that Lava holds an open-mic night on Wednesdays and thought, what the hell, I'll check it out. I didn't intend to sing, but then we met. I thought I'd have a better shot with you if you thought I could sing."

I laugh, and the sound still seems strange coming from me. "I'm not that shallow, Dylan. The reason you had a shot with me had nothing to do with your singing. It was because . . . you're a doctor."

———

After the table is cleared, I lead him to my living room and suggest we watch a movie. He lets me choose, and I settle on one starring Reese Witherspoon called *Wild.*

Once the movie is queued up, I snuggle into Dylan. He strokes my hair. With each stroke of his hand, I fall further under his spell.

"I don't want to be a downer," I say as the opening credits roll, "but I still feel a little guilty. I'm really enjoying myself with you, and my sister is . . ."

"You need to take care of yourself too. You know, like what they say before the plane takes off. Put on your own oxygen mask before assisting others."

He says this looking deeply into my eyes. I want to kiss him so badly. Instead, I decide to let him into my thoughts, to share what's going on in the hope that it'll make me feel better.

"Because I used to be a prosecutor, I know the police lieutenant who's running the case. His name is Gabriel Velasquez. He keeps me up-to-date with the investigation. At first they focused on Charlotte's boyfriend. Zach's a real asshole and initially refused to cooperate. But he's cooperating now and he passed a polygraph. There was another guy Charlotte was seeing too, named Josh. He cooperated from the very start, but Josh's polygraph was what they call 'inconclusive.' So I guess the state of play is that Zach's not a suspect but Josh still is. I've told the police that I don't think Josh did it, though. He just doesn't seem the type."

"You say that like you have a suspect in mind," Dylan says.

I begin to choke up. All I can think is that Dylan will never know Charlotte. No one I ever meet again will know Charlotte.

"It's okay," he says softly.

He pulls me in tighter. God, it feels so good to be held.

"There's another guy she was seeing," I say slowly.

With each word, I can feel my rage beginning to boil, although at whom it's directed remains unclear. Charlotte for keeping her secret? Paul for what he did to her?

And then I know. It's none of the above. I'm furious with myself. For not protecting my sister. For not being there when she needed me.

"It's my former college boyfriend. How messed up is that, right? I hadn't seen him in more than ten years, but we recently reconnected. He told me that he also knew Charlotte. And I think—more than just think, actually—I'm pretty sure that he's the guy who killed . . . or whatever . . . Charlotte."

A thought crams into my brain, and I want to keep it from Dylan. I don't want him to know the kind of person I really am. But then it comes out, anyway, as if I'm incapable of keeping a secret from him.

"You know, before this, I never considered myself a vengeful person. I mean, I was a prosecutor for a lot of years, but I was never one of the ones who relished the idea that these guys—and I prosecuted mainly men who were sexual predators—would be on the other end of that equation in prison. I just considered it a tragedy all the way around. But now . . . all I want is for Paul, this guy I once thought I was in love with, to suffer for what he did to Charlotte. Not just to die, but to *suffer*."

CHAPTER SIXTEEN

Matthew is walking along the street outside the gallery by the time I exit the building. I call out his name, regretting it instantly in case someone who knows Marco overhears. At least it gets Matthew to stop in his tracks.

"Proud of yourself?" I say when I catch up with him.

His smirk tells me the answer.

"In all honesty, yes. Yes I am, actually."

"What if I pulled a stunt like this with your wife?"

"It was harmless, Clare. In fact, I did you a favor. He's going to be happy now. He made a sale. Am I his first one?" he says with a laugh.

"It's not funny. Do you have any idea how often Marco's going to talk about this with me? Are you even going to buy that piece?"

His expression turns serious. "Of course I'm going to buy it. I meant what I said. It really is transcendentally beautiful. But that's hardly because Painter Boy is the next coming of Rembrandt. It's because you are transcendentally beautiful."

Maybe there are women who can still be angry after a man calls them transcendentally beautiful, but I'm not one of them. My fury dissipates and I can't help but smile, which tells Matthew that he's won.

———

While I'm writhing with Matthew on thousand-thread-count linens, Marco texts that he's going to go out after the show with the two other student artists. I don't see it until around midnight, when I'm already on my way home from the hotel. Since Marco didn't text again, I assume he hasn't given a second thought to where I've spent the last few hours.

Marco arrives home several hours after me. I'm awake but pretend to be asleep so I don't have to deal with him, just in case he's angry that I made a hasty exit from the show. Or worse, he wants to have sex, which I'm definitely not up for after Matthew.

———

The following morning, I wake up early and make a strong pot of coffee. I'm hoping to have some time to myself before Marco rises, and take my cup out onto the balcony. Alone, with the wind swirling around me and the beauty of the Hudson below, I reflect on what I've let my life become. When did it get so out of control? I'm a train wreck, no two ways about it. Living with a man I fear is becoming abusive while in love with a married man and sleeping with a student who might get me expelled.

I'm not outside long when I hear the unwelcome sound of Marco in the living room. He opens the glass door to the terrace and pokes his head out.

"Good morning," he says. He's wearing sweatpants, a T-shirt, and a broad grin. "I'm going to get a cup of coffee and join you, okay? Do you want a refill?"

Marco's good spirits from last night have apparently carried over to morning. He seems so cheerful that I wonder if maybe he sold another piece last night, although I find that to be extremely unlikely.

"No, I'm good."

He goes inside to the kitchen and returns a minute later, mug in hand.

"God, this coffee is good," Marco says. "I had a little too much last night. I was out with Rafael in some dive bar on a Hundred and Seventh, and we ended up closing the place."

"*Rafael?*"

"*Yeah. One of the other two students. The one at Parsons. We started out with the chick from CUNY, but she bailed at midnight. Then Rafael and I got down to some serious drinking.*"

"*How'd the rest of the show go?*"

"*Fine. I didn't sell anything else, but that one sale was more than the other students made. I don't think anyone even gave their work a second thought. Rafael's stuff is pretty—in that you could see it over a sofa in a McMansion kind of way—but there's no power to it at all. And Mercedes—she's the girl from CUNY—her stuff is so derivative she should be embarrassed.*"

"Derivative" is the worst insult Marco can lodge at an artist. "Pretty" is a close second.

"*I'm happy that you sold something and you had a nice time,*" *I say.*

"*Not just something. A ten-grand portrait of you. And I have a good feeling about that Matthew guy. Maybe he'll become a real patron.*"

I smile at Marco, but inwardly I'm rolling my eyes. This is exactly what I feared would result from Matthew's purchase. Marco sees Matthew as the Medici to his Michelangelo.

I'm saved from having to hear more by my ringtone. I should let it go to voice mail, as I usually do when Jason calls and I'm with Marco, but I'm so desperate to stop Marco from talking about Matthew that I say, "It's Tobias. I need to take it."

Marco scowls. I wonder if that's because he suspects that it's not my director who's calling, or he simply doesn't want to be interrupted.

"*Hi,*" *I say, just as I'm getting off the terrace.*

"*I need to see you,*" *Jason says. "Right now."*

"*I'm sorry, I'm in the middle of something now.*"

"*Are you with him?*"

Damn. He knows about Marco.

"*Who?*"

"I'm not doing this over the phone. And I'm not asking, Clare. You better come here right now, or my next call's going to blow up your world."

This doesn't sound like Jason. Not the Jason I know, at least. Still, I'm in no position to call him on the threat in case he's not bluffing.

"You win. Give me twenty minutes."

"Not a minute more," he replies. Then he hangs up.

DAY ONE

TUESDAY

Christopher Tyler

25.

In my wildest dreams, I never thought I'd be staring at the corpse of a woman I just fucked. But there you have it. A lifetime of being a non-murderer, gone in a flash. Never to return.

I will say this in my own defense: there was no premeditation. It just happened. One thing led to another.

That's where the choice point actually occurred. I could have called the police and turned myself in. Or I could have run. Or I could have begun the cover-up.

You know which one I chose by now.

Moralize all you want about how something like this could never happen to you, and if by some crazy confluence of events it did that you would do the right thing. That's just talk. Hell, I might have said the same thing. But when you do something without thinking—no matter how horrible—you can't really say that you could never do something like that, because, by definition, you didn't intend to do it in the first place. And once it's done, the calculus shifts dramatically. Nothing I did was going to bring Charlotte back. Which meant that the only question was the degree to which I should be punished for my momentary lapse. A little? Sure, that seems fair. But to have my life destroyed? No, that's too great a punishment for any person to self-impose. I know society is all gung ho about justice, but I don't think too many people in my position feel the same way.

———

I met Charlotte six months earlier. She was sitting in Starbucks having a fight with some black guy, who I assumed was her boyfriend. Women don't fight in public with a man they're not sleeping with. He stormed out of the place, leaving her in tears. I figured that made her easy pickings.

Up close, Charlotte was even more beautiful than from a distance. Although her eyes were tear-filled, they reminded me of a flickering flame—all blues and oranges—and her bee-stung lips were nothing short of perfection.

"It can't be that bad," was my opening line.

She rubbed her eyes with the tips of her fingers. "What?"

"I'm sorry for intruding. I've got a bit of a white-knight thing. And you're nothing if not a damsel in distress, milady."

She smiled at me and then wiped her eyes again. "I'm so embarrassed," she said.

"Don't be. I've been married for six years, which means that I've had more than my fair share of Starbucks fights, believe me. My name is Christopher Tyler."

I made the call on the fly that I'd improve my odds if I told her I was married. People in relationships like that because they think it means you have something to lose as well. It seemed to work, because I got another smile.

"Nice to meet you, Christopher Tyler." The repetition of my name was another good sign. She didn't want to forget it. "I'm Charlotte. Charlotte Broden."

"Nice to meet you too, Charlotte. Can I get you another coffee, or was your fight the kind that requires alcohol?"

I knew this was a ballsy play, but it's my experience that you need to move fast in these situations or else the woman starts to think twice about where it's heading.

"I could go for a drink," she said.

There was a very nice hotel bar just around the corner. I'm partial to hotel bars, even though they charge at least a 30 percent premium, because they're almost never crowded. I'm more than willing to pay eighteen bucks for a drink if I can carry on a conversation without either of us needing to shout to be heard.

She ordered a gin and tonic without specifying the brand, which I liked. I said, "Make it two," to start laying the groundwork that we had much in common.

Our banter was easy. We flirted a bit about how I was too old for her, and I complained about my imaginary wife to keep up with her bad-mouthing of her boyfriend. When she asked what I did for a living, I told her the truth—that I'm an investment banker—because women, no matter how independent, don't mind hearing that I've got money. She said she was studying to be a writer.

"I didn't know people study to be writers," I said. "I thought they, you know, just wrote."

"You can learn to do anything better. All it takes is someone sharing their expertise and lots of practice."

By the lasciviousness of her smile, I knew she wasn't talking only about writing.

A second round of drinks followed and then a third. When she downed this last G&T like she was a gunslinger in an old Western saloon, I suggested that we see if the hotel had any availability. She didn't even blink at the overture. Instead, she grabbed her purse and said, "Let's go."

It was great. The kind of sex you can only have with a stranger. I think the age difference also helps. You know that thing about how wives should be half their husband's age plus seven? Having never been married, I can't vouch for whether that formula predicts a lifetime of wedded bliss, but I am a big believer that an age gap leads to pretty explosive sex. I know what I'm doing in the sack, and Charlotte seemed like she'd had a lifetime of dating guys who didn't.

After, we got to the inevitable discussion about whether we were ever going to see each other again. I would have been okay either way, but Charlotte said that she'd feel less slutty if I called her. To keep in character, I went through this whole thing about my wife being super suspicious, so I'd buy a prepaid cell phone and we'd need to meet in hotels. She said she was fine with that.

And that's the way it went for six months. Charlotte and I would meet once a week or so, have mind-blowing sex, and then say our good-byes until the next time.

That is, until tonight. When I killed her.

———

The evening began like all the others. She texted my burner saying that her boyfriend—as a way of heaping further disdain on him, I never called him by his name, but just referred to him as Mr. McDouche or McDouche, for short—had left unexpectedly for a few hours, and she was hoping I could get away too.

We met in the bar of the W Hotel in Union Square, where we quickly did a couple of rounds of shots followed by two real drinks. Then we adjourned upstairs. It turned out that neither of us had eaten much that day, so we were both drunker than usual. That led to the sex being particularly good, but rougher too. She was totally into it, though, screaming at the top of her lungs. Real porn-star shit.

Then she called me by another man's name. Not her McDouche of a boyfriend's name either. A third name. There was another guy, apparently.

I stopped cold. Still inside her, I said, "What did you call me?"

She turned around. Up until that moment, her head had been buried in the sheets facing the opposite direction from me.

"Don't stop," she said breathlessly. "I'm so close."

She pushed back against me, trying to start me going again. As she gyrated, I grabbed a fistful of her hair and yanked on it, hard. This only excited her more; her pace quickened and her moans grew louder.

She called me by the right name. Over and over again, in fact. But I knew what I'd heard a moment before, and the fact that she was now screaming my name in the throes of passion wasn't going to make that go away.

When her orgasm finally subsided, I stopped too. She must have thought I had finished, because she rolled over with a satisfied smile on her face.

"I swear, I've never been fucked so good in my life," she said.

"Not even by *him*?" I asked.

"By whom?"

For a woman who had barely uttered a word that could be said on network television for the past hour, she had the most innocent look in her eyes. I wasn't buying it. Not for a minute.

"You know who," I said.

"I really don't," she said.

I said the name. Her face told me everything I needed to know.

For a moment, I felt as if I'd left my body and I was watching the scene play out. I knew how it was going to end. Badly. Very badly. And yet I didn't see any way to avoid that result.

I never hit her. Ironically, I wish I had. That might have spent my rage and maybe she'd still be alive. Instead, when the impulse to violence overwhelmed me, I grabbed her by the throat. It was a position we'd assumed before, but always during sex, when the danger excited her. This time her eyes bulged out. She knew this was not about anyone deriving pleasure.

Once, when I was a boy, I touched a lever on some kind of electrical box that was live, and my hand became paralyzed. I knew I had to let go, and if I didn't I'd die, but I still couldn't relax my grip. The circuit finally broke when I yanked my entire body back from the box and fell to the floor.

It felt exactly like that. But I didn't release quickly enough.

26.

I move Charlotte's lifeless body from the bed to under it, just in case housekeeping comes in. Then I put the "Do Not Disturb" sign on the doorknob and leave my dead lover inside.

There's no place open in Union Square at close to midnight that would sell a receptacle large enough to hide a fully grown woman's body. Although it is the last thing I want to do, I have no choice but to go home and bring back something of my own.

I walk a few blocks away from the hotel, where I grab a taxi back to my place. I pay the driver in cash. I go up to my apartment, retrieve the largest suitcase I own—which I'm hoping will be big enough for Charlotte to fit inside—and head back to the hotel. Before leaving, I scrub the valise down with a damp cloth and empty every pocket. The last thing I want is something linking it back to me.

I arrive back in the room less than an hour after I left. When I reach under the bed, I don't feel Charlotte. For a moment I think that maybe she's still alive. That she somehow got up and went home. But then I feel her hair. I slide my hand down until I grasp her shoulder. Her skin is room temperature, maybe a little cooler. Like a steak that's been left out overnight. She still feels fleshy too; I've been wondering how long it would be before rigor mortis sets in. More than the time I've been gone, I suppose.

I drag her body out. She looks like she's sleeping, although her lips are bluer than before. I give fleeting thought to dressing her, but that seems like too much work. So I collect her clothing and stuff it into the suitcase.

It's more difficult wedging Charlotte inside than I had initially thought. Her legs fit, but her head sticks out. She looks a bit like a magician's assistant right before he's about to saw her in half. I push down on her head, first with my arms, but when that doesn't yield results, I put my knees on her shoulder to leverage my body weight. That does the trick, although I hear a definite crack as I fold her in.

The suitcase lurches as I pull it, but not so much that I can't get it to roll along to the elevator and then through the hotel's marble lobby.

"Taxi, sir?" the gloved attendant asks.

I jump at the sound of a voice that's not in my own head. "What?"

"Would you like me to get you a taxi, sir?"

He's looking down at my bag. I wonder if he's seen an arm or a leg pushing out the side. I glance down myself. Everything looks fine— aside from the fact that I'm pulling such a large suitcase after midnight, of course.

"Oh. No, thank you. I'm only going a few blocks."

"In that case, would you like us to hold your luggage?" he says.

"Thank you, but I have some things in it that I'm going to need for my meeting."

If he's dubious about my having a meeting at such a late hour, he doesn't betray it. Nor does he inquire about the contents of my suitcase.

"Very well. Have a pleasant evening, sir."

In this part of Manhattan, I'm almost equidistant from the East and the Hudson Rivers. Without giving it much thought, I head east. I cut over to Fifteenth Street to avoid the traffic on Fourteenth and select the block to the north because, even though I'm not the least bit triskaidekaphobic, it feels like I'd be tempting fate by dragging a dead body along Thirteenth Street.

Once I'm off the main drag, I relax a bit. Of course, I'll have no good answer if a cop approaches and asks why I'm wheeling a suitcase large enough to hold a dead body along Fifteenth Street after midnight, but it reminds me a little of walking my dog as a kid. That feeling of being alone, but not completely so. I stifle the impulse to talk to Charlotte, to apologize for what I've done and for what I'm about to do. That won't do either of us any good.

When I reach FDR Drive, the highway that runs along the eastern shore of Manhattan, I realize that depositing Charlotte in the East River is going to be more difficult than I'd previously imagined. Before getting to the river, I'll need to traverse the FDR, which is four lanes across with a three-foot-high median between north and south traffic. It's a difficult thoroughfare to cross under the best of circumstances, but at night, with a dead body in tow, it'll be next to impossible.

I spy a pedestrian bridge a few blocks south and decide that's the better play. It has a ramp, so making it across turns out to be relatively easy. A few minutes later, I'm on the other side.

I give some thought to leaving Charlotte in the park that borders the East River but figure that, given that I've come all this way, I should see the job through as I envisioned it. So I drag the suitcase across the dirt until I make it to the railing at the river's edge.

I had originally thought that Charlotte's weight would be enough to sink the suitcase to the bottom of the river, but now I'm not so sure. Once she's in the river, it'll be too late to rectify the situation if I'm wrong. To eliminate any risk she'll float to the surface, I start collecting rocks and stuffing them in the outer pockets of the suitcase. When I can't lift the satchel above my ankles, I figure it's heavy enough that it will sink to the bottom.

My plan is thwarted when the suitcase doesn't fit under the lowest bar of the railing. Worse still, because I've loaded it down with rocks, it's now too heavy to lift over the top. Although it's the very last thing

I want to do, I have little choice but to take Charlotte out and make the transfer in phases.

Her lifeless body spills out as soon as I open the zipper. Charlotte is now contorted in a way that's anything but natural. I try not to look at her face, and instead roll her body under the fence and down the embankment, stopping just short of the water. I look around once again to make sure I'm not being watched, then scurry back up the hill to collect the suitcase.

Without Charlotte's weight, I'm able to hoist the suitcase over the top bar even with the rocks. Then I slide it down the embankment until it rests beside Charlotte's lifeless body. Once we're all reunited, I stuff Charlotte back inside.

If I want to make sure she isn't found, I know I'll need to pull the suitcase out into the river. Otherwise, I run the risk that she'll just wash up on the bank ten feet from where I've pushed her in. But after the deed is done, I'll still have to make it back home without raising any suspicions, and a soaking-wet man walking through Manhattan is something people remember. So I strip down to my birthday suit and get into the water, dragging the suitcase in after me.

The water is freezing cold. From the first stroke, I know my body isn't going to adjust to the temperature. I shiver every inch of the way. After I paddle far enough out that I can no longer stand, I feel the suitcase drop hard. I had forgotten that even though the suitcase is lighter in water than it had been on land, my leverage is much less now that I'm afloat. I originally thought I could make it halfway across, but the weight of the suitcase and the numbness in my limbs make me quickly realize I'll never get that far.

I'm a hundred feet from the shoreline when I let go of the suitcase.

Once I've released my load, I'm overcome with a sense of lightness. Not just because I'm more buoyant now without holding a dead body. It's as if the act of letting go of Charlotte's body has freed me from what I've done. My sin will also be forever buried beneath the black water.

The swim back is far easier. Without Charlotte pulling me down, I make it to land quickly. Once there, I lie low in the muck until I'm satisfied I'm outside of anyone's view. It takes me a few minutes to locate my clothes in the dark, but I eventually stumble across them.

I do my best to shake the water off before I get dressed. I'm confident that it will be next to impossible to ascertain by sight that I'd spent time in the East River. The stench is a different matter. I can't tell how rank I'll be to others, but my nostrils twitch.

I've got three options to get back home: walk, subway, or taxi. Walking renders me the most incognito, but it will take at least an hour and I need tonight to be over. The subway is faster—probably less than five minutes—but I'll be on the security cameras and in sight of other passengers, which is obviously less than optimal. With a taxi, there's only one person to worry about—the driver. So I select the least of the three evils and hail a cab on First Avenue.

Other than giving the driver my address, I don't say a word. I try my best to hide my face, but still can't shake from my mind the image of the cabbie—a Mr. Mamadou Iqbal, according to his license—on the witness stand, testifying that he picked up a guy after 1:00 a.m. on the night Charlotte Broden went missing who reeked like he'd just gone for a swim in the East River.

Needless to say, I pay in cash.

Once inside my apartment, I step into the shower and let the hot water rain down on me. It feels like a baptism, washing away not only the chill in my bones, but also what I've done.

DAY TWO

WEDNESDAY

27.

After the strenuous work of disposing of Charlotte's body, I have no problem falling asleep. There's no tossing or turning, racked with guilt. Nor do nightmares invade my slumber. Like the rest of me, my subconscious is at peace.

After my good night's sleep, I wake up, shower, put on my best Kiton suit and tie, lace up my Berluti cap-toes, and head out into the world. My plan is simple: go about my business as usual. In my case, that's as an investment banker, where I specialize in providing financing for midsize companies trying to make the jump to the big time.

As it happens, I'm ass-deep in a deal that's beginning to crater. My client is an underwear company called The Pouch. Seriously. They have a patent on some technology that enhances the male package. Think of it as a push-up bra for men. To paraphrase the old saying, no one ever lost money investing in the insecurity of the American man. The company can't keep up with product demand.

The CEO of The Pouch is named Paolo Amoroso. He's based in Milan and looks it, right down to the perpetually maintained three-day growth of beard. During our initial meeting, Amoroso told me that the company's goal was to raise $100 million without giving up more than a third of the equity. That meant they were looking for a banker who could convince people smart enough to have millions of dollars available for investment that The Pouch was currently worth $300 million.

That was going to take a lot of salesmanship. The company's revenues in the last fiscal year were only slightly north of $20 million, and the industry multiplier was ten times the trailing twelve—which meant that most people on Wall Street would value The Pouch at $200 million, tops. Numbers don't lie, so all the other banks were likely quoting Amoroso an IPO price of around $8 per share. To get the business, I told Amoroso that I could get him at least $10. Guaranteed.

That was six months ago. Amoroso has flown in from Italy because he's finally realized that I lied to his face.

———

Amoroso is impeccably dressed, as always: pin-striped suit that looks as if it were sewn onto his body; a single sleeve button open on each arm to signal to the world that they're functional; a white shirt that's likely never been worn before, the collar standing at full attention; and a patternless silver tie. His stubble is the same length as always, and his thick head of black hair is gelled straight back.

Knowing what's coming, I had suggested we meet for lunch. My thinking was that a meal would make him my captive audience for an hour, so after he chewed me out I'd still have some time to dissuade him from firing us. He said he'd prefer to meet in my office, which I took to mean that he didn't want to spend a second more with me than was absolutely required.

The first good sign of this encounter, though, is that he's come alone. Usually he travels with flunkies, but he must have thought ripping me a new one would be humiliating enough without an audience.

"Paolo," I say as if we're still best friends.

He stares at my outstretched arm, and I fear he's going to leave me hanging. But then he shakes it.

Even before I can offer him a seat, Amoroso says, "Let me tell you why I'm here."

We're now in the awkward pose of me standing in front of my desk with him facing me, although there is an array of perfectly comfortable chairs in my office going unoccupied.

"Want to sit down?" I say with a smile.

"No," he says flatly. "This should only take a minute."

His accent is slight. Just enough to enforce he's Italian, but not so much as to make it difficult to understand him.

"Okay, then. Shoot."

"I'm not going to spend time going over ancient history, but just so we're on the same page, when you were pitching me, you told me that you could raise the hundred million dollars by offering ten million shares, and you guaranteed—that was your exact word, *guaranteed*—an offering price of at least ten dollars a share. And now you're telling me that the best the market will bear is somewhere between seven and eight. That puts us in the position of either raising twenty to thirty million less than we need, or giving up more of the company to get up to the original hundred million. Needless to say, neither are attractive alternatives to my board."

"I understand, Paolo. Believe me that I do, but—"

He talks over me. "I've heard your BS before and, *believe me*, I didn't fly across an ocean to hear it again. Just let me say what I came to say, and then you can go about your day lying through your teeth to some other client, no doubt."

He's right. Better for me just to shut up and let him finish. So I nod that the floor remains his.

"I've taken meetings with other banks, and everybody tells me that your read of the market, at least, is correct. As a result, the company is resigned to the fact that our stock is going to be valued in the seven-to-eight-dollars-a-share band at offering. And believe me, I'd go to another bank in a heartbeat to finish the deal if it weren't for the fact that we're thirty days out with you guys and they're all telling me that they'd need six months, minimum, to get us to market. Of course they can't guarantee today's pricing will still be there six months down the road."

I try not to smile, but I know this means we're in. He can't fire us without putting the company at risk.

"Where that leaves us is that we'll stay with you, but only if we get some concession on the fee to compensate us for the shortfall. Since we're taking a twenty to thirty percent hit, the fee has got to be reduced accordingly."

By now I've assumed a more relaxed posture, leaning against my desk. Paolo tops out at five seven—thanks to the two-inch heels he sports on his alligator-skin shoes. Even slouching, I still maintain a considerable height advantage.

I'm not going to reduce our fee. Given my bait-and-switch to get Amoroso to sign on in the first place, the odds are awfully good that The Pouch isn't going to be a repeat customer. That means that any gesture of goodwill on my part now is simply throwing money away.

Of course I can't say that. So I launch into classic banker double-speak.

"Look, I want you and your board to be happy. We don't build on this relationship if you're not. But we clearly have different recollections of our initial discussions. I'm not going to do a whole he-said/he-said thing, but you act like I'm some sort of magician. The market pays what the market pays. Now, if this were a situation where our mistake cost you money, I'd have no problem discounting the fee. But we didn't do anything wrong. Nobody can get you ten bucks a share. You know that's right because you've been shopping this deal. So the beef you have is that you came away from our initial meeting thinking that price was doable, and now the market won't pay it. And I feel the need to remind you that we *never* guaranteed a price. The contract is quite clear that our only obligation is to use best efforts to get you a reasonable market price based on conditions at the time. We're delivering exactly that. Besides, let's be honest here—you know as well as I do that if the market rallied and the offering went off at eleven or twelve, you weren't going to pay us a dollar more than the fee in the contract. It's a two-way street, I'm afraid."

"You certainly are a smooth talking son-of-a-bitch, I'll give you that." Amoroso shakes his head in obvious disgust to be in my presence. "But no matter how you spin it now, you know and I know that you lied to me when you promised us ten dollars a share. I'd understand if the market dropped, but that's not what happened. The realistic market price back then was the same as it is now. You knew it then, and you know it now. When you quoted me ten, it was just to lock up our business. Everyone else at the time was telling us seven to eight."

I want to point out to him that he's just as big a liar as I am. I remember him distinctly telling me that the reason he chose our firm was because he valued the personal chemistry between him and me. He never once mentioned everyone else's market estimate had come in at least two bucks a share under mine. It's his own greed that put him in this spot. He knows as well as I that he would have done business with Satan for an extra buck a share. Still, name-calling isn't going to advance the ball here.

"I'm sorry, Paolo. There's no give on the fee. That's a nonstarter. If you want to move the business to someone else, just tell me where to send the file. But if you stay with us, we're ready to bring you to market in four weeks."

We stare at each other for a moment. The primate thing—wondering, if it came to it, which one of us would be able to kill the other.

He leaves my office without saying another word. The truth is that I'm surprised he's able to walk at all, considering that I have his balls in a vise.

———

Less than an hour later, I get a call from the office of the firm's CEO. I'm told by his assistant that "Mr. Freedman wants to see me right away."

I've given so little thought to Charlotte Broden today that it doesn't even occur to me that Freedman might be calling me in to be arrested for murder. Instead, I'm certain that Amoroso pulled rank and now it's Freedman's turn to ream me out.

"What the fucking fuck?" Freedman asks when I enter his office.

The guy actually talks like that. Like he's in a Quentin Tarantino movie.

"I'm sorry, Mr. Freedman," I say. "What the fucking fuck about what?"

One of the odd things about Wall Street is that it's one of the few places where you *don't* want to be the boss. The goal is to make money, not to be in charge. Supervisors get fired, or worse, indicted. To be sure, Joel Freedman makes a shitload of money. More than I do. But that won't be the case in a few years. It's like being a professional athlete who plays for a marquee head coach. When you're starting out, the coach may make more money, but that doesn't mean that you're angling to be the coach. You just want to stay on the field as long as you can so someday you can buy the whole goddamn team and retire to a Caribbean island. Right now Joel Freedman's tax return might have a bigger number than mine, but he's also sixty-seven years old and doesn't live on a Caribbean island.

"Don't play dumb with me, Tyler," he says. "You fucking well know what."

"You talked to Paolo Amoroso, I'm assuming."

"No. I didn't talk. He talked. No, that's not right either. He fucking screamed at me for twenty minutes."

"The guy's upset that the numbers we're seeing from investors are below what he had hoped for."

"No fucking shit, Sherlock. Why the fuck is that?"

Just like I knew overpromising Amoroso would lead to his chewing me out, I also knew that I'd eventually wind up in Freedman's office on the receiving end of a profanity-laced tirade. It was a price I was more than willing to pay. My bonus last year reflected bringing The Pouch into the firm. Besides, if I had come to Freedman back then and told him it would take lying to Amoroso to land the business, he wouldn't have hesitated to tell me to do it. No, that's actually not true. He would have fired me for asking such a stupid question in the first place. His hand-wringing now is all about him pretending to be holier than thou.

"As I explained to Amoroso this morning, my price quote was provided six months ago. At the time, the market was stronger in the underwear sector. Now there's a lot of uncertainty. Also, there was an IPO just last month, granted, it wasn't an underwear company, but it was in the sportswear space, and the market didn't react well to it. I think that's also dampening interest at the levels we're trying to achieve."

"I only care about one fucking thing, Tyler. So I'm going to ask you about that one thing, and I want a one-fucking-word answer out of you, and then I want you to get the fuck out of my office."

I know better than to say anything, so I wait for the question. I'm reasonably sure I know what he's going to ask. It's the only question that matters on Wall Street.

"You gonna fucking bring in the full ten-million-dollar fee?"

"Absolutely," I say.

———

I had been confident that Amoroso would be back with his tail between his legs by the close of business, but at quitting time, I still haven't heard from him. For the first time all day, my thoughts return to Charlotte. More precisely, why I haven't heard anything about her disappearance.

Like everyone else in the United States, I'm well aware of the nation-wide manhunt for Jennifer Barnett. I assumed Charlotte too would become a fixture on the 24/7 news cycle as soon as she was reported missing. In fact, given that Charlotte's father is a hotshot lawyer, her disappearance should be twice as newsworthy as Jennifer Barnett's.

So why hadn't the news broken?

CHAPTER SEVENTEEN

I always visit Jason's apartment at night, when there's no one else around. Even though it's far more innocent to come in broad daylight, I'm more nervous than ever entering his building. I keep looking over my shoulder to see who might be watching.

He opens his front door with a smile. "I'm so glad you came."

"I wouldn't have except that you made very clear that I didn't have much of a choice. So what's so important?"

"Come in and have a seat," he says, still all smiles.

"I really don't have time for this, Jason."

"Please, I insist," he says.

His grin is still fixed, but it now looks frightening. Almost maniacal.

I do as directed and enter his apartment. The moment I'm seated on his ratty futon, I say, "Now I'm in. Tell me."

"No. You tell me, Clare."

"Tell you what?"

"Who is he?"

"Who is who?"

"The guy you've been fucking behind my back."

For the briefest of moments I consider coming clean. I could tell Jason about Marco and thereby shift the dirty work of this breakup from me to him. But I quickly banish that thought. Even though his question suggests he already knows, there's a big difference between suspecting your girlfriend is sleeping with someone else and knowing for certain.

"Oh, for God's sake. There is no other guy. But this juvenile behavior makes it crystal clear to me that we're done."

I've gone too far. There's an anger in his eyes I've never seen before.

He reaches into his pocket. For the briefest moment I'm worried it's to get a weapon of some sort.

He pulls out his phone. A few scrolls later, he pushes the screen into my face.

"Who the fuck is this, then?"

It's Matthew. More precisely, Matthew and me. And to be even more exact, Matthew kissing me.

Jason doesn't know about Marco. He thinks I'm cheating on him with Matthew!

His discovery is that much more ironic because Matthew and I almost never engage in any public display of affection. In fact, I remember this kiss in part because it was so rare. We were entering the Four Seasons. It was kismet that we had both arrived at precisely the same time, coming from different directions. Without thinking, he greeted me with a kiss.

"Jason, have you been stalking me?"

"Answer my question, goddamn it, or I'll do a hell of a lot worse than that. Who is he?"

I sigh to show him that I find this to be beneath his dignity. And mine.

"He's just a friend. And I've had enough of this. I'm out of here."

I move toward the door. Jason runs around me, blocking my exit with his body.

"Just a friend? A friend who you go to hotels with, you mean."

"Get out of my way," I say and push him aside.

———

When I return home, I'm determined to tell Marco it's over. If Jason confronts Matthew and Matthew believes him, Matthew could well tell Marco. At the very least, I can contain some of the damage by making sure that Marco isn't living with me when he finds out I've been cheating on him with two other men.

Marco's watching television in the bedroom when I come home, lying atop the covers. Before I can say a word, however, he kisses me. Not a welcome-home peck, but a prelude-to-sex cue.

"Not now," I say. "There's something I want to talk to you about."

"We can talk later," he says, and pulls me back into him. This time his tongue goes deep inside my mouth, his hand moves to my breast.

"Hey, slow down there, cowboy," I say. "Let me catch my breath for a second. Okay?"

He does just the opposite, however, pushing himself on top of me so that I fall back onto the bed. I can feel his erection. I push back hard to get free, but barely move him.

"Get the fuck off me!"

He grabs my right wrist, squeezing it tightly. With my free hand, I strike him hard on the back, but it has no effect. I do it again, and this time his only reaction is to laugh in my face.

"It looks like someone needs to learn her place," he says.

I'm fighting against him with all my might, but from the smile on his face and his stiffness I know my resistance is meaningless to him. I'm trapped.

All I see above me is as sinister a smile as I can imagine. There's usually a hint in Marco's eyes that he's in control. What frightens me most is that I don't see that now.

"Now tell me," he snarls. "Who the fuck is Matthew?"

"Get off me and I'll tell you," I bark back.

He hesitates for a moment, apparently considering the proposal. Then he rolls away from me and jumps to a standing position, but the sick smile on his face tells me that this is not over. He's going to turn violent the moment he hears my confession—or my denial, if I go that route. Which means I need to figure out a way to get out of here.

I pick myself up off the bed, and move over to the end side opposite Marco so at least the mattress separates us. Unfortunately, he's closer to the door, which means I'll have to get past him to reach freedom.

"I'm off you," he says, feigning calm. "So tell me. Who is he?"

I'm looking around the room for a weapon. Or my phone, even, to call for help.

"I'm waiting, Clare. And running out of patience. I'm going to ask you one more time. Who the fuck is Matthew?"

Jason must have known about Marco too. Maybe all along. And now he's exacting his revenge by sending the photo of Matthew and me to Marco.

"He's . . . just a guy I know."

"You're nothing but a fucking slut, Clare. You know that, right?"

"I'm leaving."

I declare this as if there's nothing Marco can do to stop me. Then he says the one thing that does.

"I don't think Matthew Harrison is going to be too happy to see you because the moment you walk out of here, I'm calling his wife. What do you think she's going to say when I tell her that you've been fucking her husband?"

I try to show that the threat doesn't frighten me, but it's a losing effort. As I make my way the twenty feet to the door, it feels as if I'm passing through a gauntlet. With each step I'm expecting Marco to knock me back onto the bed.

But he doesn't. When I reach him, he steps aside as if he's actually being gracious.

I walk by him as fast as I can and then through the bedroom door and out of the apartment. It's not until I'm in the apartment stairwell that I break into an all-out sprint.

———

As soon as I'm far enough away from the apartment that I don't fear Marco jumping me, I text Matthew.

MARCO KNOWS ABOUT YOU AND YOUR WIFE!!!

MEET ME AT THE BENCH.

Matthew knows the bench. We had sex on it in Central Park one night when there wasn't enough time for a hotel. Officially, it's called the Waldo Hutchins Bench, a fifteen-foot white granite sculpture capable of seating at least ten near Seventy-Second Street on the east side of the park. After using it to quench our sexual desire, I Googled it to find out what its inscription meant, which is how I learned that it actually had a name and that Waldo Hutchins was a member of the original board of commissioners for Central Park.

Alteri vivas oportet si vis tibi vivere, it says. "One must live for another if he wishes to live for himself."

I never told Matthew about the inscription, but I found it more than symbolic. I suppose I didn't share it with him for fear he wouldn't find it as meaningful.

Matthew is one of those guys whose cell phone is glued to his eyes. Granted, he might not carry the burner with him at all times, especially when he's with the missus, but he also must not keep it very far away. I get a response within five minutes.

I'll be there.

———

I see Matthew as he approaches. He's wearing jeans and, even though the weather is warm, a leather jacket. It's different from the one he wore at the museum that night we first met. This one is brown whereas that one was black, but it looks no less expensive. I'm struck by the thought that I don't think I've ever seen Matthew in anything but a suit and tie since then. Oh, and when he's stark naked, of course.

He looks over both his shoulders before sitting down beside me on the bench. Then he checks behind him once more before kissing me hello on the cheek.

"Thank you for coming. I'm so sorry."

He's clearly in no mood to comfort me. I suppose that's fair, but then again, it's not like he didn't know this was a possibility.

"So what does Painter Boy think he knows?"

"I'm not sure. Your name. First and last. And he said he'll tell your wife about us, so I assume that means he knows you're married."

"What did you say?"

"Yeah, I'm fine. Thanks for your concern."

"I'm sorry, Clare. I am concerned. I'm just trying to process the state of play here."

"Well, I didn't say anything. I got the hell out of there."

"How the hell did he find this out?"

Clearly Jason told him. Admitting that, however, opens up an entirely different can of worms.

"I don't know," I lie.

He slumps back. I've never seen Matthew in any situation in which he wasn't in total control. But now he looks . . . scared.

"It's going to be okay," I say, trying to provide some comfort. "I really think Marco was just trying to scare me. I don't think he's going to tell your wife."

"Easy for you to say. It won't cost you your marriage and . . . I don't know how many millions of dollars in alimony in a divorce."

"I know this is terrible for you, but I also know that I love you. And if the end result of all this is that we're together, isn't that all that matters?"

I can tell at once that this is not all that matters to Matthew. In fact, his expression makes me wonder if it matters at all.

"I can't think about happily-ever-after now," he says. "I need to fix this immediate problem."

"How do you propose to do that? Short of killing Marco, I mean."

From the look in his eyes, it's clear to me that Matthew's already come to the same conclusion but does not consider the possibility as outlandish as I do.

"Ask him to meet you here," he says.

"Matthew . . . no. That's crazy talk."

"It isn't. You know it isn't."

"The hell I do. There's no way I'm going to be a party to anything like that. I love you, Matthew. I truly, truly do. But not enough to help you kill someone."

I get up off the bench, but Matthew grabs my wrist and pulls me back down onto the hard marble seat.

"That hurt," I say, more to register my displeasure with him than because it actually caused me pain.

"Listen to me, Clare. I'm not going to sit back and just let him ruin my life. If it comes down to him or me, it's going to be me. Every fucking time. And I expect you to support that, or you'll end up just like him."

I stand again. This time he doesn't reach for me, but he joins me on the path. At six foot two, he towers over me. For the first time in my life, I'm afraid of him.

"Are you threatening me?" I ask.

"No. I'm warning you. And you'd best take my warning to heart, because I mean it."

———

I leave the park in a daze. How could it be that three men—each of whom had told me that they loved me within the last week—had threatened my life in the last hour?

That thought is the last one I remember in my life.

DAY SEVEN

MONDAY

Ella Broden

28.

After telling Dylan that I want to torture and then kill my college boy-friend, I slide back into his arms. On my television, Reese Witherspoon is hiking somewhere, for reasons that I don't fully understand.

"Do you have any idea where she's going or why?" I ask.

Dylan laughs, and I thoroughly enjoy the sound.

"No. No, I don't. But she looks like she could really use a shower."

The phone rings.

Somehow, I already know what awaits me on the other end of the line. It's as if I'd previously dreamed the conversation and now it's coming true.

From the look in Dylan's eye, he knows too.

"Hello," I say.

"Ella, it's Gabriel. We found a body matching Charlotte's general description . . ."

I don't hear another word he says.

———

Less than five minutes after Gabriel's call, I'm in the back of a taxi that's hurtling through the streets of downtown Manhattan. At this hour, there isn't any traffic and the trip takes less than ten minutes. I must not have realized we'd arrived, however, because the cabbie says, "This is it, right? One Police Plaza?"

I'm in that same fog when I enter the building. I show my ID to the cop manning the downstairs security checkpoint.

"Ms. Broden? I asked who you were going to see?"

I look up. The cop asking the question is Steven Lassiter, a guy who's held this job for as long as I've been a lawyer. I didn't even recognize him at first.

"Um . . . Gabriel . . . Gabriel Velasquez."

Lassiter calls upstairs and then leads me to the elevator bank. He even presses the button for the eighth floor.

Gabriel is standing at the elevator when the doors open. Lassiter must have suggested I could use some assistance. I step off the elevator and into Gabriel's arms.

"Come with me," Gabriel whispers into my ear.

I know that means that I should let go and follow him to his office. But I can't move. I actually grip him tighter. He shifts my position to his side and then we begin to move together, a slow, four-legged beast.

Once we enter his office, Gabriel lowers me into his guest chair and closes the door. Rather than take his usual seat behind the desk, he drops down to his knees beside me. My head slumps.

"Ella, do you want me to call your father?"

I want to answer him verbally, and try to say something, but words don't come out. I mutely shake my head to indicate that I don't want my father to know yet.

"Are you sure it's her?" I finally manage.

This is my last sliver of hope. That the corpse the police had found was someone else's sister, daughter, wife, or mother. That it isn't Charlotte.

"It's her," Gabriel says. "I'm sorry."

———

I don't know how I got from Gabriel's office to the morgue in the east thirties, about two miles away. I'm sure we traveled by squad car, probably with the sirens blasting, but there's a hole in my memory from the moment Gabriel took my hand to lead me out of his office to a second ago, when we entered the morgue.

The room is large, the size of a banquet hall, with too-harsh fluorescent lighting and a smell that's an affront to the senses. Some type of cleaning solution. Despite that, everything looks dirty. The walls are dingy and the concrete floor is stained an offensive rust color, which I assume is the remnants of blood. There are a number of empty gurneys, and the walls are lined floor to ceiling with compartments, silver handles sticking out. Bodies lie inside.

Beside Gabriel stands a man in his twenties, in a white lab coat. He's too young and wears too vacant an expression to be a medical examiner. I presume he's a tech of some kind. The guy in charge of making sure none of the corpses escape.

I have borne witness to my fair share of dead bodies. Gruesome ones too. Gunshot wounds, stabbings, drownings. I've seen a decapitation and an old lady who had been rotting in her home for almost three weeks before she was found. Even so, I know that my prior exposure to death will not prepare me for the horror of seeing Charlotte's lifeless body.

"Remember what I told you," Gabriel says. "Because your sister was in the East River for several days, there's going to be extensive bloating and skin discoloration. The suitcase she was in didn't keep out much water, and so she looks kind of . . . blue."

"Suitcase?" I say.

He gives me a patient look, but overly so. Like when you're explaining something to a three-year-old for the second time.

"Yes. As I told you back at the station, Charlotte's killer put her in a large Tumi suitcase. We consider the suitcase to be a major lead, and for that reason we're not going to release that detail to the press. I also asked that you keep it a secret too. It's a way for us to root through the tips we get. It'll also give the killer a sense that we don't have him in our sights."

I don't remember him saying any of this previously. Not about the suitcase or even that Charlotte was found in the East River—which is about as far away from Charlotte's apartment as you can get and still be in Manhattan.

I try to imagine Charlotte blue and bloated, and the image that pops into my head is of Violet from the original *Willy Wonka and the Chocolate Factory*. Charlotte and I watched that movie so many times when we were kids that we knew most of the dialogue by heart. She never failed to giggle when Augustus fell into the chocolate river or when Veruca went down the bad-egg chute, and she especially enjoyed it when Mike Teavee became tiny. But "the big blueberry girl," as Charlotte called her, always made my sister cry. *Violet, you're turning Violet!* Eventually it became a running joke between us, as in: *One more word out of you and I'll show you a picture of the big blueberry girl!*

"Are you ready?" Gabriel asks.

I don't answer. The tech pulls open drawer number eighteen anyway.

When we were younger, Charlotte would come to my bedroom in the middle of the night and we'd have what we called sister sleepovers. She'd climb into bed next to me and whisper, "Sister snuggle." Our parents would find us the next morning, wrapped tightly together.

Gabriel later tells me that I tried to get into the drawer with Charlotte. That's something else I don't recall.

———

After, Gabriel drives me to my father's apartment. He offers to come upstairs with me, explaining that my father might have questions I can't answer. I thank him, but tell him that it's unnecessary. He's already done so much, and I know there is still more for him to do tonight.

"Is your father expecting you?" Leo the nighttime doorman asks.

"No," I say, pulling out my phone. "I'll call up now, just in case he's asleep."

My father's "hello" reveals he's wide awake.

"Ella?" he says, curling the last syllable of my name to bend it into a question.

"I'm downstairs. I'm going to come up."

"Okay."

He doesn't ask me why I'm visiting at such a late hour. His lack of inquisitiveness makes it clear that he knows exactly why I'm there.

———

A minute later, my father greets me wearing a bathrobe over his pajamas. His face looks as if I've already told him. A mask of unfathomable grief.

Still standing in the open doorway, I say, "The police found Charlotte's body. I just came from the morgue. She's dead, Daddy. Charlotte's dead."

Telling my father that his little girl is dead is the hardest thing I've ever done. It feels like I'm killing him. As the words leave my lips, the light goes out in his eyes.

For the third time tonight, I embrace a man with all my strength. This time, however, I'm the ballast keeping him upright.

I don't know who told him about my mother's passing. A nurse, I suspect. He told me, and it was something of a relief when he did. For the last few weeks of my mother's life, the three of us—my father, Charlotte, and I—had stood vigil in the hospital, taking shifts sitting at her bedside. Throughout, my mother lay there unresponsive. The only sign of life was when she writhed in pain, curling her body in the most unnatural positions with each moan. No one could bear witness to such suffering and not hope for its end.

My father's reaction to the news of Charlotte's death is different. Against all odds, and contrary to his professional training, he has been holding out hope that Charlotte would come back to us. He's now paying the price for clinging to that dream.

After our hallway embrace, I deliver him back to the living room. I offer to make us some tea but he shakes the suggestion away, still unable to speak.

Finally, he says, "You're all I have, Ella."

My father is very precise with language. *Words are my business*, he often told us when we were growing up. And yet, the truth of the matter is that I'm not all he has. He has his work to sustain him. If history is any guide, he'll immediately throw himself into Garkov or some other high-profile case, and thereby allow himself to heal—or at least to focus on something else.

It's me, not my father, who actually has nothing now.

DAY THREE

THURSDAY

Christopher Tyler

29.

On Thursday morning, the sun is shining brightly and a cool wind blows. It's one of those days that makes you happy to be alive, and I wouldn't otherwise have a care in the world except that, thirty-six hours ago, I murdered my lover.

I stop at the newsstands in front of my office to peruse the headlines. It's the usual nonsense: some type of explosion in Syria that killed six; the death of some scientist I'd never heard of; Mets win; Yankees lose.

No mention of another missing young woman in Manhattan.

At 8:00 a.m. on the nose, I'm sitting at my desk, staring at my Bloomberg terminal. Underneath the market quotes is a news ticker, like the one you see on the bottom of CNN. The top bar runs the stock quotes, and beneath is a news scroll. I watch the words pass across the screen.

Still nothing about the disappearance of Charlotte Broden.

———

Bill Fitzgerald is a beefy Irishman with a thick head of brown hair. He might have been a half-decent trader if it weren't for the fact that—ever since I've known him, which is going on fifteen years now—he's been desperate for a big payday to get him out of debt. Any gambler will tell you—from Kenny Rogers on down—that if you want to win, you can't think about the money. It's the same thing with trading. You make the trade because of the opportunity. If you focus on the risk or the payoff you're always going to blow it, either by pulling out too soon or not getting in early enough.

The investment bank that employs Fitzgerald and me is called Harper Sawyer. When I first joined, I spent time in the trading group before I realized that private equity is where the big boys ended up. But Fitzgerald and I remained friends even after I switched departments—at least in the way that guys who work together are friends. I know Bill is twice divorced and in the process of getting a third because he talks about the alimony payments he makes all the time, but other than that I don't have the first clue about his life.

"There's the man in his big corner office," Bill says.

"Bill, my brother. How's the market treating you?"

"Like a hammer treats a nail."

Fitzgerald is always saying stuff like that.

"Can't force it."

"Easy for you to say. I got two kids in college and one about to go."

Bill Fitzgerald has kids. At least three. Who knew?

Out of the corner of my eye, I see it come across the screen. Two o'clock on the button. Probably some PR flack's idea that right after lunch will maximize publicity.

TERROR LAWYER'S DAUGHTER MISSING . . .

I make Fitzgerald a promise that we'll go to a strip club next week—on me. When that doesn't do the trick of getting him out of my office, I tell him that I'm late to a conference call with the coast and ask him to shut the door behind him on his way out.

The moment Fitzgerald steps out of my office, I start clicking on news stories like a madman. The idea is that—in the event that someone later searches my computer to see what I was reading just as news broke of Charlotte Broden's disappearance—it'll look as if I took a respite from the markets to catch up on what was going on in the world. I wade through sports headlines, political stories, and then the article about the Syrian mess before I click on the only one that matters.

TERROR LAWYER'S DAUGHTER MISSING

The youngest daughter of criminal defense attorney F. Clinton Broden has been reported missing. Charlotte Broden, twenty-five, a graduate student at New York University, was last seen on Wednesday morning in her Upper West Side apartment. Ms. Broden's father is currently representing Nicolai Garkov in connection with charges of securities fraud. Mr. Garkov has also been linked to the Red Square Massacre, but has not been charged in connection with that terrorist attack. The police did not comment on whether foul play was suspected in Ms. Broden's disappearance or whether there is any connection to the case of Jennifer Barnett, the twenty-two-year-old financial analyst who was reported missing when she did not report to work at Maeve Grant on Tuesday.

Last seen Wednesday morning. Mr. McDouche is even more of a douche than I previously gave him credit for. As I contemplate why he'd claim to have been with Charlotte on Wednesday, when I'm reasonably sure *he* was not at the bottom of the East River, my phone rings.

It's Amoroso.

"Paolo, how are you, my man?" I say as if we didn't have a massive blowup the day before.

"My board met last night. Needless to say, there was a lot of support for firing your ass and suing."

"I hope cooler heads prevailed. I know you're a smart enough guy to tell them that it's in the company's best interest to make a shitload of money on this IPO, instead of pissing it away on lawyers."

"I don't need you to tell me what's in our best interest. We still may wind up suing you, but for now, we're going ahead with the IPO as planned."

Victory. I don't care about happy clients. I only care about paying clients. Still, I have to show the guy some contrition to make sure he remains that.

"Look, I get why you're upset. And I'm sorry if there was a misunderstanding between us. But you're making the right call. We're going to do a successful offering for you guys, and it's going to bring in the money you need to expand. A year from now you're going to be sitting on top of fifty million dollars in revenues, and by that time I guarantee that you and I are going to be best friends."

He doesn't say anything in response. That's not like Amoroso. He's a talker.

"Paolo, you there, man?"

Still nothing. I pull the phone away from my ear to find that the call has been disconnected. I assume he hung up on me right after he was done talking, before my crap about us walking hand-in-hand together into the sunset.

———

The rest of the day, I try to keep myself busy by answering e-mails, making some calls to fund managers I think might be interested in throwing six or seven figures into The Pouch. None of those guys answers his phone, so I leave my pitch as a voice mail message, even though I know that they're also too busy to listen to their voice mails. I'll have to reach out to their secretaries tomorrow to set up in-person meetings.

At five, my assistant Beth knocks lightly on my door. I motion for her to come in.

"You have a second?" she asks.

She looks frightened. More or less the same look she gets when she hears rumors that the firm is doing a round of layoffs. But I haven't heard anything along those lines. Something else has her spooked.

"Sure. What's up?"

She steps inside and closes my door behind her. Then she sits down.

"I don't know if you heard that there's a second girl who's gone missing. Another one like Jennifer Barnett."

"Okay . . . ," I say tentatively, not sure where Beth is going with this.

"Well, on the Internet they're saying that there's a serial killer out there. And he's targeting white women in their twenties . . ."

Beth is a white woman in her twenties. Naturally, she thinks she's next to be abducted. I'm tempted to point out to her how many women in this city fit that description, but I know that's not going to make her feel any safer.

"I'm pretty sure that security downstairs screens for serial killers, Beth," I say with a smile.

"I'm not worried about being here. I just . . . if it's okay with you, I'd like not to work any overtime for the next few days. So I can leave at a normal time, while it's still light out. Is that okay?"

"Yeah, that's fine."

The fear leaves her eyes. She's now certain that she's safe, even though she's less than four feet away from the man who murdered Charlotte Broden.

DAY FOUR

FRIDAY

30.

On Friday morning, I repeat the same mantra in my head: every day from here on out will be easier than the last. The trick is to go on living my life and, soon enough, the murder of Charlotte Broden will recede into the background until it's indistinguishable from a dream, unclear, even to me, whether any of it had actually happened.

Of course, all that depends mightily on my not being caught.

On my way to work, I again stop at the newsstands. As I had expected the previous day, this morning the New York City tabloids are running Charlotte's picture on the front page. The headlines both go with the same motif—that a serial killer is on the loose.

ANOTHER ONE! is the *Post*'s effort. The *Daily News*'s banner is COPYCAT OR SERIAL? Even the paper of record, the *New York Times*, devotes front-page real estate to Charlotte's disappearance. Bottom left, below the fold, under the headline: DAUGHTER OF FAMED LAWYER MISSING.

I plunk down a few bills and grab the *Times*. The story cites anonymous but "high-ranking" sources inside the NYPD stating that there is no evidence of any connection between this most recent disappearance and the prior reported case of Jennifer Barnett. The middle of the article focuses on Charlotte's father's legal representation of Nicolai Garkov, recounting the crimes for which Garkov has been indicted as well as the Red Square Massacre, which he's only suspected of masterminding, and then leaves it to the reader to connect the dots that anyone *that* evil could be behind Charlotte's disappearance too.

The bottom line is that the police have nothing. Less than nothing, in fact, because they're apparently barking up the wrong tree with Garkov.

Still, that could change quickly. Or maybe the newspapers had it wrong.

Which is why the most important fact I learn from the press accounts is that the police will be holding a press conference today at noon. That's when I'll hear what the cops have, and know how to plot my next moves.

———

At noon, I tell Beth that I'm about to begin a conference call with Europe that I expect to last for an hour and that I'm not to be disturbed. I take my phone off the cradle so it will light up as in-use at Beth's desk—and not ring audibly at mine—and I click my mouse so that it pulls the press conference up on my computer. It's being broadcast live on NY1, the city's news station.

The shot on my screen is of an empty podium, a young reporter with glasses standing beside it. He's saying that someone from the NYPD will be making a statement any minute now and then will be answering some questions.

The live shot is replaced with the photograph I'd seen about a million times before of Jennifer Barnett. She's on the beach, crystal-blue water behind her. Her photo vanishes from the screen. In its place is the picture of Charlotte the tabloids ran. It's not one I've seen before. She's in a restaurant, wearing a black T-shirt. Her hair is down and loose and she's got the classic Charlotte smile front and center.

The TV image returns to the podium. Now a man is standing behind it. He looks to be Hispanic, about my age, dressed in all black and not wearing a tie, which strikes me as odd for some reason.

"My name is Lieutenant Gabriel Velasquez," he says. "I'm going to make a brief statement, and then I'll take some questions. Charlotte Broden, a twenty-five-year-old graduate student at New York University, has been missing since Wednesday morning. Although it's early in the investigation, we've already developed a short list of people of interest in the disappearance. Let me say at the outset that we have absolutely no reason to believe that there is any connection whatsoever between Ms. Broden's disappearance and the previously reported disappearance of Jennifer Barnett. Now, I know that some of the more irresponsible members of the press have raised the possibility that someone might be targeting young women in our city. There is absolutely no evidence to support that conjecture. Obviously, I cannot share with you the leads we have uncovered in either investigation, but I will tell you that at the present time we have a limited number of suspects in both matters, and I can further state that there is no overlap between the two suspect lists. Now I'll take a few questions."

The camera stays on the cop, so the questions come from disembodied voices. Despite the cop's disclaimer a minute earlier, the first reporter asks whether the disappearances of two young women might be the work of a serial killer.

The cop is having none of it. He quickly shoots down any suggestion, reiterating that the police believe they are looking for two different people, one responsible for each crime.

Next up a woman's voice asks whether the police are going to impose a curfew. This question merits only a one-word response: "No."

"Can you identify the person or persons of interest in the Broden case?" another woman asks.

I can feel my heart rate spike. I can't help but imagine that he's about to say my name.

Instead he says, "No. Not at this time."

"What can you tell us about the suspects, then?"

"I can tell you that there are a limited number of people who are, at the moment, our primary focus. And I can say that each one was personally acquainted with Charlotte Broden."

A few more questions follow, but none of them adds anything until someone asks, "Do you believe Ms. Broden is still alive?"

The question hangs in the air. Even I'm anxiously awaiting the cop's response, which makes no sense at all. I know the answer.

"We pray that she is . . . and we have no evidence that she's not," the cop says.

In other words, they don't have the first clue what's happened to Charlotte. I feel my body relax. It's all good.

The cop says, "Now I would like to turn the microphone over to Charlotte Broden's father, F. Clinton Broden, to say a few words."

The man who enters the screen looks like the very epitome of grief. His face is almost frozen in shock. He says something I don't quite catch and then shakes his head, clearly unable to utter a word more.

A woman comes to his rescue. A moment before, she was nowhere to be seen on the screen. She's wearing a black business suit and her hair is pulled back tight into a ponytail. The resemblance to Charlotte is striking.

"My name is Ella Broden. Charlotte Broden is my sister. My father is obviously overcome with emotion, as we all are. We miss Charlotte so much. On behalf of our family, I want to thank the NYPD for all the work they're doing to find my sister. I also want to announce that tomorrow we will be holding a search for Charlotte at Riverside Park. It's open to the public, so please join us. We will be meeting at Ninety-Sixth Street and Riverside Drive at noon. Our family has also established a reward of one hundred thousand dollars for any information leading to Charlotte's safe return."

She pauses and then looks directly into the camera. If I didn't know any better, I might have thought she was looking right at me.

"If anyone knows anything about my sister's whereabouts, or has any information at all, please call the police . . ." She pauses, and for the second time I think she might address me personally, but then she says, "And if you're out there, if you can hear me, Charlotte, please know that we love you . . . that *I* love you, Char-bar."

———

I click off the link and place the phone receiver back on the cradle. It immediately starts ringing, but I leave it for Beth to answer.

My focus is on the police. What do they have? How close are they to me?

I'm hardly an expert on criminal justice, but when a young, affluent woman living in a doorman building in a $1,000-per-square-foot neighborhood vanishes without a trace, even I know the police are going to zoom in on the "boyfriend" as the most likely suspect. And when the boyfriend is black and the victim is white, well, the police probably don't look any further. I smile to myself that I'm making Mr. McDouche's life even more miserable. Of course, the irony isn't totally lost on me that my vitriolic dislike of the guy was because he treated Charlotte so poorly, and here I'm the one who killed her.

And what about the other guy? Strange how Charlotte's utterance of his name had set me into a murderous rage and now I can't even remember it. Jason? Jared? Something lame that started with a J. The mysterious J-man must have left evidence of the relationship. Maybe he's been to her apartment, which means fingerprints, and quite possibly DNA. Unless he's married, he likely didn't use a burner phone, so there'll certainly be phone calls and texts if nothing else. That means he'll wind up being suspect number two.

The question in my mind is whether I will become suspect number three.

DAY FIVE

SATURDAY

31.

Saturday morning, I learn that America's now second-most-famous missing twentysomething woman is dead. My only reaction to the news about Jennifer Barnett is the concern that law enforcement will now focus greater resources in finding Charlotte, which only reinforces my need to keep one step ahead of them.

And that's why I head to Riverside Park.

I arrive ten minutes before the advertised noon start time. I had expected there to be twenty or thirty people in attendance but, looking around, I find the volunteers number in the hundreds. On virtually every tree hangs a pink leaflet with Charlotte's picture, offering a reward of $100,000 for information leading to her safe return.

I wade through the crowd until I come upon an information booth manned by three people. Two of them look to be twentysomething. I assume they were friends of Charlotte. The other has a definite law-enforcement vibe: closely cropped hair, clean-shaven, highly starched shirt.

As my bad luck would have it, the cop becomes free when it's my turn. "Thanks for coming out today to help us find Charlotte Broden," he says.

I wonder if finding Charlotte is truly the purpose of today's event. I would have thought that the goal would be *not* to find her lying dead in Riverside Park.

"Glad to help," I say.

"Good. Here, put this on."

He hands me a rubber bracelet. It's silver and says CHARLOTTE BRODEN in white letters.

As I'm sliding the band around my wrist the cop says, "Please sign in, sir."

A clipboard is on the table in front of him. The paper on it has four columns: name, address, e-mail, and cell phone. I hesitate for a moment, but quickly conclude there isn't much risk in giving out phony information.

"Thank you," the cop says after I've completed the form. "Please wear the bracelet as much as you can. In about ten minutes, there's going to be some brief introductory remarks by Mr. Broden."

The snippets of conversation I hear among the volunteers almost all concern Jennifer Barnett. How terrible it is that she's dead, and what an absolute horror it must be for her family.

The crowd continues to thicken. It feels a little like going to a concert, a throng of people just standing around waiting for the music to start.

Charlotte's father takes the mic. Even from a distance, I can clearly see the man has been suffering. I have taken away his daughter and now I'm putting him through the further agony of not knowing—for no reason other than my own self-preservation. Nevertheless, I don't consider for a moment reversing my path.

What I'm doing, no matter how heinous, I do for self-preservation. It's no different from those stories you hear about survivors of shipwrecks resorting to cannibalism. You can't judge unless you've been there.

He squints, and for a moment I wonder if he's going to be able to speak at all, or if it will be a repeat of what happened at the press conference. But then he smiles and says, "Thank you all for coming today. I can't tell you how touched I am by the outpouring of love for Charlotte.

Of course, it doesn't surprise me. Everyone who met Charlotte instantly fell in love with her. So thank you. Thank you all from the bottom of my heart."

My team leader for the search identifies herself as Eva, claiming she's a classmate of Charlotte's at NYU. She has thick, curly red hair and freckles, which I suppose some men like, but I never have. She speaks very quickly, and there's something about her that makes me doubt that she and Charlotte were actually friends. More likely, I suspect, this is just another do-gooder cause that Eva has glommed onto.

"Our team has been assigned section twelve," she says, "and our street coordinates are Eighty-Sixth to Seventy-Second. We're the team closest to the river. The way we've been told to do it is to fan out about three feet from one another and then just walk. Obviously, we hope that no one in our group finds"—she gives a theatrical sigh—"Charlotte. But if anyone comes across anything suspicious, please call out my name. Again, it's Eva. I'll come to you and blow my whistle. That'll cause a supervisor to come over to check it out. Sound good?"

I scan my fellow section-twelve volunteers. No one voices any objections to walking ten blocks and raising your hand if you see a dead body.

"Good. When we've reached Seventy-Second Street, we're going to move over one chain length. So whoever is on the easternmost end of our group will then move over five feet and become the westernmost walker, and then we'll head back to Eighty-Sixth Street that way. We're supposed to do four passes, and it's expected to take about two hours. When we're done, there will be refreshments back where we originally all met. The place Mr. Broden made his remarks. Any questions?"

One of the men in our group asks if there will be water available. He's an older guy, so I cut him some slack. Eva tells him that there are stations set up along the search, and he can always leave the group to find a water fountain or to buy a bottle of water from one of the vendors in the park.

"I guess that's all the instructions," Eva says. "But, like Charlotte's father said before, I also want to thank you all for coming out today. I don't know how many of you knew Charlotte, but we were in a creative-writing seminar and she's so . . ." Eva starts to break down, which strikes me as a bit over the top.

Without further delay, the walking begins. Every so often there's a shrill piercing of the silence. Everyone comes to a complete stop, waiting in place to see if the search is now over because the whistle means someone has found Charlotte's corpse.

Of course, I'm the only one there who knows that each whistle is a false alarm. But I stop like all the rest and look around anxiously.

After one whistle stoppage, the man to my left tells me he'd never met Charlotte, but had a case with her father once. "It's so weird, right? I mean, you don't want it to be her, and yet . . . there's this odd sense that maybe it would be best if they found her already. You know, to give her family some closure."

"I guess it depends on whether you think there's any chance she's still alive," I reply, because I assume that's what someone like me would say if he didn't know for a fact that Charlotte was dead and at the bottom of the East River.

In all, there are probably seven or eight whistles. After the first three or so, I no longer see the anxious looks—the fear in people's eyes—that a gruesome discovery is at hand. Now it's more like when a penalty is called in a football game. Just a break in the action.

By the time the volunteers are corralled back to Ninety-Sixth Street, I have worked out in my head what I'm going to say. I find her greeting the volunteers as they enter the refreshment tent.

Ella looks shocked to see me. Shocked, but happy.

"Dylan?" she says before I can say anything to her.

CHAPTER TWENTY-THREE

There are things that are too strong even for death to steal away.

I suppose I always knew that. It's a common lover's refrain to profess that you'll love each other forever. Matthew and I would say that to each other. I'll love you for all eternity. That kind of thing. I think he said it half in jest, as if we were characters in some melodrama on Lifetime. But I meant it. Jason never used such language, but I'm certain he thought it was true. He could never imagine an existence in which his love for me was not the defining feature. Marco, of course, never made such a sweeping pronouncement, nor did I toward him. It wasn't true for him, and if I'd said it, he wouldn't have hesitated to call me a liar.

It's not to any of my lovers that I'm still bound after death. It's only to Emily that I feel such a magnetic pull. In fact, my connection to my sister now feels stronger than ever, as it's undiluted by any other.

I take comfort in the knowledge that my father will survive my death, although whether he'll be the same man on the other side is unclear to me. I hope that he is, and at the same time, that my death changes him too. A contradiction permitted to those no longer of this world.

It's ironic that, in my life, I parceled out my time to three men, and now, with eternity stretching before me, I have no interest in such meaningless pursuits. Even I am struck by the absence of any need for revenge. It is not present in me at all, no matter how deeply I search.

That's because I'm more convinced than ever that there is no such thing as justice. Many things happen—some good, some bad, some tragic, some retributive—and if you try to match them up against one another, you can convince yourself that there's some balance, especially if you eliminate the ones without any logic to them whatsoever—the thirty-year-old mother of three who is mowed down by a hit-and-run driver, the terrorist who kills scores of children—as merely part of God's unknowable plan, but the truth is that there's a terrible randomness to life, and no cause and effect to give any of it meaning.

Even if I could whisper the identity of my killer into Emily's ear, letting her believe that it came to her in a dream, I would not do so. I keep my silence not out of any complicity with my attacker, but because I refuse to devote even that much energy toward him.

It no longer matters. Nothing of that kind matters any longer.

But I know it matters to Emily. For her, it's all that matters now. She will not rest until my murder is avenged.

In the end, if I could whisper anything to her, it would be to let go of that pursuit. To honor my life by being happy. And I'd tell her that my greatest fear is that, if she is not careful, my murderer will end her life too.

PART TWO

DAY FIVE

SATURDAY

Christopher Tyler

32.

"Hello, Ella," I say like I'm James Bond.

Everything about the woman standing before me is the opposite of Cassidy: her hair is pulled back, her clothing hangs loosely, and aside from lip gloss she appears not to be wearing any makeup. Nevertheless, I can see Cassidy clearly. She's behind Ella's eyes—that dead-on stare that signals she won't be denied what she wants.

"I'd wanted to get in touch with you, but I'm such an idiot," I say in my best, aw-shucks way, just as I rehearsed it. "I never got your number the other night, and you never gave me your last name. I thought about dropping by your apartment building, but that seemed kind of stalker-ish. I was just about to leave you a note at Lava, when I saw you on the news and decided that I'd come here to see you. I hope that was okay."

I know I'm playing with fire with this gambit. More than that, I'm doing so while wearing a suit made of gasoline. If somehow Ella learned that Dylan Perry, do-gooder doctor, was actually Christopher Tyler, and that Christopher Tyler knew Charlotte . . . that would be all she wrote. But I'm convinced the potential rewards outweigh the risk.

When I made the decision to seek Ella out at Lava, it was because I needed to know why Charlotte's death hadn't been on the news. I figured that if Ella were singing at Lava, then that would mean that *no one* knew Charlotte was dead.

My approach today is the next logical step. I need to learn what the police know, and Ella is in a position to tell me.

I'm certain Charlotte never imagined that when she shared with me a little gossip that a high-school friend had been at open-mic night at Lava and said that one of the performers looked like Ella in heavy makeup it would lead to my seeking her sister out at the lounge. But it's long been a firm belief of mine that information isn't just power, as the expression goes. It's freedom. It's money. It's knowledge. It's . . . everything.

There's a tremendous irony in the fact that I suspect Charlotte only shared the story about Ella's secret life with me to assuage her own guilt. Here she was keeping secrets from everyone in her life—McDouche, the J-man whose name she called out the night I strangled her, me, and, of course, Ella. She must have felt some comfort in knowing that *everyone* keeps secrets, even her perfect older sister.

I'm fixated on an entirely different secret, however. Did Charlotte tell anyone about me?

She swore that she hadn't, but I can't be certain of that. The one thing I know for sure is that if she *had* shared, it would have been with Ella.

"Yes. I'm really glad you came, Dylan," Ella says.

I actually came up with the name Dylan Perry on the fly. I was thinking of a rebel. My first choice was to go with Dean James, but I worried that was too obvious. I'm embarrassed to say that the next image to pop into my head was of Luke Perry, who played a character named Dylan on *Beverly Hills, 90210.* I couldn't remember the character's last name, so I went with the hybrid.

"I'm so sorry about your sister," I say. "I can't imagine what a nightmare this must be."

I've never considered acting to be one of my strengths, but I think I'm doing a passable job. I sound sincere, even to my own ear.

"Thank you," she says. "It's been really awful."

I'm not a sociopath. A sociopath lacks any empathy for others, whereas I understand Ella's suffering, and feel badly for her. Just as I feel remorse for killing Charlotte. I'd take that back in a second if I could, and I'd also ameliorate Ella's pain by confessing—if the repercussions were minor, but they're not. The undeniable fact is that no matter how much Ella grieves, her pain will still be much less than mine if I have to spend the rest of my life in a maximum-security prison. So, in the end, you could say that I am a relativist, and that is why I continue on with my prepared speech to Ella.

"I know this is going to sound odd because we don't really know each other at all, but if there's anything I can do, please just ask. Even if it's just to talk."

I wait a beat, hoping that she's going to ask for my number, or at least give me an opening to ask for hers. Instead, she makes a comment about the rubber bracelet. I decide that I need to push a little harder.

"Normally I'd ask for your number, but I don't want to reach out to you until you're ready, so why don't I give you my number instead? That way, you can call me whenever you want. No pressure, though."

She nods and takes out her phone. "Ready."

I recite the digits of the burner phone I purchased that morning on my way to Riverside Park for precisely this purpose. The same number I put on the sign-in sheet. She punches them into her phone.

I programmed "Under Pressure" as my ringtone. She laughs when it comes through, which was my intent in choosing the song.

"No pressure, huh?" she says, laughing.

By the way she looks at me—as if she's remembering our night together and wishing for more—I know that I won't have to wait long to hear from her.

DAY SIX

SUNDAY

33.

On Sunday mornings, my usual routine is to go for a run. I do a five-mile loop along the Hudson River, starting out at Jane Street and making the turn at the *Intrepid* Museum, a World War II battleship docked permanently at Forty-Second Street. The path tends to be crowded, filled with joggers and cyclists, but I enjoy the cold wind whipping up from the river—the Hudson Hawk, they call it. Then I walk back home, the sweat trickling down my back and the sun on my face as I watch the other runners grunting by me.

Today, however, when I leave my building, I jog to the east. I hadn't given it any true forethought. It's almost as if my mind has tricked my body, or perhaps it's the other way around. Whichever is in charge, I find myself heading to the East River. Returning to the scene of the crime, as it were. Well, not the crime exactly, but the cover-up.

I run from Chelsea through the East Village and then into Alphabet City, that part of Manhattan where the streets are lettered rather than numbered. On nearly every tree I see Charlotte's smiling face staring back at me from that pink leaflet.

It takes me no more than twenty minutes to bisect Manhattan and arrive at First Avenue. From there I head north, watching the numbered streets tick by—First Street to Second to Third. My destination is Fourteenth, where I'll enter East River Park, just as I did six days ago.

Only this time, I'm without Charlotte's dead body in a suitcase.

I haven't formulated any sort of plan for what I'll do when I arrive. Nor have I really thought about whether my presence is well advised. For all I know, the cops are staking out the area. But if I see a horde of police, that'll be helpful information I didn't have before, and I'll just turn around and go home.

Nothing looks familiar in the park in daylight. In fact, it's a joyous place on this Sunday morning, a bustle of activity. Couples hand-in-hand, people walking dogs, the ball fields filled with Little Leaguers, and the playground bursting with the bright colors of the outfits of the children running around. Best of all, no cops.

I walk down the embankment to the East River, stopping at the fence separating the park from the water. I recall how formidable it seemed, but without a suitcase filled with Charlotte's dead body, it only takes a half jump to scale it. On the other side, the ground is soft and muddy even though it hasn't rained over the last few days. There's no evidence of footprints and certainly nothing to indicate wheels or a heavy item being dragged.

I look back into the park. No one has taken any notice of me making my way down to the river. Perhaps this is something people do—try to get close to the water.

The river is calm, barely a ripple on the surface. It's what lies below that concerns me, of course.

I can feel Charlotte with me. It's not that I actually *see* her dead body rise from the river, nor do I feel a ghostly presence. Rather, she has invaded my consciousness somehow.

Although I thought I'd succeeded in intellectualizing away my breaking of the "Thou shalt not kill" commandment, her presence suggests otherwise. Needless to say, she takes the opportunity to make clear that she's not supportive of my choices.

"You're not going to get away with it, Christopher," she says. "You think you're smarter than anyone, but you're not. Ella's twice as smart as you. She'll figure it out."

I respond audibly, albeit in a whisper. "She hasn't so far."

"She will. And when she does, she'll make you pay."

———

At ten, my phone pings. A text. The only reason I even move to read it is because it's my burner.

Ella.

If she had let the weekend pass without reaching out, I would have begun second-guessing everything I had thought about her interest. Worse than that, I would have become suspicious that she knew I'd killed her sister. But any thought of that is erased when I read her message.

The words almost completely fill my screen. Full sentences, complete with punctuation. Not the phonetics and emoji-heavy gibberish most women text.

Hey there. Wondering how you're doing.

I'm good. And you?

I've had a crappy day, to tell you the truth.

Sorry. Anything I can do?

I stare at the screen, awaiting her reply. Ten seconds pass. I no longer even see the ellipses that indicate she's typing her next message.

But then my phone rings.

"Hello?" I say, as if I don't know it's Ella calling.

"Hi, Dylan. It's Ella. Call me old-fashioned, but I'm just not that into texting."

"Me either." Of course, that's a lie. I text all the time, usually preferring it to actual conversation. "I was really hoping that I'd hear from you."

"I have to be honest," she says, "I've been struggling with the whole can-I-meet-someone-new-while-my-sister-is-missing thing."

She laughs. A nervous laugh. I try to put her at ease. To let her know there's nothing wrong with her becoming close to me.

"I totally understand. Timing . . . couldn't be worse. But I'm a big believer that things happen for a reason . . . at least sometimes. We met, we really clicked, and then this terrible thing happened to your sister. I think . . . I don't want to get all higher-power on you, because I'm not religious, but I do consider myself spiritual and, well, I think the universe does send us messages. And yes, I know that makes me sound like someone dressed in pajamas giving out daisies at the airport, but I believe it."

She laughs again. This time it isn't nervous. It's the sound of comfort.

A few moments of silence tick by before I finally ask the question again: "Is there anything I can do? To make things easier on you, I mean."

"In fact, there is," she says. "Would you mind terribly keeping me company tomorrow night? I'm just going crazy here all alone and I don't want to do it again another night."

"It would be my pleasure. Do you have a favorite restaurant?"

"I don't think I want to be in a restaurant. You know, out in public."

This is music to my ears. I don't want to be out with her in public either. Unfortunately, I also don't want her knowing where I live. I have a lie on the tip of my tongue—I've been having some painting done and the smell is awful—when she spares me.

"So, could you come to my place? Seven? Do you remember where I live?"

I do, but I think better of admitting it. "I know it's close to the Lava Lounge, but I have to confess I don't remember exactly where."

She gives me the address. Then she says, "I figured I'll order in some pizza. Is that okay?"

"Who doesn't like pizza?"

"Great."

"Thanks so much for calling, Ella. I'm looking forward to seeing you again."

"Me too. Bye, Dylan."

DAY SEVEN

MONDAY

34.

From the moment I wake on Monday, my thoughts are about seeing Ella that evening. I'll have real time with her, in her apartment, aided by alcohol, hopefully. That should get her to open up to me about the police investigation, her sister's love life. Who knows what else?

But until then, I have to pass the day at work and not raise anyone's suspicions that I'm the man at the center of the biggest missing-persons case in New York City history.

"Morning, Beth," I say to my assistant when I enter the firm. "Keeping safe, I hope."

"Not funny," she replies. "I didn't go out all weekend. I just had friends come over to my place."

"Don't worry. You're safe here with me."

I go in my office and shut the door. I click on the Excel spreadsheet that lists the potential investors I'm circling for The Pouch. The levels I'm seeing are not good. Amoroso is going to be apoplectic when I tell him that interest is below eight bucks. One of the biggest players in this space, a hedge fund appropriately called Bottom Feeder, told me early on they were willing to invest upward of $40 million, but yesterday reduced their buy to $25 million, and they now refuse to pay more than $7.75 per share.

I call the fund manager, Brian Weinberg. I'm told he can't come to the phone, and my call is rerouted to Seth Shapiro. Seth's a decent enough guy, but the fact I can't get to the head honcho means that things are even worse than I thought.

"Seth, my man. How's it going?"

"No complaints," he says. "What can I do you for?"

"Looking at the circles on my spread. I have you guys at twenty-five mil at seven seventy-five. We had originally talked about forty at eight."

"That was two weeks ago. Ancient history."

"But the market is up two, three percent."

"That's a tech pop, Christopher."

I'm not bullshitting him. I really don't understand why they're skittish at eight bucks.

"What's going on, Seth? Really."

"You want the truth?"

"Hell yeah, I do."

"Brian went to Bergdorf Goodman's and bought a pair."

"What?"

"You heard me. He went to Bergdorf's and bought a pair of your client's product. Dropped a hundred fifty bucks. He had them on yesterday."

"And . . . ?"

Seth laughs. "I take it that you've never worn them."

I could lie, but what's the point. "I'm a Jockey guy."

"Well, suffice to say, you're lucky we're buying at all."

"That bad?"

"Brian's balls itched all day."

———

Either the other big players in the market have stronger testicles or haven't decided to do their own market research, because their circles remained at the eight-buck level. It didn't much matter, though. They each had favored-nation status, which meant that they got the best price I was willing to offer anyone else—and if Weinberg's itchy balls meant that Bottom Feeder was only going to pay $7.75, that's the price everybody else would get too.

Amoroso is going to shit when I tell him that he's going to be short on the total raise. But that conversation can wait.

Today, I have much bigger fish to fry.

I arrive at Ella's apartment right on time, wearing what I consider my not-trying-too-hard outfit—jeans and a long-sleeved, collared shirt. On the way to her place, I picked up a bottle of wine, a cheap one, to vary things about myself so as to better pull off my alter ego of Dylan Perry, mild-mannered, altruistic doctor.

Ella's hair is loose, reminding me of the way she wore it at Lava the night we first met. That's where the similarities to Cassidy end, however. Tonight, she's dressed casually—black jeans, loose-fitting white T-shirt—and, as when I saw her at Riverside Park, she's not wearing any makeup aside from lipstick.

I hand Ella the bottle of wine. "I don't know much about wine," I say, trying to sound humble, "but the guy in the store said that this was good."

"My motto is that every wine goes with Italian food," she says. "There's this great little place I always order in from. They have pastas and small pizzas, so I thought maybe we'd have a carbfest and do one of each."

"I'm in your hands," I say.

She calls in our order. After hanging up, she reports there's a backup at the restaurant, so it's going to take an hour for the food to arrive. Then she sits beside me on the sofa, even though her living room has other seating options. I'm about to inquire about the investigation when she asks me about the one thing I did not want to discuss: myself. Or more accurately, Dylan Perry.

"So, give me the whole Dylan Perry story. From birth to right now."

I've prepared for the question, just in case it came up, going so far as actually writing down my fake biography. I'd also double-checked my data through Google, to confirm she couldn't disprove any of what I might tell her. At least not without some serious background checking.

In my alternate life, I'm a farm boy—born in Wyoming, because I assume she's never been there—but the son of intellectuals. Reared in Kansas because that's where my made-up father taught English at the university. I almost screw up by making an off-the-cuff joke about Manhattan, Kansas, before realizing that I'd told Ella I live in Brooklyn, not Manhattan, but I cover it well enough. I give myself a fancy pedigree—Duke undergrad and Johns Hopkins for medical school—although it's less impressive than my actual Ivy League education. I'd already told her about Doctors Without Borders when we met at Lava, but now I gild that lily by saying how rewarding my work has been, even amid the horrors I've seen.

After reciting my too-good-to-be-true biography, I feign interest in Ella's life and I hear all about how she chose to go to law school rather than pursue a career in music. This leads to the inevitable question of what she was doing performing at Lava under an alias, at which time she gives me the sad story that Charlotte had mentioned before. How her mother wanted her to pursue her talent in music but, after she died, Ella chose the safer path of law school to please her father. The one part that Ella adds that Charlotte never told me is how Ella's choices had left her with so much regret.

Dinner finally arrives, during which we finish the bottle of wine. After, Ella suggests we watch a movie. She scrolls through the Netflix selections and asks if some Reese Witherspoon flick is okay. I couldn't care less what we watch, so I tell her it sounds great.

Once the movie is queued up, she snuggles beside me.

"I don't want to be a downer, but I still feel a little guilty," she says. "I'm really enjoying myself with you and my sister is . . ."

This is my opportunity. If I approach it right, I'll be able to get Ella to open up to me.

"You need to take care of yourself too," I say. "You know, like what they say before the plane takes off. Put on your own oxygen mask before assisting others."

I wait to see whether she'll go for the bait I'm dangling. She doesn't at first, and I'm left petting her hair as the credits roll.

Just when I think that this is going to be a waste of my time, she breaks the silence. And when she does, it's music to my ears.

"Because I used to be a prosecutor, I know the police lieutenant who's running the case," she finally says. "His name is Gabriel Velasquez. He keeps me up-to-date. They were initially focused on Charlotte's boyfriend. Zach's a real asshole and initially refused to cooperate. But he's cooperating now and he passed a polygraph. There was another guy that Charlotte was seeing, named Josh. He cooperated from the very start, but his polygraph was what they call 'inconclusive.' So I guess the state of play is that Zach's not a suspect but Josh still is. I've told the police that I don't think Josh did it, though. He just doesn't seem the type."

There's so much in this download, I don't know where to begin. First, they've been polygraphing suspects. Second, McDouche has apparently been cleared, but this other guy Charlotte was screwing— the guy whose name she called out on the night I killed her—flunked the poly. And third, if Ella's ruling this second guy out, does she believe it's someone else?

I need to press further. "You say that like you have a suspect in mind," I say, hoping I'm not being too obvious.

She begins to cry. It's soft, and she's trying to hold it back, but I can see that I've touched a nerve. It's good for me, the vulnerability. So I pull her closer to me.

"It's okay," I say softly.

"There's another guy she was seeing," she says.

This cuts way too close to home. I try to maintain a calm exterior, but inside I'm in a full-fledged panic. I need her to tell me what she knows about this other guy. I'm formulating how to coax the information out of her without making her suspicious, but then she just comes out with it.

"It's my former college boyfriend. How messed up is that, right? I hadn't seen him in more than ten years, but we recently reconnected and he told me that he also knew Charlotte. And I think—more than just think, actually—I'm pretty sure that he's the guy who killed . . . or whatever . . . Charlotte."

It's not me. That's all I hear. She has a prime suspect and *he's not me*.

I watch her expression change. Her grief has receded, and she's taken on a different cast. Angry. Defiant, maybe.

"You know, before this, I never considered myself a vengeful person," she says. "I mean, I was a prosecutor for a lot of years, but I was never one of the ones who relished the idea that these guys—and I prosecuted mainly men who were sexual predators—would be on the other end of that equation in prison. I just considered it a tragedy all the way around. But now . . . all I want is for Paul, this guy I once thought I was in love with, to suffer for what he did to Charlotte. Not just to die, but to suffer."

I swallow hard. I need to make sure that never happens.

35.

Ella's phone rings a few minutes later. She'd resumed her position cradled under my arm, but when it rings, I can actually feel her clench up beside me. It's not just that she's startled, though. I know what she fears on the other end of the line. Truth be told, it's what I fear too.

"Hello," she says tentatively.

The way the blood drains from her face confirms that our mutual concern has been realized. Charlotte's body has been found.

The conversation is short. Less than two minutes. When she puts down the phone, her eyes are unfocused, almost as if she's been hypnotized.

"Ella, are you okay?" I ask.

She doesn't answer. I ask again.

"Ella, was that about your sister?"

"The police . . . ," she starts slowly and then stops. After a deep breath, she provides the information I've been waiting for. "They found Charlotte. She's dead."

Ella falls into my arms. Her face is buried deep into my chest, and I can feel her convulse. As she sobs, I'm reduced to patting her on the back, an effort to provide some comfort for what I've taken from her.

After a moment, she pries herself off me. Sitting up but breathing heavily, she looks at me quizzically, like she can't quite place how she knows me.

"I . . . I need to go to the police station," she says.

I walk her out of the building, keeping my arm around her, almost as if I'm holding her upright. The right thing to do, of course, would be to accompany her to the police station, but that's not even a consideration. There's no way I'm letting the police see my face or let them learn that I know Ella.

I flag down a taxi and then open the door for her. Before shutting the door, I lean in to the backseat.

"Promise me that you'll call the second you're done with the police, okay?" I say.

"I promise."

As I watch the cab pull away, I contemplate whether running is now the smart move for me. With the discovery of Charlotte's body, it'll become a murder investigation. Should I get on the first Amtrak to Canada? Or better yet, board a plane for some country without an extradition treaty with the United States?

Just a little longer, I tell myself. *Keep Ella in play for another day or so.*

I know I sound like one of those guys in Vegas wanting to play just one more hand in a losing game, but breaking contact with Ella now means a lifetime of waiting in the dark for the police to show up at my door, and that simply isn't an option I'm willing to entertain.

I walk a few blocks away from Ella's building before getting into my own taxi. I don't want a cab driver to be able to tell the police he picked someone up in front of Ella's home at precisely the time she left for the police station. I continue the subterfuge on the other end, asking the cabbie to drop me three blocks away from my apartment.

During the ride home, my mind swirls with the thought of possible loose ends I've left untied. The affected accent of Hercule Poirot plays in my head. *"It was almost perfect, except for one little thing. One minor detail you overlooked . . ."*

What is the one little thing I've forgotten? The minor detail I've overlooked?

I imagine the movie version of my life. Shots of me lying in bed intercut with the evidence that will lead to my arrest. But what is in the second image? Her body? The suitcase? Someone who works at the W Hotel?

I decide to think about it methodically. To go over each piece of new evidence now in the police's custody.

First, there's Charlotte herself. Now the police know that she's certainly dead, and they'll undoubtedly test her body a million ways to see if it yields any clues that will help to identify her killer. We always used a condom, so my semen, at least, won't be inside her. But could they find something else linking to me? My fingerprints? A strand of my hair?

No, I tell myself. Not after a week in the East River. All her corpse will tell the police now is that she died of strangulation.

Then a different thought hits me. Another thing the police now have that they didn't know before: Charlotte's body was disposed of in the East River. That means that the police's best lead might be to canvass the area for someone who remembers a man pulling a large suitcase the night she went missing.

But I didn't see another soul in the park that night, so I can't imagine that someone saw *me*. And even if there was someone at a distance that I hadn't noticed, at most they saw a silhouette. There's no way that anyone could identify my face from that night. It was pitch-black.

Last is the suitcase. I scrubbed it clean, but could I have missed something? A hair caught in the zipper? I try to take solace in the belief that immersion in the East River for a week would destroy anything linking back to me, but I have no idea whether that's actually true.

The discovery of the suitcase also gives them the brand. I remember Marcia Clark's famous claim that the bloody footprints belonged to O. J. Simpson because they were made by "rich man's shoes." I wonder if Tumi will be considered "rich man's luggage." Does Tumi change models every couple of years, like car manufacturers? With any luck, they've been selling the same model I used as Charlotte's coffin for years. Tens of thousands of people might own one exactly like it.

I try, without success, to recall where I bought it. I remember it was purchased shortly before I went on a twenty-one-day African safari. What year was that? 2012? 2013? I went with Stephanie and broke up with her the week we returned. Would she remember that I had a Tumi suitcase that matched the one Charlotte was found inside? For the life of me, I couldn't remember *her* luggage. Why on earth would she remember mine? Does she have any photos? Us at the airport, surrounded by our bags? Our jeep with the luggage in the back, secured by a bungee cord?

Get a grip, I tell myself. A million things would have to happen before the cops start looking at my ex-girlfriend's old photos for proof that I once owned a large Tumi suitcase.

What about the bellhop at the W hotel? Will he remember I had a large Tumi suitcase? Is it unusual in his line of work for a man to wheel a large piece of luggage out of a hotel after midnight? Would my refusal to ask for a cab be something that would stick in his mind? What about my not checking the bag? Then again, how many large suitcases does that guy see in a day? A hundred? A thousand? And I'm certain the brand couldn't have registered. Why would it? Besides, what are the odds he follows the news close enough to realize that a dead girl was found in a suitcase? And even if he knew this fact, would he want to get involved in a high-profile murder investigation? Is he the kind of guy who would reach out to the police?

But if he does, it would be the beginning of the end for me. I'm on the hotel registry. My real name. My American Express card is on file. A copy of my driver's license. The hotel's surveillance cameras would show Charlotte and me entering the hotel. A few hours later, I'll be on camera leaving by myself, only to return an hour after that with a large, black Tumi suitcase. Then an hour after that, the video will show me leaving yet again, this time with that same suitcase—with it looking much more difficult to handle.

And, of course, the cameras will never show Charlotte leaving.

———

Once I've returned to my apartment, the realization that things could be closing in on me causes me to immediately go to the liquor cabinet. My good friend Mr. Johnnie Walker is front and center. I pour myself a double. Drink in hand, I settle into my living room and reflect on what I've wrought—and what might follow.

Eventually the alcohol does its job. I fall asleep in my chair. I might have slept through the night had it not been for the ringing of my phone. My burner phone.

Ella.

"Hello?" I say.

I can hear the drunkenness in my scratchy voice. *Sober up and focus,* I tell myself. *There's no room for error here. One slip with Ella and I'll make myself a prime suspect.*

"I'm sorry. I didn't mean to wake you."

"No, it's all right. Where are you?"

"At my father's. I'm going to stay here tonight. I don't want him to be alone."

"Okay. How'd it go with the police?"

She starts to answer, and then her voice cracks. When she begins again, she says, "I saw her, Dylan. I saw Charlotte. I saw what that animal did to her. I'm never going to get that image out of my mind. And I swear to God, I'm going to . . ." Her voice trails off into sobs.

"Is there anything I can do?"

I know that there's nothing she'll ask for. At least not tonight. So I feel safe in making the overture. Still, I prepare a lie if she actually calls on me to perform any service.

"No. Thank you, though. Actually, there is something. I'd like to see you tomorrow. I know this sounds . . . I don't know . . . we barely know each other, but I guess there's something about our not having any history that makes it easy for me to escape from all this for a little bit when we're together. Is that okay?"

It's better than okay. I need to know more. Has Charlotte's body revealed any additional evidence? Do the police have any new leads? Most important of all: do they know anything about Christopher Tyler?

"I want to see you too. How about if I come to your place after work tomorrow? I have a meeting at five. I can be there around six thirty or seven."

"A meeting? I didn't know doctors had meetings."

Shit. "It's with my practice leader. I'm not sure exactly what it's about, but I think he's going to ask me to go back to Peru with him."

"I hope not too soon."

"I hope not too. I'll find out more tomorrow."

"Okay. I'll see you tomorrow at around seven, then."

"Good night. And Ella . . . I'm so sorry."

"I know you are. And like I said, thank you. I don't know if I'd be able to handle this without you."

DAY EIGHT

TUESDAY

Ella Broden

Christopher Tyler

36.

I wake up on Tuesday morning at 6:00 a.m. I can hear my father puttering in the kitchen. The aroma of freshly brewed coffee fills the air.

"How long have you been up?" I ask.

"I'm not really sure," he says. "An hour, I guess. Do you want some coffee?"

"Please."

My father is wearing his robe, and it appears he has not yet showered or shaved. If he plans on going to work today, he'll have to start that process shortly. I've already decided that's not how I'm going to spend my day.

"I just can't come to the office today," I say.

I don't tell him that I'm never going back, although I suspect he already knows that my career in the practice of "real law"—as he puts it—is over. I simply can't defend the Paul Michelsons of the world any longer.

"I totally get if you want to go in," I add. "Either to make sure everything is under control, or simply to take your mind off everything."

"I need to make arrangements," he says.

It isn't clear if that means he's going to the office. He could just as easily make the funeral arrangements from home.

"Do you want me to help you with that?"

"No," he says. "I'll do it. It's my obligation. I hope it's a very long time before you have to do anything like that." Then he laughs. "Unfortunately, I doubt I'll be able to help you then, as I suspect those arrangements will be for me."

I weakly smile at his attempt at humor. The last thing I want to think about, however, is his death.

"But there is something you can do for me, Ella."

He says this grimly. He's not going to ask for a favor, but impart a life lesson.

"Of course. What?"

"I want you to focus on yourself more. You don't need to be there for me."

"Okay."

"No. I mean it." He offers me a soft, albeit sad, smile. "I'll be okay, Ella. I promise."

———

On my way to Maeve Grant, I buy the *New York Times* from the newsstand a few blocks from my apartment. I haven't read the news from my computer, or even my phone, for fear I'd be leaving evidence. It takes me a moment before I find what I'm looking for. It's in the Metropolitan section. Front page. The headline: BODY OF MISSING LAWYER'S DAUGHTER FOUND.

I scan the newsprint looking for the word *suitcase*, but it's not there. I go back to the top and read it more carefully. The story reports that Charlotte's corpse was found in the East River and that the working police theory is that she was killed elsewhere and then deposited in the water, likely on the day she went missing. My careful read confirms that there's nothing about the suitcase.

They must not have it, I think. *Maybe, somehow, the suitcase tore open under the water and Charlotte floated to the top alone.*

I breathe a deep sigh of relief. Without the suitcase, the police barely have any more evidence than they had before. All they know is that she was thrown in the East River. The *Times* article made no reference to witnesses, and the newspaper didn't suggest that there was any DNA, fingerprints, or anything else that the police were testing.

Only one weak link remains. The only possible way the police will be able to tie me to Charlotte's murder: Ella.

The path forward is now clearer than ever before. I'll see Ella again to ascertain with certainty that the cops haven't found the suitcase. Once that's established, I'll kill her and thereby tie up the last loose end. With her death, Dylan Perry will never have existed, and Christopher Tyler can go back to living his life.

———

I return to my apartment before nine and immediately climb back into bed. I had thought that I might be able to escape into sleep, but no matter what I do to calm my mind, I can't shake the image of Charlotte's lifeless body lying in that morgue drawer. When I try to focus on something else, anything else, it only results in my conjuring an even grimmer image regarding Charlotte's final moments. How terrified she must have been. Did she cry out for help? Did thoughts of being reunited with our mother provide her any comfort?

In my toughest cases back when I was an ADA, when I was truly stymied, I'd close the door to my office, pull out a yellow legal pad, and scribble. I didn't do flow charts or diagrams but simply jotted down the evidence. Then I'd stare at it the way you'd look at one of those optical-illusion images that hides a 3-D picture within it. Relaxing my vision in hope that all would be revealed.

I pull myself out of bed and go to my dining table. There, I take a yellow legal pad from my briefcase and begin to list the evidence the police have uncovered:

Tumi suitcase
East River
Missing since Tuesday

To that, I add the things I know about the fictional Matthew Harrison:

Tall, black hair, handsome
Banker
Patek Philippe watch
Art gallery/topless out-of-focus photo
Married
Scar/initial/hip

———

I call Amoroso at 8:00 a.m. my time, which means it's about 2:00 p.m. in Milan. With any luck, he's still having his espresso in some café and I'll get to leave a message.

I'm not in luck. His assistant tells me to hold.

"*Pronto,*" Amoroso says.

"Paolo. Christopher Tyler."

"Oh, Tyler," he says, switching to English.

"I've got a good news/bad news situation."

He doesn't state a preference for which he'd like to hear first. I get the sense that he feels as if he's losing a piece of his soul every second we interact and just wants to get the call over with.

"Good news first, then," I say. "I got the financing in place. In fact, the offering is oversubscribed. So that gives us some flexibility if you want to sell more."

"No," he says. "The point is to raise the hundred million but keep as much equity as possible."

"And that leads me to the bad news. The price is going to top off at seven dollars and seventy-five cents. So to get to the hundred million you want, you're going to have to give up more equity."

———

As I'm still staring down at my evidence list, the phone rings. It's Gabriel.

"The ME has a cause of death," he says.

I brace myself until he says it.

One word: "Asphyxiation."

Even though I know the answer, I ask the question. "How?"

"The ME said her windpipe was fractured. He thinks it was probably done by hand."

"She was choked to death?"

"That's the preliminary determination, yes."

"My God."

"I know, and I'm sorry." He waits a moment, likely for me to say something, but when I don't, he says, "We're canvassing East River Park. From Battery Park to Thirty-Fourth Street, showing Charlotte's photograph and asking if anyone saw a man with a suitcase last Tuesday night. Hopefully that will give us a hit. Someone wheeling a large suitcase in the park late at night is not the usual occurrence."

I'm in no mood to be optimistic. It seems like hope is simply a luxury I can no longer afford. And even though I know Gabriel is just trying to help, I want to make that clear to him.

"Homeless people do it," I say.

"Not thousand-dollar luggage. We've also followed up with Josh. He let us search his place. He has a set of luggage, but it's not Tumi. The local cops even got the okay from his parents to look through *their* home. Same story. No Tumi luggage."

"They could have tossed it," I say.

"They could have, but Josh and his parents had different luggage. Much lower-end stuff and all the pieces—even Josh's—were from the same set. I'm not saying that they couldn't have had one larger piece that was high-end in addition to a complete set that was low-end—or even two completely different sets, and like you said, they tossed the Tumi—but that's not the way most people are. And don't get me wrong, I'm also *not* saying that we've cleared Josh on this, but I *am* saying that the luggage doesn't point to him."

"So what's it going to be, Paolo? Do the hundred-million raise? Or can you live with less?"

I'm sure the answer he wants to give me is "none of the above." Actually, that's probably his second choice, right after "Fuck you, Tyler."

"I need to talk to my board," he says. "I'll get back to you within the hour."

The 21 Club is almost a caricature of a power spot. It's housed in a former speakeasy on Fifty-Second Street, just west of Fifth Avenue. Diners are greeted by thirty-three porcelain statues of jockeys standing on a ledge on the exterior of the building, all wearing bright colors. The famous barroom—where Charlie Sheen lunched with Michael Douglas in *Wall Street*—features assorted sports-related memorabilia hanging from the ceiling. Much of it was donated by famous patrons: Willie Mays's bat, John McEnroe's tennis racquet, Jack Nicklaus's golf club.

Paul is already seated when I arrive. As I'm led by the maître d' to his table in the back, I scan the faces of my fellow diners. Not more than a handful of women, no people of color. As per the dress code, every man is in a jacket, with most wearing neckties.

Paul stands when I arrive and greets me with a kiss. It takes all my energy not to wince.

"Thank you for bumping your real date on such short notice," I say.

It was comically easy to get Paul to cancel on whomever he was supposed to meet at 21 today for lunch. All it took for him to rearrange his schedule was the suggestion that I might end up in bed with him after the meal.

My plan isn't much of one. I'll suffer through lunch and then accede to his request to go back to his place. Once there, I'll search for Tumi luggage while he no doubt prepares for sexual conquest. I don't have an exit strategy, not a small detail considering I suspect Paul of being a murderer—possibly of two women—but I'll deal with that later.

"My pleasure. After all, you're much better looking than him."

Paul gives me a smile that I bet he thinks is sexy as hell.

"This wouldn't have been my first choice for lunch with you, as it's kind of a guy mecca," he says. "But I hate to cancel a reservation, given that I have special table status here."

It's ironic that we're at 21. When Charlotte and I were little, my father would take us here for our birthdays. It was very exciting for us to order a twenty-one-dollar burger. I remember how impressed Charlotte was that the ketchup came on a little dish and not in a Heinz bottle.

The waiter approaches and asks if there's anything we'd like to drink.

"I normally don't at lunch," Paul says, "but I'm game if you are."

I want him drunk. It will help later.

"I have nowhere to be this afternoon," I say with what I hope he perceives as a flirty smile. "What do you think goes well with an overpriced burger?"

"I'm thinking a cabernet," Paul says. He peruses the wine list, which is as thick as a novel. "Yes, we'll take a bottle of the Brunello di Montalcino La Torre 2009."

———

Amoroso calls back thirty minutes later. "We need the full hundred million," he says, then hangs up without uttering another word.

I take it as a sign that everything is heading in my direction. The Pouch deal will come through, and that will put me in line for another big bonus this year. And today I'll turn the corner on the Charlotte situation by killing Ella.

———

After the wine is poured, when the waiter has stepped away, I tell Paul that my sister's body has been found. He acts as if he hadn't heard, which must be a lie—unless Paul is purposefully shielding himself from all forms of media because he doesn't want to be reminded of his crimes.

"I'm so sorry," Paul says, as if he had nothing to do with it. His feigned empathy lasts about a second before he gets to what he really wants to know. "Do you think they'll be able to find out who did this now?"

I tell him that there has been a break in the investigation, but I'm not at liberty to share it just yet. I want him to sweat. From the smug look on his face, it hasn't worked. I suppose killing two women hardens your nervous system. Then again, maybe Paul was always immune to guilt.

A few minutes later, our entrées arrive. By then Paul is droning on about this deal he's working on, without any awareness that I couldn't possibly care any less about it. All I want is for this part of the plan to be over so I can move on to phase two.

When the waiter comes and asks if we'd like any dessert or a digestif, I use the request as my opportunity to get into Paul's apartment. Once there, I'll be able to find out if he has a matching Tumi suitcase.

"Is that lovely cognac you mentioned at Sant Ambroeus still available?" I ask.

"In fact it is," he says, "but it's not cognac. It's Armagnac, which, in my humble opinion, is far superior. So you're in for a real treat."

He gives me a cocksure smile. I smile back because he's expecting me to, but I can't dislodge from my mind that the same smirk was probably on full display when he choked Charlotte to death.

—

Paul's apartment is exactly as I'd imagined it. It reminds me of Patrick Bateman's place in the movie *American Psycho*, minimalist and stylized to the very last detail. The walls are a stark white and the floors a dark stain. The furniture complies with the monochromatic scheme—black leather sofa, white chairs, black-and-white photography on the walls.

"You have a lovely home," I say.

"Thank you," he says, seeming proud of himself. "I've been here for about five years. I have one of the smallest places in the building . . . because my place isn't quite fourteen rooms. It's what's known in the prewar world as an 'Edwardian five,' which is a one-bedroom with a full dining room, and a second, very small bedroom designed to house a maid. An apartment for old-world bachelors who entertain."

"Or latter-day investment bankers with commitment issues," I say.

"Yes, that seems to be the market today," he says, laughing.

I look around the living room, although I don't really expect to find Tumi luggage beside his Mapplethorpes.

"Allow me to pour us that Armagnac," he says.

"While you're pouring, I'm going to excuse myself for a moment. Which way to your bathroom?"

He points down the hallway, past the dining room, and then heads to the kitchen to open his fancy liqueur.

I walk past the bathroom and smack into his bedroom. A king bed with an enormous headboard is front and center. It's the only furniture in the room aside from an ultramodern glass desk under the window. Paul apparently doesn't watch television in bed—or maybe he does it on a laptop.

His closet is the size of my bedroom, with at least twenty-five suits, all on padded hangers, assorted by color, looking a little like a paint palette at the hardware store, the grays going from dark to light. His ties are similarly arranged by hue on a rack on the door, and his shoes are stacked floor-to-ceiling. In the back is an array of sweaters so plentiful it evokes that scene with Leonardo DiCaprio in *The Great Gatsby*.

But there it is. On the top shelf. A medium-size suitcase made of space-age-looking black material:

Tumi.

I unzip it. Inside is another suitcase of the identical design. Paul has a set. The small and medium sizes are here, but the large is not. It's no doubt now in the police evidence room.

"Hey, where'd you go?" Paul calls out from the other room.

"Coming!" I shout, as I scamper back to the living room.

Paul is standing at his counter, snifter in hand. I walk over to him with murder on my mind. But how?

"This is Armagnac, which is often confused with cognac, but they're actually completely separate drinks," he says—pontificates, is more accurate. "In fact, Armagnac predates the invention of cognac by seven centuries," he continues. "The main difference is that Armagnac is only distilled once, whereas cognac goes through the process a second time. The result is that it's more flavorful."

He hands me my glass of Armagnac, but I don't take it. Instead, I grab a chef's knife from the butcher block and brandish it as if it were a gun.

His eyes widen, and he takes a step back. "What the hell, Ella?"

"Pull down your pants."

"What?"

"You heard me. Pull down your goddamn pants!"

He looks even more terrified than before. Undoubtedly afraid I'm going to go Lorena Bobbitt on him.

"Do it!" I scream.

He slowly reaches for his belt and unfastens it. Then he pulls down the zipper. Finally, his pants drop to the floor, leaving pin-striped boxers.

"Those too," I say.

"Ella, please."

I can't deny that I like seeing him so defenseless. I take half a step closer to him and jab the knife. "Now!"

His boxers drop to his ankles. He looks about as ridiculous as a man can look. From the waist up, he's dressed in full business attire—pressed white shirt, silk black tie, jacket—while from the waist down he's naked as the day he was born, his flaccid penis hanging between his legs like a sad bird.

I walk backward toward his door, continuing to wave the knife. He doesn't move toward me, clearly relieved that I'm retreating.

———

A moment later, I'm on the street. I still have Paul's kitchen knife in my grip. I slide it into my purse as I reach inside to retrieve my cell phone and call Gabriel.

"I just came from Paul Michelson's place. He has Tumi luggage."

"You saw it?"

"I did. In his closet."

"That'll be enough for a search warrant for sure. We'll pick him up right now."

I come close to telling him the other part—that Paul doesn't have a scar on his hip. I withhold it for two reasons. First, I'm convinced he killed Charlotte, and therefore there's no reason to sow any doubt in Gabriel's mind. The scar could have been fiction, but nearly everything else matches—he's a banker, he wears a Patek Philippe, he met Charlotte at the museum, just like she described in the book. And he has the same Tumi luggage.

Second, it's too humiliating for me to admit to Gabriel that I held Paul at knifepoint and made him pull down his pants. I assume that Paul will explain this to Gabriel when they pick him up, but then I assuage that concern with the realization that Paul's been coached well enough—by me—that he'll know to exercise his right to remain silent.

"Ella . . . are you okay?" Gabriel asks.

"I . . ." I stop in midthought. Gabriel's not the person to confide in that I'm angry with myself that I didn't kill that son of a bitch. I wanted to, I truly did. And if he had the scar, maybe I would have. But at the last second, I lost my nerve.

"Ella . . . ?" Gabriel says again.

"Yeah . . . I'm fine. It's a lot, you know?"

"You did great. Be proud of yourself. Your sister's going to receive justice."

I know he means to comfort me, but his words have the opposite effect. I had the opportunity to deliver justice in the biblical sense, and I failed.

37.

Dylan knocks on my door at seven. I'm not sure exactly what comes over me, but all the emotion I've been bottling up, not only since I learned that Charlotte was dead, but from the moment Zach called to say she was missing, suddenly bursts free. Rather than debilitating me with sorrow, it manifests by my ravishing Dylan.

"Are you sure?" he says when I start kissing him. "I mean, we can just talk . . ."

I can barely catch my breath. "No, I need to do this. Now."

It isn't more than thirty seconds later that we're in my bedroom, groping at each other in the dark. I almost feel badly for Dylan as he tries to keep up with me. I can't recall ever being so overwhelmed by desire. It feels like needing a fix. I have to escape one existence and enter another.

———

Ella barely lets me enter the apartment before her mouth is on mine. It reminds me of the night we met at Lava—how Ella knew exactly what she wanted and wasn't going to be denied.

I would have preferred to talk first. After all, I'm here for information, not to get laid. But she literally pulls me into her bedroom. The room is so dark that I can barely see her face as she reaches for my pants. I decide to give her what she wants—then I'll get what I'm after.

Dylan understands that I'm not interested in foreplay. It's only a matter of seconds before he's inside me.

From the first thrust, I'm cast into another dimension. In no time at all, I'm over the edge. Seconds later, I'm there for a second time.

Left to my own devices, I would have taken things more slowly, but Ella's on her own timetable. She pulls me on top of her. A moment later, she lets out a shudder. Her head rolls back and her arms flay to the side, tightly gripping the sheets.

Charlotte was extremely vocal during sex. At times, it felt almost like she was narrating. Ella is her opposite in that regard. Almost mute. If I didn't know better, I might think that she's just going through the motions to get things over with. But I *do* know better. I can feel each of her orgasms, until they start coming in waves that won't stop.

When it's over, we lie there in a heap. The thick scent leaves no doubt what's just occurred. My sheets are soaking wet.

"Jesus," he says.

I laugh. "I'm sorry for taking such advantage of you. I don't know what came over me."

He gives me a sideways glance. "I don't think you're really sorry."

He's right, and I tell him so. "Not even a little bit. In fact, I'm actually more thankful than sorry."

"I'm going to get some water," he says. "Do you want any?"

"If you're getting it. Sure."

He climbs out of the bed and I watch his perfectly formed ass walk away.

———

I don't even bother to try finding my underwear in the dark. Instead, I stroll out of the bedroom as naked as the day I was born.

The contrast between Ella's darkened bedroom and the brightly lit living room is so stark that I'm initially blinded. It takes a moment for my pupils to adjust. When my eyes can focus, they catch sight of a yellow legal pad on the dining-room table.

It takes me only a second to scan the page.

Tumi suitcase
East River
Missing since Tuesday
Tall, black hair, handsome
Banker
Patek Philippe watch
Art gallery/topless out-of-focus photo
Married
Scar/initial/hip

I know immediately what I've just read. Ella has written down clues about Charlotte's murderer.

How does Ella know I own a Patek Philippe? I've never worn it around her, as it doesn't seem to be the kind of accessory an altruistic doctor would possess. And why on earth does she think that Charlotte's killer owned one?

Tumi suitcase. The cops found it, apparently. But if they could trace it back to me, I would have already been visited by a swarm of New York City's finest. It must be a dead end, just as I'd thought. The police seemingly also know that she went missing Tuesday, not Wednesday. McDouche must have changed his story to pass the polygraph.

But why has Ella concluded Charlotte was killed by a married banker? Only the banker part applies to me. And what does *art gallery/ topless out-of-focus photo* mean? That isn't me. I never took a photo of Charlotte topless, and we never went to an art gallery—or anywhere in public—together.

It's the last entry—*scar/initial/hip*—that stops me cold. Somehow, Ella knows that Charlotte's killer has a scar in the shape of his initial, and yet her phrasing indicates that she doesn't know the letter it forms, which means she still doesn't know the killer's name. How could she know that? Maybe Charlotte told her . . . but then wouldn't she also have shared the name that goes with the initial?

Relax, I tell myself. *Even though the police have a lot more than I thought, neither they nor Ella know the one thing that matters—that I killed Charlotte.*

But is that right? Is it possible that she hasn't realized that I have a scar on my hip in the shape of a *C*? Even though she thinks my name is Dylan, if she notices a scar in the place she believes Charlotte's murderer was so marked, that certainly would be too much of a coincidence for her to overlook.

This is the second time I've been naked before her. Both times, it was in her dark bedroom. Clearly, she hasn't noticed. After Lava she was drunk and, just now, we went at it so fast and furious that I'm certain she didn't see it.

But maybe that's not right. Could it be that she didn't know after our first session, but this time she's seen it?

"Hey, did you get lost out there?" Ella calls from the bedroom.

"Just a second," I shout back.

———

Dylan returns to the bedroom a minute later with two glasses of water, one in each hand. He holds one in front of his genitals, as if he's embarrassed. He has nothing to be shy about, however. Far from it. A point that's driven home by the fact that a highball glass doesn't remotely cover him.

But then I feel a sharp pain in my brain. I now understand why Dylan's suddenly become so modest.

I can see it through the glass. On his hip is a scar. It's smooth, almost as if it were created with a scalpel. It's in the shape of the letter *C*.

It's like a bolt of lightning has struck me. Paul didn't kill Charlotte. The naked man in front of me is my sister's murderer.

Dylan matches the physical description of Matthew Harrison and now shares Charlotte's fictional lover's most defining feature—a scar on his hip. What Gabriel surmised must be right. Charlotte used the meeting with Paul in her book, but there can be only one explanation for why she decided to give Matthew a scar on his hip: She knew Dylan. More than just knew. She'd seem him naked.

Dylan Perry does not have a cyber footprint. Everything I know about him—including his name and his occupation—is based solely on what he's told me himself. I think about what Gabriel said—how sociopaths like to stay close to the investigation. What better way to do that than to get close to *me*?

I'm instantly consumed by rage. All I want to do is leap out at Dylan and strangle him with my bare hands. Or grab the lamp on my nightstand and crack his skull. Instead, I suppress all impulses to attack—not because of my more charitable instincts, but for the least Christian reason of all. I'm concerned that I'll fail.

He's twice my size and obviously capable of choking the life out of a woman with whom he's recently had sex. If I lunged at him now, he'd make quick work of me for sure. And grabbing the table lamp will not serve me well. It's likely not heavy enough to do the job, and this is certainly one of those situations where I'll only get one shot. If I try but don't manage to kill him—or at least sufficiently stun him so that I can follow up with another blow—Dylan will surely kill me.

I scan the room for something else to bring the odds more in my favor. Everything else I see is soft or too unwieldy: fabric-covered chairs, clothing, my television, the cable box. None of those things converts well into a weapon.

And then I remember. My purse. It's on the nightstand. And inside it is a knife.

———

I had thought about bringing a knife into the bedroom upon my return but decided against it because, given my nakedness, I had nowhere to hide it. I considered briefly dropping it in the water glass, but concluded that the element of surprise would be of greater advantage than a blade.

So when I reenter the room, I hand Ella her water, careful to keep the second glass at my hip. If she hasn't noticed the scar up until now, I aim to keep it that way. If all goes according to plan, she won't have anything to fear from Dylan Perry—until my hands are around her throat.

———

I take the glass of water he's offering. The other remains in place, blocking his scar.

"Thank you," I say.

He nods that he's heard me, but doesn't say anything. That's when a second, horrifying thought hits me: Dylan knows that I know that Charlotte's killer has a scar on his hip. That's why he's trying to shield it from me.

He saw my notes. That's the only explanation. Like an idiot, I left them on the dining table. He must have seen them when he got the water. I might as well have written him a letter saying that I know he killed my sister.

Stay calm, I tell myself. *Relax your breathing. He'll know if your demeanor toward him has changed.*

I slowly move to leave the bed. To grab the knife.

"Where do you think you're going, young lady?"

"I'm cold," I lie. "I'm going to get my sweatshirt."

"I've got a much better way to keep you warm," he says.

———

I slide between the sheets, careful to keep my torso twisted so Ella cannot see my hip. After I've placed my water glass on the nightstand, I turn to Ella.

———

I move to grab my handbag, which means closing the distance between Dylan and me. He must think I'm engaging, however, because he takes the opportunity to press his lips onto mine, ramming his tongue into my mouth. It's as disgusting to me as if he'd vomited.

Then he pushes me back onto the bed, his hands pressing down on my shoulders, effectively pinning me down.

———

I position my body on top of Ella's, careful to make sure that my weight immobilizes her. The irony strikes me that I choked Charlotte to death without meaning to, and now I'm worried that it might be difficult to do the same thing to Ella—even though this time I'll be acting with clear purpose.

———

Dylan's weight makes it impossible for me to move. I struggle to shift my shoulders off the mattress, trying to get any part of me out from under him.

He doesn't seem to notice my hand reaching over to the nightstand. Instead, he's focused on getting himself to his goal. As he does, I slide slightly away from him, each time moving a little closer to my own.

My arm extends as far as it can, feeling the hard wooden corner of the nightstand. Dylan has entered me, which allows me one final movement. He undoubtedly thinks that I'm bucking with him, rather than trying to reach the weapon with which I'm planning to kill him.

———

I'm fully submerged, and she's defenseless.

I move my right hand to her throat. Then my left.

———

All of a sudden, both of Dylan's hands grasp my throat.

I abandon all thoughts of my purse and enter survival mode, grabbing his wrists to break his hold, but I'm no match for his strength. His grip tightens.

———

I can feel her submission. Her eyes are bulging, as if she can't believe that it's actually happening. It is nothing like killing Charlotte. Then it seemed to move in a flash, but this time everything is in slow motion.

I press down harder. It will be over very soon.

———

I can't break his hold on my throat. My only chance now is the knife.

My hand flails for the table, knocking aside a framed photograph of Charlotte and me, and the glass Dylan just placed there flies to the floor. His grip tightens further around my neck. I can actually feel myself slipping away. My fingers splay out, reaching as far as I can.

The touch of the purse's leather strap gives me a renewed strength. I stretch every inch of my limb, from the shoulder socket to the finger joints, until, at last, I'm wrapping my palm around the knife's smooth grip.

In one swift motion, I whip the blade up and plunge it as hard as I can into Dylan's side.

He screams in pain. The force of my thrust pushes him off me.

I pull the knife out of him. He looks relieved, as if I've just saved his life.

Then I drive the point as hard as I can into his throat.

He gasps and begins to shake. I let go of the blade, leaving it in his neck as he rolls onto his back.

It's his eyes that stay with me to this day. The shock in them. I wonder if that's what Charlotte looked like as he strangled her to death.

After spending nearly my entire adulthood prosecuting criminals, I finally understand the rush of adrenaline that accompanies taking a life. Dylan Perry—or whatever the hell his name really is—is sprawled on my bed with blood pouring out of his neck and his side, and all I feel is the exhilaration of knowing I've avenged my sister's murder.

38.

I sit beside Dylan's body for more than a half hour. The first—I don't know how long—five minutes or so, before he succumbed to the inevitable, I didn't do anything but stare at him, watching the blood flow from his wounds. A thick river of red pooling on my white linens.

All that time, I didn't say a word. No screams of anger. No cursing his name. No shouting about what he'd taken from me. I've communicated all I had to say with the blade.

He gets the message. Enough to know that asking for help is futile. His eyes remain fixed on mine, though. So much so that they don't move when he expires.

That's when I call Gabriel.

"You need to come to my apartment. The guy who killed Charlotte just tried to kill me, and now he's dead."

I say it like that. Cool and collected. As if I was giving someone directions to the market, rather than admitting to the police that I'd just taken a man's life.

I expect him to remind me that it was only a few hours ago I told him Paul Michelson had killed my sister. In fact, he might be interrogating Paul at this very moment.

"I'm going to call a patrol in the neighborhood," Gabriel says instead. "They'll get to your place before me, but I'm going to tell them not to question you. And if they try, you tell them that you want to speak to your father and mention that he's a lawyer. Understand?"

I understand perfectly. He's protecting me.

———

After the call, I put on a T-shirt and sweatpants and wait for the police to arrive.

The cops show up only a few minutes later. A man and a woman in full police blues. The man is about my age. Big, with red hair and pasty, white skin. His badge says McKeege. His partner is younger, a Latina. She's barely five feet tall and with the bulletproof vest looks like she might fall over. Her name is Rosario.

McKeege is the lead, apparently, because he's the one who speaks first. "Are you Ella Broden?"

I nod. "Come in. Thank you for getting here so quickly."

I lead them into my bedroom and directly toward the dead body splayed on my bed. The knife is still sticking out of his neck.

Rosario must not have been to many gory crime scenes because she instinctively turns away. McKeege looks on as if nothing's amiss.

"Are you okay, ma'am?" McKeege asks.

For some reason, I find the use of the term "ma'am" comical. Like McKeege is a character in some 1950s police drama.

"As well as I can be, all things considered."

McKeege turns back around to look at my bed. "Did you move anything?"

I shake my head that I haven't, but, because he's still not looking at me, I follow up the nonverbal communication with a quiet, "No."

"Lieutenant Velasquez will be here any second now," McKeege says, turning back around to face me. "Our instructions are to wait with you until he gets here. Is there anything we can do for you in the interim?"

"Do you mind if we sit in the living room?" I ask. "I don't . . . I don't want to see him anymore."

———

Gabriel must have flown over from One PP, because he arrives only a few minutes after the uniformed cops. He's a sight for sore eyes. So much so that I immediately embrace him.

His professionalism, however, is front and center. He pushes me back. "Are you okay?"

"Yeah, I'm fine. Shaken . . . but feeling very lucky to be alive."

"You are lucky, Ella. Wait here. I'll be back in a moment."

Gabriel walks into my bedroom with McKeege a step behind him, while Rosario is left to babysit me. Through the open doorway, I see Gabriel reach into his pocket and pull out latex gloves. He says something that I can't hear to McKeege, which causes McKeege to reach into his own pocket and toss Gabriel what appears to be a leather wallet. I don't recall him taking it from Dylan's pants, but he must have. I can't imagine McKeege giving Gabriel his own wallet.

Gabriel catches it with one hand and then, with the other, he pulls out a few cards. After a quick examination, Gabriel returns the cards to their sleeves and hands the billfold back to McKeege.

"His name is Christopher Tyler," Gabriel says when he returns to me. "He's a banker at a firm called Harper Sawyer."

"Matthew Harrison . . . ," I say. "It makes perfect sense. Classic Charlotte."

"I don't follow."

"She was always playing word games. William Henry Harrison was an early president. He's most famous for dying a month after taking office. His vice president and successor was John Tyler."

Gabriel looks over his shoulder at the uniformed cops. In a whisper, he says, "You know as well as I do that presidential wordplay is not evidence that he killed your sister. And you were right—Paul Michelson's luggage is the same model and color as the one the killer used."

"Paul didn't do it. This guy did."

I explain it all in less than a minute. How he told me his name was Dylan Perry when he approached me at Lava, the second meet-up at Riverside, the notepad I'd stupidly left on my dining table, and his effort to kill me before I killed him in self-defense.

Then I tell him the clincher. "He has a scar on his hip. It's in the shape of his first initial. Just like in my sister's book."

Gabriel's eyebrows arch and he hurries back to my bedroom. I watch as he slides down the sheet, exposing Christopher's lower abdomen. He doesn't look at it long before he turns to walk back out to me.

I'm about to ask Gabriel if he believes me now when my father enters the apartment.

"Dad?" I say, confused by his presence.

"I called him," Gabriel says.

My father walks more quickly than I've ever seen him move, rushing to embrace me.

"Oh my God, Ella. Are you okay?"

"I'm fine, Dad. It's all over," I whisper in his ear.

He's slow to release me, and I take a moment to enjoy the sensation of his hug. When he lets go, he looks at me with tears in his eyes.

"What happened?" he asks.

"He was having an affair with Charlotte. I met him before Charlotte went missing. Actually, it was after he'd killed her, but before I knew she was missing. He gave me a fake name and must have sought me out to shadow the investigation. I had no idea he knew Charlotte . . . but, like I said, it's over now. He killed Charlotte, and now he's dead."

"Do you know why he killed her?"

"No. Not really. Jealousy, maybe."

My father considers this. He'll never know why this man took his daughter from him. He looks as if this reality is yet another assault. The not knowing.

"We're almost finished here," Gabriel says.

I can see my father's antennae perk up. His lawyer hat is back on.

"Did Ella give a statement?" he asks.

"In a matter of speaking," Gabriel says.

"What's that mean?"

"It means she said it was self-defense, and I believe her. It didn't go further than that."

"It's okay, Dad," I say.

Gabriel nods. "I'm going to leave you two alone for now. I can't guarantee that I won't need to get back to you about some things, but I'm going to try to limit that as much as I can. In the meantime, Ella, if you need anything, anything at all, please call me." He smiles. "And that's not just something I say. I mean it."

I'm touched by Gabriel's offer. I know it's not just something he says.

"Thank you. For everything, Gabriel."

He nods again and then places his hand softly on my shoulder. He doesn't say anything further, just walks back over to his colleagues.

By now, the police tech crew has arrived and put the body in a bag on top of a gurney. They wheel my sister's murderer away.

Gabriel is the last of them to leave. He waves as he shuts the door, and I wave back at him.

DAY TEN

WEDNESDAY

Ella Broden

39.

Charlotte's funeral is held two days after I killed her murderer, ten days after her own death.

It's raining. Not a driving storm, but more than a romantic mist.

Had it been any other day, I likely wouldn't have minded, or even noticed. But today it seems like yet another form of divine punishment. I wanted my last day with Charlotte to be gloriously sunny, as if her warmth had descended from the heavens to envelop the earth.

When my mother died, my father purchased a matching burial plot beside hers, intended as his final resting place. With tears in his eyes, he asked if I'd mind it if he gave the space to Charlotte. "It'll make it a little easier for me if I can see Charlotte next to your mother."

I couldn't hold back my own tears. "Of course," I said. "I think . . . no, I'm certain, that they'd both like that. And it'll be nice for us too, to be able to visit them together."

As far as I know, my father has never visited my mother's gravesite. I never liked coming here either. I preferred to talk to her when I was lying in bed, or walking in Central Park, or even on the subway. Still, Charlotte and I came out every year on my mother's birthday. It was Charlotte's idea, of course. She'd always bake a cake, even that first year, when Charlotte was only thirteen and I didn't think she even knew how to boil water. We'd have a picnic right on top of my mother's grave.

When we got older, champagne was added to the event, and Charlotte would balance a flute on our mother's headstone.

For today's burial, my father had wanted only the two of us to attend. He didn't even see the need for an officiant to be present. But I told him that we needed to be more inclusive. Others loved Charlotte too, and they deserved the opportunity to say good-bye. In the end, we invited a few people and relied on the grapevine to get the word out to the rest.

I sit beside my father in the back of a Lincoln town car on the way to the cemetery, holding his hand for most of the drive. Early on in the ride, he shares with me what he thinks is news.

"I got the strangest call yesterday. Paul Michelson has decided to retain new counsel."

"Did he say why?" I ask.

"No. Just that, given everything that's going on with us and Charlotte, he needs someone more focused on him."

I stifle the urge to laugh. No need to share with my father that I held his client at knifepoint.

"No great loss there," I say instead.

He looks at me with a resigned air. But I know he doesn't care about losing Paul as a client—especially because the retainer was nonrefundable.

"I have the strong feeling that it's going to be hard for you to truly believe the whole innocent-until-proven-guilty thing after this."

"We don't have to discuss it now, Dad."

"I think that maybe we do. I don't want to make the same mistake twice."

"What do you mean?"

"When your mother died, you were the glue, Ella. It should have been me, but it was you who held it together for Charlotte . . . and for me too. And I know that had your mother lived, you would never have become a lawyer. She wouldn't have let you. I hope you don't think I pushed you in that direction. I truly never meant to do that. What I meant to do was stand back, allow you to make your own decision."

"I just wanted you to be proud of me."

"I could never be anything but proud of you, sweetheart. But what will make me most proud is if you live your life on your own terms. Not for me. Not for what your mother would have wanted. And please don't do it now for Charlotte. Nothing would make me happier, or prouder, than for you to be who you want to be, Ella. And I'm confident that on this point I speak for your mother as well."

I know he's right. I just wish I had known it years earlier.

———

After that we barely say a word, but I imagine our thoughts are identical. The tragedy that Charlotte will never fall in love, get married, or have children. The utter injustice that the world is forever going to be diminished by her absence. People who never knew Charlotte even existed would be deprived of the words she would have written, and the lucky few who would have met her had she lived will now be less for not knowing her.

I keep imagining a man. In my mind's eye, he's blond, although Charlotte rarely went for fair-haired men. He's not from New York City, but California. San Francisco, maybe. He's smart and kind and handsome, and his friends and family can't, for the life of them, understand why he's never married—even he wonders why no woman has ever captured his heart. I envision him meeting Charlotte on some hiking expedition somewhere, and them marrying within a few months of first casting eyes on each other.

I feel sorrow for him too, even though he is merely an imaginary placeholder. Whoever was destined to be Charlotte's soul mate has no idea of the tragedy he's suffered, and he never will. From that perspective,

I count myself as supremely fortunate. At least I had twenty-five years to bask in Charlotte's love.

———

Trinity Cemetery was established in the 1840s, and is the only remaining active burial ground in Manhattan. Located on 155th Street and Riverside Drive, it's less than three miles from Charlotte's apartment and offers mourners the same sweeping views of the Hudson. The cemetery is affiliated with the famous Trinity Church on Wall Street, where George Washington prayed after his inauguration. It didn't occur to me when my mother was laid to rest, but I'm certain my father had to use all his considerable influence to get a plot there.

The mass takes place in a large church. My father and I are allowed to sit in a waiting room and enter just as the service is about to begin. When we do, I see far more people than I had expected. A standing-room-only crowd. I take only the briefest scan of the faces, noting some cousins and aunts, scores of Charlotte's friends—and Zach, who looks away from me when we make eye contact.

The minister is right out of central casting. An elderly man, tall and thin, with white powder for hair and small, circular, wire-framed eyeglasses. He spares us the effort of pretending he knew Charlotte and immediately leads the congregation through the scriptures that tradition dictates must be recited.

"In light of the weather," the old minister says, "I thought we would all be more comfortable if the eulogies were delivered at this time. That way, those who would rather not have to brave the inclement weather can take their leave after this service. And so, at this time, Charlotte's father, F. Clinton Broden, would like to say a few words."

My father once again reminds me of the larger-than-life figure of my childhood. I know he's not 100 percent yet, but I feel sure that he'll eventually get there. Charlotte's death will not break him. He may not throw himself back into work as earnestly as he did after my mother's death, but he will return to being the man he was before. Even now, he shows signs of the command he held in the courtroom as he addresses the audience.

His remarks are brief but poignant. He tells a story about Charlotte as a small child that I've heard before. We were at the dinner table and Charlotte hit me. My mother told her that if she hit me again she'd have to go to her room. Without missing a beat, Charlotte responded, "Where do I go if I hit Ella when I'm *in* my room?" When the laughter subsides, my father says he felt sure back then that, with that type of mind, Charlotte would enjoy a prosperous career in the law. This elicits even more laughter, after which he segues to her gift for the written word, which became her true passion.

"I thought it would be fitting to end my remarks today by reading a short passage that Charlotte wrote, and which was selected by the person who knew Charlotte best—her sister, Ella." He looks up and smiles at me. "Everyone who ever discussed writing with Charlotte knows all too well that Charlotte was famous for saying that her work was fiction and any resemblance to real people and events was purely coincidental. But in this case, I think, even maybe Charlotte would have conceded that some truth made its way into her prose."

He pulls out a single sheet of paper from his breast pocket and smooths the page on the lectern. Then he reaches into his other jacket pocket to retrieve a pair of reading glasses.

My murderer has deprived me of very little. There are the years I will not live, but set against the vastness of eternity, the time I've lost is but a moment. What is forever is the same as if I'd lived another sixty years or more: those I loved will always be a part of me, and I will never cease being a part of those who loved me.

I did not want to speak at the service. I've said my good-byes to Charlotte in private, and I expect to speak to her daily for the rest of my days.

This means that, after my father's words, the congregants pour out of the church and into the rain. It's now coming down in torrents, and a sea of umbrellas burst skyward.

At the doorway to the chapel, I'm greeted by my old boss and mentor, Lauren Wright. I introduce her to my father, and she offers him the half smile befitting the circumstances.

"Thank you so much for coming, Lauren," I say. "And for everything you did to help with the investigation."

She nods, but this time doesn't smile. "Of course. You're family to me, Ella. I only wish . . ."

I know what she wishes. I wish it too. It's the only wish I'll probably ever have again.

———

The downpour is enough to dissuade all but a few from venturing to the gravesite, but approximately twenty people begin the trek to follow Charlotte's casket, which is being wheeled across the muddy ground. My father holds an umbrella aloft for both of us. My arm is around his waist, both to be sheltered from the rain, but also because I enjoy feeling so connected to him. We walk like that for about a minute when I see the small tent set up at the grave. The ground is open, and men are placing the casket onto the bands that will be used to lower it to the bottom.

I feel a tap on my shoulder.

"I'm sorry to accost you like this," a man says. A boy, really. "You don't know me, but I was a friend . . . a very good friend of Charlotte's."

I do know him. It's Josh Walden. It's funny to think that we've never actually met, as all my encounters with him were from a distance. First through Charlotte's description of his alter ego, Jason, then through the monitor when he was interrogated and polygraphed, and finally off in the distance at the Riverside Park event.

He looks like he's wearing his father's suit. It hangs off him in the shoulders, and the shirt puckers around the neck. His umbrella is one of the cheap ones sold on the street for five bucks. It barely covers him, and his shoulders are wet.

I turn to my father. "Go sit down. I'll join you in a minute."

When my father steps away, Josh places his umbrella over me. I lean closer to him so it covers at least part of him too.

"Thank you for coming today. I'm Ella."

"Josh Walden," he says. "I just wanted to say that I'm so very sorry for your loss. Your sister . . . she was the most amazing person I've ever met."

"Thank you for saying that. She was amazing."

"Did she ever say anything to you about me?"

I consider his question. Of the three men in Charlotte's life, Josh alone did the right thing. Zach only cared about protecting himself. And Christopher, well, he got what he deserved. Although Charlotte's fictional Jason was hardly a paragon of virtue, I have to remind myself that Josh is not Jason. I could be wrong, but I want so much to believe that Charlotte was right in letting Josh into her life.

"She did. She said that she thought you were a gentle soul and an amazingly talented writer. She also told me that she was very happy when she was in your company."

He seems pleased by my white lie. He smiles again. "Thank you," he says and then allows me to seek refuge under the awning.

———

The overhang at the gravesite provides shelter only for the two chairs reserved for my father and me. The minister pokes his head under its protection as well, but the rest of the mourners remain in the steady downfall, with only their umbrellas to shield them from the rain.

It's only after I'm seated that I see Gabriel. He's wearing a suit and tie, which I'm not sure I've ever seen him in before. His badge is nowhere to be seen. I smile at him and he returns the gesture, following it with a courtly bow of his head.

The graveside service lasts only a few minutes, and then Charlotte's coffin is lowered into the hole. As I watch it descend, I can't help but think about her first burial—in the suitcase in the East River. Although I had been determined not to cry today, I fail in that resolution.

Finally, it's over. The minister dismisses us, and I walk out into the rain toward Gabriel. He quickly closes the distance and pushes his umbrella over my head until it's covering far more of me than him.

I kiss him on the cheek. In that touch, I remember so vividly when our lips locked those years before.

"Thank you so much for coming today. It means more to me than I can tell you."

"They say that this is the worst day, and it'll get easier from here."

"That is what they say."

I nod to my father that he should go on ahead, and Gabriel and I walk together toward the parking lot.

"I come with good news," he says after my father has put about ten feet between him and us. "Both investigations have been closed. Christopher Tyler definitely killed your sister. His credit card led us to the W Hotel on the night of the murder, and the security cameras leave no doubt that they both entered, but that he later left wheeling the suitcase."

It hurts all over again. I know that's foolish as there's no doubt in my mind that's what happened. Yet, just thinking about Charlotte being imprisoned in that suitcase moves me to tears—even though she's now encased in a box buried underground.

"I'm sorry," he says. "I didn't mean to upset you. I thought you'd—"

"No, I want to hear. You said *both* investigations are closed. Do you mean Jennifer Barnett?"

"No. That's gone to Missing Persons. There's no evidence that Christopher Tyler knew Jennifer Barnett, so he's not responsible for that crime. No, I meant that we officially ruled Tyler's death to be an act of self-defense."

I nod. I hadn't really given much thought to a different outcome. But of course, t's have to be crossed and i's dotted whenever someone stabs someone else through the neck.

"Thank you."

"What's next for you now?" he asks. "Back to work?"

"No. I need . . . a change of focus, I think. Did I ever tell you that, before law school, I always wanted to be a singer?"

He smiles in a way that makes me smile back. "No, I would have remembered that."

"Yeah. Long story there, but I think I'm going to try to turn back time a little bit and see if I can't make a go of it."

"You'll have to tell me when you get your first . . . do they still call them gigs?"

"I actually don't know. But I'll do more than tell you because . . . one of the other mistakes of my former life that I'd like to remedy was not returning your phone calls way back then. So, if you're not seeing anyone at the moment, can I turn back time on that too?"

He hesitates, and I fear I'm going to get shot down. But then he says, "I'd really like that too. I know this sounds corny, but I've always thought of you as the one who got away."

It is corny. But I've thought about him that way too.

"Chalk it up to me being an idiot. I like to think I'm much smarter now."

"How about if we start again on Saturday night?" Then he quickly adds, "Unless that's too soon."

"No. No, that sounds absolutely perfect."

By now we've reached the parking lot, and I can see my father leaning against the town car that brought us here. He's no longer holding an umbrella, and I realize that the rain has stopped.

"The sun is coming out," I say.

Gabriel closes his umbrella and shakes the excess rain onto the ground. "Look," he says, pointing up.

It's a rainbow, filling the sky. The kind that makes you stop and take notice.

I'm normally the cynic who would say that it's just a coincidence. That it's not a sign from God or my sister smiling down on us. But that's another thing I'm ready to change. Today, I'm certain that it *is* a sign from God. And my sister *is* smiling down on us.

ACKNOWLEDGMENTS

Thank you so much for taking the time to read *Dead Certain*. Please e-mail me at adam@adammitzner.com with your thoughts about the book. I love to hear from readers, and I write back!

Dead Certain is my fifth book, and the most fun to write. I hope my enjoyment came through on the page, and I hope that you enjoyed it too.

Writing in my house is a family affair. My wife, Susan Steinthal, is the best editor, sounding board, and critic any writer (or husband) could have. All that and she's responsible for my being happier than I ever dreamed possible. I dedicated *Dead Certain* to my daughters, Rebecca and Emily, not only because they are my world but because at the heart of the book is the relationship between two sisters, and that part is modeled on my daughters' bond, which never ceases to amaze me. My stepson Benjamin gives the best comments of anyone (and is my first reader), and Michael is always willing to explain technology and global politics to me. Finally, I miss my parents, Linda and Milton Mitzner, more with each book that they never got to read.

I owe an incredible debt to all my friends and family for their enthusiastic support. I'm looking at you: Jessica and Kevin Shacter, Jodi (Shmodie) Siskind, Jane and Gregg Goldman, Lisa and Eric Sheffield, Matt and Deborah Brooks, Beth Miller, Bonnie Rubin, Ellice Schwab, Abby Doft (who lent her name), Leslie Wright, Paolo Amoroso (who lent his name), Kelly Nelson (who lent her name), Margaret Martin, and Ted Quinn.

I want to single out Clint Broden for thanks. Clint is a real person and a real criminal defense attorney of the first rank in Dallas, and in my fictional universe he is a fictional person and a fictional criminal defense attorney of the first rank in New York.

This is my first book for Thomas & Mercer, and the experience has been nothing but spectacular. Liz Pearsons has been a joy to work with, and I was thrilled to be reunited with Ed Stackler, my very first editor. Ed made many insightful critiques about *Dead Certain* that made it far better than it would otherwise have been. Also a big shout-out to everyone on the Thomas & Mercer team, many of whom I sadly never met, but each of your contributions truly makes the book better.

My agent, Scott Miller of Trident Media, is the man who starts it all going, and without him I'd still be printing my books out for just my family to read. My thanks also go out to Scott's colleague, Allysin Shindle, and to Jon Cassir of CAA, who I have faith will one of these days bring my books to film or television.

When I'm not writing, I'm lawyering as a partner at Pavia & Harcourt. Everyone at my firm is enormously supportive, especially Diane Pimentel, Olga Sushko, and George Garcia.

One of the creative sparks that gave rise to *Dead Certain* was that people who know me assume that there is a great deal of autobiography in my fiction. Like Charlotte, I disabuse them of that notion, and like Ella, my friends and family roll their eyes when I do. But if readers want to glean anything about me from my writing (and I recommend that they don't), it's that my family means everything to me—that and I have pretty good insight into how a sociopath thinks, apparently.

Again, thank you all so very much for your readership! It means more than words can say.

ABOUT THE AUTHOR

Photo © 2016 Matthew Simpkins Photography

Adam Mitzner is a practicing attorney in a Manhattan law firm and the author of several acclaimed novels. *Suspense Magazine* named *A Conflict of Interest* one of the best books of 2012, and in 2014, the American Bar Association nominated *A Case of Redemption* for a Silver Gavel Award. He and his family live in New York City. Visit him at www.adammitzner.com.